THE HONEYWOOD SETTLEMENT

THE HONEYWOOD SETTLEMENT

H.B. Creswell

Academy Chicago Publishers

Published in 2007 by
Academy Chicago Publishers
363 W. Erie Street
Chicago, Illinois 60610

First Published in 1930.

Printed and bound in the USA.

Library of Congress Cataloging-in-Publication Data

Creswell, H. B.
  The Honeywood settlement / H.B. Creswell.
    p. cm.
  Sequel to: The Honeywood file.
  ISBN 978-0-89733-566-9 (pbk.)
  1. Architectural practice—England—Fiction. 2. Architects and builders—
England—Fiction. I. Title.

  PR6005.R55H67 2007
  823'.912—dc22

                    2007028562

TO

P.H.K-K.
P.B., M.T, E.C.

PREFACE

The Honeywood File described the building of a house, and the present volume carries the history to conclusion ten months later when the last defect has been remedied, the last dispute settled, and the last account paid.

The aspirant to architectural practice—unlike the general reader—is more interested in building houses than in occupying them; but the proof of a pudding is in the eating, and by showing the consequences that flowed from events recorded in the earlier book, *The Honeywood Settlement* completes the lesson of *The Honeywood File*.

H.B.C.

CONTENTS

INTRODUCTORY REMARKS

The matter before us purports to be a correspondence file from the office of James Spinlove, a young London architect. The file is concerned with the building of a country house for a certain Sir Leslie Brash, and consists of a folder within which are clipped, in order of date, letters received and carbon copies of those dispatched. The colours of the picture presented are necessarily somewhat brighter than life; the characters are also entirely imaginary and the episodes inventions; yet, since the whole of the didactic value of the book and much of its interest depends upon the reader's acceptance of the picture as true to life, it has been the author's particular concern to make it so by enhancing verisimilitude. The detachment of the commentator is, however, no such elaborate affectation as appears; for the commentary has been provoked by the reaction of characters to the events, and new events have had birth in those reactions so that the author is, in general, identified with the commentator in not knowing, from one page to the next, what is going to happen.

The file we are about to open is the second and last of those covering the history of the building of Honeywood Grange. In the closing commentary of *The Honeywood File* it was mentioned that somewhere in the architect's office there must be a second Honeywood File, for the first file ended when the folder would hold no more papers, and the circumstance that the last letter coincided with the completion of the house was merely an example of

1

Author's luck, for if the business of building a house ended when the workmen left it, this world would be a happier place than it is for owners, architects, and builders.

There is the vexed question of defects which, in a greater or less degree, manifest themselves in all new buildings, and which, so far as they appear within a certain time and are due to improper workmanship or materials, the builder has to make good under the terms of his contract; or, so far as they are due to negligence on the part of the architect, the architect is responsible for under his. Then, the builder's final Statement of Account has to be dealt with. This is likely to include charges for extras and to raise questions of fact long gone out of memory. When these disputes have been settled it devolves on the architect to reconcile his client to those extra charges that are due to his interferences, and to those others imposed on him by the oversights or afterthoughts of his architect. Lastly, there is the architect's account for balance of fees due. As this account includes items for expenses and disbursements, and special charges for services—additional to those directly involved by the contract work; and as, besides, these expenses and charges are based on the architect's status and style of living and the cost to him in time and trouble, and are to be justified only by their reasonableness, it sometimes happens that owner and architect discover, perhaps for the first and only time, that their ideas of reasonableness differ.

It is such matters as these that make the existence of a second file inevitable; but the bulk of that before us is exceptional and is not explained by Spinlove's habit of writing unnecessary letters which provoke unnecessary replies. Every reader of *The Honeywood File* will, however, recall that Spinlove is involved in more ways than he is aware of. He has, for instance, given his client light-hearted estimates, some of which have been wildly astray; and, although the contract lays down that no extras shall rank unless the claim be made and accepted at the time the work is done, Spinlove was not particular in enforcing the builder's observance of this rule. Spinlove is also unconscious that he has fallen into a trap set for him by the persons who supplied the facing bricks, and who have thereby established a claim for extra payment.

Spinlove warned his client not to give orders direct to the builder's people, and laid stress on the dangers of the extras that would attend any interferences with the work; but Brash's attention to this excellent advice wandered, and when her Leslie was gunning in Scotland Lady Brash began pulling down work that afterwards had to be restored—one of the least economical ways of building known to the trade.

Trouble is also promised by Brash's insistence on the interior of the house being decorated with a new, untried, patent paint called Riddoppo, against his architect's advice and in spite of the builder's objections. Riddoppo is advertised in tube lifts as a New Novelty Super-Paint, fire and acid resisting, proof against assaults of boiling water and super-heated steam, and capable of receiving a high polish; but these rare merits have not prevented it from showing such a marked tendency to "creep" or flow downwards, that Grigblay, in a private letter to Spinlove—in which his incorrigible, ironic humour veils a natural annoyance—describes "Riddoppo Super" as getting ready to crawl out of the front door and off home.

Sir Leslie Brash, his wife Maude, and his daughter Phyllis—who prefers to be known as "Pud"—occupied Honeywood Grange on 10th February 1926. The house backs upon a spinney through which the entrance drive passes to the adjoining highway, and looks out over a terrace upon a fine prospect to the south, east, and west, marred only by a pump-house chimney two miles away which reacts unfavourably on the nerve-centres that serve Lady Brash for brains. It is a brick gabled house, with leaded lights in iron casements set in solid oak frames; and the design has affinity to Tudor architecture. The oak floors and staircases and the oak panelling and open brick hearths and fireplace surrounds to the reception rooms, are in sympathy with the same tradition. Brash, however, allowed a friend, who was a director of the paint company, to persuade him to paint each bedroom out in a different colour, thus turning the upper part of the house, as Spinlove complained, into a colour-cure asylum for lunatics.

Sir Leslie Brash, the building owner, is a man in advanced middle-age. He is an accountant and financial expert of some importance whose native generosity of heart is veiled by pomposity and irascibility. His architect, James Spinlove, is about thirty: he is well-qualified and is painstaking and conscientious, but temperamental; and he lacks experience of life and of affairs, so that he is apt to turn for guidance when in difficulties to the builder, John Grigblay. Grigblay is a provincial builder of good standing and repute, and high integrity.

The last sheet in the first file was a copy of a letter of Spinlove's acknowledging a warm message of appreciation and thanks from Brash, who had just gone to live in the house. This letter was dated 14th February 1926, and when we open the second folder we find the following:

SIGNS OF DAMP

Dear Sir,   23.2.26.
    I should like your Statement of Account at once. When may I
expect it?

                                            Yours faithfully,

It is a pity Spinlove—like the rest of us—does not get his deserts, or
he would receive by return a postcard bearing the words "Say, Please,"
and obtain great benefit from the hint. He is on the best of terms with
Grigblay who has taken great trouble to make the house a success and
whose friendly help and advice he has acknowledged on several occa-
sions and been indebted to on many more, so that his gracelessness is
merely a habit with Spinlove in addressing those under his direction. It
is a bad habit, and one that has already got him into difficulties he might
otherwise have avoided.

Dear Mr. Spinlove,   28.2.26.
    I very much regret to have to intimate that my anticipations
anent the windows at Honeywood appear to be now eventuating. You will recall that I previously communicated to you, on
behalf of Lady Brash and myself, our strong preference for big
sheets of thick glass in place of little thin sheets all jointed together

with narrow strips; but you persuaded us to adhere to the present device. The consequent results are precisely what I anticipated. The rain percolates freely through the glass, which is very thin, cheap glass; and also, I apprehend, through the joints where it is connected by the little strips which are so weak that *iron bars* have in some cases been found necessary to fortify their strength. Every morning the maids have to remove the accumulated wet that collects on the new oak window-boards, which are exhibiting stains in consequence, and the water even runs over the edge on to our new carpets! The situation of Honeywood Grange is excessively exposed to the weather, and it is clearly obvious that large continuous sheets of thick glass is the appropriate desideratum, as—if you will permit me to remind you—I previously prognosticated.

We continue to be delighted with the house and to appreciate the anticipatory forethought of its architect. We notice no signs of damp other than that above intimated except in the boxroom, the outer wall of which was lately found to be streaming with water; and the domestic staff complain of wet marks near the ceiling over the fireplaces of their domain on the uppermost story.

I desire that you will intimate to Mr. Grigblay that these matters require immediate attention. There should be no difficulty in cutting the glass to appropriate sizes and effecting substitution of one pane at a time so as to avoid unnecessarily exposing us to the weather.

Yours sincerely,

Brash certainly takes these disasters in an accommodating spirit. He is evidently well satisfied with the house.

SPINLOVE TO BRASH

Dear Sir Leslie Brash,   1.3.26.

It is not possible, I assure you, for rain to beat through the glass quarries, which are not, as you suppose, unduly thin. Iron saddle-bars are essential to leaded lights. Large sheets are made thick for purposes of strength only. It is certainly possible for heavy driving rain to find its way in through the joints with the leadings, but this cannot be the case with your windows. Messrs. Watkins, who did the work, are most reliable people; and it happens that, knowing the house was exposed on the south and west, I spoke to their man on this particular point and found that he was already jointing the quarries to the cames, or leads, with a mastic stopping—a precaution not in ordinary found necessary.

I have no doubt whatever that what you describe is merely *condensation*. In a quite new house the moisture in the walls, due to the large amount of water used in bricklaying, is continually being evaporated, and the warm air becomes charged with steam which condenses on the cold surface of the glass. If the windows are left a little open the trouble will diminish, and it will entirely disappear for good and all with the summer.

The wet surface of the boxroom wall is due to the same cause. This is a solid wall, and the plaster was finished with an ordinary steel-faced float and so left. The window and door should be kept open for the next few weeks.

With kind regards,

Yours sincerely,

P.S.—You will find that wet will collect on the windows irrespective of rain, and on the boxroom wall only when mild, humid weather immediately follows cold.

Spinlove is evidently informed by experience or he could scarcely write with the assurance he exhibits—which, however, does not extend to explaining the cause of the damp in chimney-breasts. It will be noticed he says nothing of this. The reasons he gives, and the advice he offers, are sound—but we may suppose that Brash has raised a great shout over a very small matter, for the conditions at Honeywood Grange are such as least favour condensation. The brickwork was built during the summer months and the outer walls are formed of a 4½-in. inner and a 9-in. outer wall, with a 2-in. space between, so that evaporation must be relatively small. In houses that specially favour condensation—such as those built in the winter and stuccoed or rough-cast on the outside as well as plastered within, so that water is bottled up in the walls—the evaporation induced by the warmth of the occupied house is so considerable as to produce most disquieting conditions of damp. Water collects in puddles on window-boards and runs down walls to form pools on the floor below, and under such conditions of weather as that described in Spinlove's postscript, wallpapers covering outside walls may become soaked with water.

Brash's boxroom is a mild instance of this phenomenon; and when Spinlove speaks of "steam," and mentions that this particular wall is built solid and its plastered face left as finished with a steel float, he gives the explanation of it, though Brash may not know what he is talking about for he probably recognizes steam only as the vapour from boiling water (which is not steam), and has no idea that steam is invisible, or that atmospheric air is charged with steam which comes into evidence as vapour, or "condensation," only when pressure is reduced or temperature lowered.

The inner 4½-in. lining of a hollow wall speedily dries out and acquires a temperature approximating to that of the room, so that condensation cannot take place upon it. A solid brick wall, on the other hand, tends to retain its moisture and is therefore a better conductor of heat than a dry one, and, as there is no hollow space providing an insulating blanket of air, the warmth of the room is dispersed into and through the wall which, in consequence, remains cold and invites condensation. If this boxroom wall had been papered—and in the degree that the paper was thick and porous—condensation would have been discouraged and for the reason that explains Spinlove's reference to a steel float. A steel float which gives a compact, smooth, polished finish to plaster, promotes condensation by the abrupt transition of temperature presented at its surface; but a float faced with felt leaves an open grain behind it so that the air invades the interstices of the plaster surface; there is a gradual transition from the temperature of the room to the temperature of the wall, and condensation will not then take place under any conditions likely to arise in a house. Incidentally, distemper lies well on a felt-floated wall: it looks "solid," as a house painter would say—a result that can be otherwise got only by papering before applying distemper. In using the ordinary method of fin-

ishing with a steel float in the boxroom and other back quarters, Spinlove was observing a right principle of economy.

GRIGBLAY TO SPINLOVE

Dear Sir, 2.3.26.

As proposed to you by Mr. Grigblay, we held off with metalling the entrance drive until the owner had got his furniture in, and our foreman tells us that the heavy lorries have done a lot of damage to the bottoming. Mr. Grigblay looked in yesterday and thinks you ought to see what has been done, as we must make a claim for restoring and Mr. Grigblay thinks the best thing will be to put a 5-ton roller over the 9-in. pitching and then level up with 4-in. chalk rubble before laying the 3 ins. of metalling, as the present bottoming is rather light.

Bloggs will be on the site till middle of next week finishing the paths, etc., and clearing up. We have an expert ganger who will look after the road.

Bloggs says there are various little jobs her Ladyship wants done in the house, and we are attending to them. We propose to put these in a separate account.

Yours faithfully,

Heavy motor lorries are a great tax on private roads, which require better foundations than were formerly necessary. Spinlove is indebted to Grigblay for having warned him to postpone the finishing of the road: it would otherwise have been badly broken up. The additional layer of rubble was in any case desirable.

It will be noticed that Grigblay says nothing of Spinlove's demand for the Statement of Account. In point of fact, the reason Spinlove wants the account at once is a good reason why Grigblay should wish to hold it back. However exact Spinlove's methods may be—and we have no evidence that they are particularly exact—they will fall far short of the orderly, detailed records which are a necessary part of the daily routine of a builders' office, so that Spinlove will have to depend in great part on his memory

*in determining that certain charges are justified and in fortifying himself
to disallow others. Thus, if a builder delays rendering his account, the
architect is at a disadvantage in fulfilling his duties as arbiter of what is
just and unjust, and is more or less at the builder's mercy. There is also a
psychological reason favouring delay in making claims, of which everyone
is conscious and which seems to depend upon repugnance to reopening old
disputes or returning to forgotten battlefields. When an owner is in bland
enjoyment of his accomplished ambition, and his architect immersed in
fresh activities (and anxieties), neither has much appetite for renewal of
controversy. In addition to this, a builder is obviously in a bad position
if he renders his account before he knows what may be required of him in
the matter of making good defects; for if he is to be met by exacting and
crotchety demands he will be inclined to reimburse himself by claims for,
doubtful extras which he otherwise might prefer not to raise, or if, by some
misfortune, he is involved in a demand for costly restitutions that become
the cause of an action for damages, he will wish, as an offset to the claim
against him, to be free to inflate his account to the full limits that plausibil-
ity and legal ingenuity can effect. Thus there are good reasons why a builder
should delay sending in his account till the time within which he is under
contract to make good defects—usually nine months—has expired, or is
on the point of expiring; and this no doubt explains why protracted delay
in rendering the final statement of account is common. It must be remembered, however, that a builder does not make out his statement of account
until he has brought up to date his prime cost account which shows what
the actual value of material and labour is; and as some invoices reach him
only months after the materials have been delivered, an early rendering of
the Statement of Account would dislocate his organization.*

SPINLOVE TO GRIGBLAY

Dear Sir,   3.3.26.
   I will go on to the site on Monday and settle what is to be done
to complete the entrance road.
   I understand that the work Lady Brash has asked you to do
relates only to fittings. This, as you propose, should be rendered

in a separate account. You will, of course, let me know if any kind of structural alterations, or decorations, are asked for.

I shall be glad to know when I may expect your Statement of Account.

Sir Leslie Brash mentions that damp is appearing on the chimney-breasts of the second floor. Will you therefore leave necessary ladders on the site so that I can examine the listings?

Yours faithfully,

Spinlove is wise in directing the builder to make a separate account of the odds and ends of work which are necessary to enable an owner to fit himself and his belongings into his house, but he will have to see that none of this work is work that should properly be included in the contract to "complete" and make good defects. Such accounts are otherwise apt to become inflated by a carpenter employed to fix coat-rails or shelving, charging against that work time spent unhanging and easing doors.

(TELEPHONE MESSAGE) BRASH TO SPINLOVE

11.20   4.3.26.

B. notes you on site Monday. Hopes stay night. White tie. Phone. R.S.P.

Tell him *Yes*. J.S.   4.3.

O.K.   R.S.P.   4.10.   4.3.

Spinlove has begun to record and file telephone messages, as he ought to do—though not quite in this manner. We recognize in—R.S.P.—his assistant Pintle, whose style, even in these few words, also identifies him. He is an excruciating person and ought to be sacked, unless—as his toleration by Spinlove might suggest—he has on some occasion saved his master's life.

We noticed before that Spinlove had established intimate social relations with the Brashes and as Brash is precisely the sort of man who would be well aware of the disadvantage of this intimacy should his architect let him down; and as he is, besides, somewhat a self-important, unapproachable person, the thing is not exactly what one would expect.

GRIGBLAY TO SPINLOVE

Dear Sir,   4.3.26.

We have not overlooked that you wish our Statement as soon as possible, and we will press on with this work, which is in hand. In the meantime we shall be glad to receive a certificate, for, say, £3,500 on account. We may remind you that we sent you a rough approximate Statement on 31st January, which we think must have escaped your attention.

Yours faithfully,

THE DRAINS SUSPECTED

Dear Mr. Spinlove,

It is dreadfully close here, the house always smells stuffy and the drains must be *very* bad for I have tried disinfectant but it only makes it worse instead of better so something will have to be done or I am afraid we shall all be *affected!* There was a *horrid* smell the other day and I am sure it was the scullery sink or something and it might get into the larder though I told them always to keep it shut as tainted food is *not pleasant* and I am *most* particular even the dogs are not allowed to and it is *specially* at night though Leslie will not believe me.

How peaceful after all the stormy weather we have been having!
Thursday.   Yours sincerely,

Lady Brash complained of a bad smell on an earlier occasion before the house was finished. That, after some trouble, was found to be the pungent aroma of the new, untreated oak, which the lady did not like. Spinlove apparently did not answer this letter. He was, as we know, going to the house a day or two later.

SPINLOVE TO GRIGBLAY

Dear Sirs,   6.3.26.

Yes, I set aside your letter of 31st January, as the work was then not completed and you were not entitled to a certificate. The matter has since escaped my attention, and the Statement covered by your letter cannot be found in this office. I am at a loss to understand how you justify a certificate for £3,500, and shall be glad if you will let me have a copy of the missing Statement.

Yours faithfully,

A lame business! Spinlove seems to have put aside the Statement without looking at it, or he would have questioned it at the time.

SPINLOVE TO GRIGBLAY

Dear Sirs,   9.3.26.

I enclose specification for work in completing entrance road. I ought to have your estimate of the extra cost, as Sir Leslie wants to know this.

I am annoyed to find that wet gets into the chimneys and shows on the second-floor breasts. I could see nothing wrong with the listings, and Bloggs assures me the soakers were properly lapped and turned up—in fact, I saw the work being done. It is, therefore, evident that the water strikes through the cement and runs down behind the upturned edge of the soakers, and I learn from Bloggs that the cement was *not* waterproofed with Puddlyte. The listings will have to be replaced in Puddlyte cement as specified. The work should be put in hand at once, a small bit at a time, as weather allows; and care taken to keep tarpaulins rigged to prevent rain getting in.

Lady Brash tells me she finds the house "stuffy," and that she has not felt well since she went to live in it, and that two of the servants have been unwell. She suspects something is wrong with the drains. This is not possible, but, as a fact, did the District Surveyor test the whole of the drains and give you a formal certificate of acceptance of the sanitary work? If so, kindly send me the certificate by return.

Yours faithfully,

It seems that Spinlove employed lead soakers laid in with the tiles and turned up against the brickwork where roof slopes butt up against chimneys, but replaced the usual lead cover-flashings, turned into the brick joints and covering the upturned edges of the soakers, with cement fillets in the angle between tile and chimney-face. These "listings" are a perfectly sound, water-tight device, although they are associated with the tradition of humble buildings—rather than of important works of architecture. Spinlove, we remember, had several knowing ideas for a sham medieval roof which he could not get carried out; but he seems to have had his own way in this matter.

The Local Government Board's model bye-laws secure that all drains shall be planned on established scientific principles of sanitation, so that architects are relieved of the preoccupation of trying to save money by following ideas of their own, and inspections and tests by District Councils' Surveyors reduce—in practice though not in law—the architect's responsibility for seeing that the work is properly carried out. Spinlove's letter suggests that he is in need of evidence of this official approval to enforce the assurances he offered Lady Brash of the soundness of the drains. His urgency will be readily understood by those who read The Honeywood File. *If Lady Brash gets the idea into her head that something is wrong with the drains, nothing less than a course of hypodermic injections is likely ever to get it out again.*

GRIGBLAY TO SPINLOVE

Dear Sir, 10.3.26.

The whole of the drains were duly tested with water and the pipes with smoke by Mr. Gallop, the drain Inspector; and the whole were inspected on two occasions by the District Surveyor, Mr. Potch, whose certificate of approval we enclose. We are sure there

is nothing wrong as the work was done under the supervision of
Bloggs; and as Mr. Potch could not find fault with it no one else is
likely to be able to. [*This letter was evidently dictated by Grigblay.*]
As regards the listings, this is not in our opinion the best
method of flashing to chimneys; but we have no reason to think
that the work at Honeywood is defective, as it was carefully carried out to your instructions. We have respectfully to point out
that Puddlyte to listings was not, as you state, ordered by you.
Puddlyte cement is specified for bedding and jointing weathered
brick members only.

We do not know to what the damp in chimney-breasts is due,
but Mr. Grigblay expects to be that way on Friday and will take
the opportunity.

We have noted your provisional acceptance by telephone to-day
of our estimate of £64 12s. for remaking entrance road. We have
ordered the pitching and enclose details of our measurements and
rates on which our estimate is based for you to check.

Yours faithfully,

*Spinlove is making a muddle of things. He ought to have asked the
quantity surveyor what the approximate value of the work on entrance
road was and left it to be measured and valued at settling-up. Apparently he accepted Grigblay's estimate so that the work could be put in
hand, but subject to measurements being checked and rates agreeing
with the Contract Schedule. This, however, is a task for the quantity
surveyor, and in any case Spinlove had no business to learn what those
rates are, for the priced bills of quantities, which constitute the Contract
schedule, are properly kept under seal. A builder has a right to expect
that they will be so kept, as otherwise the architect is in a position to
vary the contract in the interests of his client, and unprofitably for the
builder, by substituting work for which the builder has included a low
price for that for which he has allowed a good one. Such a proceeding
by a building-owner is manifestly unfair and, by an architect, dishonest; for the architect is, by the terms of the contract, constituted arbiter
between client and builder.*

It is not usual for the District Sanitary Inspector to test with smoke, but he has the right to do so and there were reasons why Mr. Potch, the District Surveyor, should instruct him to so test at Honeywood.

SPINLOVE TO LADY BRASH

Dear Lady Brash,   11.3.26.

As I promised, I enclose the formal official certificate of the Local District Surveyor showing that the whole of the drains conform with the regulations of the Local Government Board and Public Health Acts; and that the pipes, both below and above ground, have been subjected to smoke and water tests; and that the whole of the work was approved as sound and to his satisfaction. I hope that this will entirely banish any doubts you may have. May I assure you that I have none whatever myself? As I told you, I personally overlooked the whole of the arrangements, and you may rest assured that everything is safe and sound. Even if a defect had developed in the drains since they were tested and passed, which is unbelievable, it could not by the remotest possibility lead, as you imagine, to contamination of the air in the house. With kind regards,

Yours sincerely,

P.S.—Will you please return the certificate when you have done with it?

Here we see our young friend making his old mistakes. In his anxiety to emphasize his assurances, he represents sanitary security as a very difficult and dangerous matter to arrange and a still more difficult matter to prove—which are the particular things he should have avoided. He also depicts himself as persuaded, only, of the purity of Honeywood: he does not, as he should, assert a fact, but reasons his conclusions although he knows that the person he addresses is incapable of reasoning and unable to weigh the evidence if she were. On the top of all this he actually admits the possibility of a defect and, without knowing what that defect may be, pledges his word that it cannot set up unsanitary conditions. It would probably have been better if he had left Brash to open the subject, as he would do were it more than a figment of his lady's imagination. Why the exasperating fellow cannot hold his tongue, after all he has suffered from unnecessarily wagging it, is beyond understanding. It is inconceivable that there can be anything wrong with the drains, but Spinlove has given his client reason to think it possible.

DEFECTS APPEAR

Sir,   12.3.26.

I looked in at Honeywood when I was passing to-day. You can take it from me that there is nothing wrong with the listings and, if there were, they would not let water into the flues to run down and lie in puddles on the back hearths of fireplaces as it has been doing. There had rightly ought to be a damp course across the chimney, and flue pipes in the stacks; for the rain drives across from the S.W. something cruel, and the proper thing to live in up at Honeywood is a submarine, but I can make all right with a bit of soap. The house is dry, but the water drives right through the 9 inch, that's certain, for the wall at the bottom of the hollow is soaked; but nothing is showing inside, though the maids were quack-quacking about a bit of sweating there which is only what you must expect in a new house. [*"Sweating" is here loosely and inexactly used by Grigblay to signify condensation.*]

The matter I am taking the liberty to write to you privately about is this New Novelty Super-Paint the old gentleman insisted I use and which is going to be a bit more of a novelty than he bargained for. The ripple is much more than it was, and is forming in ridges. Sir Leslie may think it looks pretty so, but he will change his mind when it begins to fold over on itself and break away in flakes—which is what comes next, for I found a place behind a radiator in the bathroom where it is doing a bit of private rehearsal. The worst place is on the wall of the kitchen where the furnace flue goes up behind. The maids have brushed it over and washed it down till there isn't any paint left, scarcely.

As you know, sir, I refused to take responsibility for Riddoppo and gave warning before the painters left the job that it would all have to come off again—except what came off of itself—and I hope you will bear it in mind, because when Riddoppo gets a move on and shows how super it knows how to be (and we shan't be long now) the dogs will begin to bark; and as I don't want to be bit, and you, I take it, don't want it either, and as I have perhaps had a little more experience of mix-ups of this kind than has happened to come your way, I take the liberty, with all respect to your superior judgment, of dropping you a friendly hint—which is just to take no kind of notice; and if the old gentleman says anything or makes any complaint, to hold out that the paint is no concern of yours any more than it is mine, for I understand you objected to Riddoppo and only carried out instructions in passing on Sir Leslie's orders to me. Please be very careful, sir, what letters you write to Sir Leslie; and do not write any if avoidable, for lawyers are wonderful fellows at proving words mean the opposite to what they do.

I hope no harm done by me addressing you, but thought best, as I am afraid there is trouble ahead.

I am, sir,

Yours faithfully,

For a builder to write such a letter to an architect is most unusual, although the understanding established between Grigblay—a builder ripe in years and experience—and Spinlove—an architect mature in neither—would render it easy for Grigblay to make the same communication in conversation; for Grigblay's individuality is masterful, and Spinlove, although he has great tenacity and can show spirit on occasion, impresses us as lacking personal force. Grigblay has, however, formed the habit of dissipating the evening preoccupations of his active mind in well-purposed letters to Spinlove, which, though intimate and fatherly in tone, are perfectly respectful, and that is all there is to say about it. It is necessary to call attention to the oddness of the circumstance, or an experience few architects are ever likely to have might be supposed usual.

The meaning of the letter is that Grigblay, in visiting the house, is reminded of the imminent failure of the inside paint work; and that he is uneasy. Apparently, he feels that his original disclaimer, and Brash's acceptance, of responsibility for Riddoppo, does not perfectly secure him; and he is afraid that Spinlove may be led, by characteristic exuberances, to countenance an interpretation of the facts prejudicial to Grigblay's position. Spinlove, of course, cannot by anything he may write or say commit Grigblay, but he may readily mislead Brash as to what Grigblay's obligations are, and thus foment contest.

FIRST NEWS OF EXTRAS

GRIGBLAY TO SPINLOVE

Dear Sir,   12.3.26.
Our estimate for certificate is as follows:

Amount of contract. . . . . £ 18,440
Less 5 per cent retention. . . . . £   922
Received on a/c . . . . £ 15,500

                                                             £ 16,422

                                                             £ 2,018
Add balance variations account, say . . . . £ 1,500

                                                             £ 3,518

We shall be glad to receive your certificate as this matter has
been standing over some time.

                                                    Yours faithfully,

*On completion of the work to the architect's satisfaction—an event
which befell on 10th February—the retention of 10 per cent of the value
of work done was reduced, under the terms of the contract, to a 5 per
cent security for the builder's performance of his covenant to make good
defects appearing within nine months. Grigblay was at any time entitled
to require the value of extra work to be included in the computation of
Spinlove's certificates, but does not appear to have asked for it.*

GRIGBLAY TO SPINLOVE

Dear Sir,   13.3.26.

Mr. Grigblay visited Honeywood yesterday and is of opinion that the damp on chimney-breasts is due to rain driving into the brickwork of the chimney. It also drives through the parging into the flues which may account for complaints made to Bloggs of the flues not drawing. We think that the trouble can be cured by treating the face of the brickwork with soap, unless you prefer application of some special waterproofing. If you will let us know what you wish we will estimate cost of same.

Yours faithfully,

Grigblay's proposal to supply an estimate is intended to make it clear to Spinlove what he is slow to discern for himself, namely, that the architect, and not the builder, is responsible for the architect's mistakes. Having regard to the exposed situation and the extreme, though not exceptional, porosity of the facing bricks, Spinlove ought, as Grigblay says, to have put dampcourses through the stacks and piped the flues. He will, no doubt, on the next occasion when a similar conjuntion of circumstances arises, benefit by this experience; but it was no part of the builder's duty to foresee the trouble: a builder has preoccupations enough without thinking for the architect; and though he would, for his own credit and in a spirit of collaboration, warn the architect when he saw dangers ahead, he may have learnt that such interferences are not always welcomed and that when they are, and the precaution proves ineffective or for any reason is afterwards regretted, the trouble he puts himself to lands him in trouble he could do without.

Perhaps this is Spinlove's first experience of building with sand-faced bricks in an exposed position. In that case he will have good reason to appreciate the device of the hollow wall which he has apparently carried out with exact care. If the ties binding the 4½-in. inner wall to the 9-in. outer wall were not of a particular pattern, the rain, which Grigblay discerned to stream down the inside of the outer wall when driven by heavy wind, would creep across to the inner, and if the clearing-battens, hung in the space between the walls when the bricks were being laid, had not been carefully maintained, droppings of mortar would have lodged on these ties with the same result. If, also, Spinlove had neglected to carry the hollow space down through the damp-course which stops water rising from the ground into the wall, or had mortar droppings been allowed to accumulate at the bottom of the hollow, the water flowing down the inner face of the outer wall would have soaked across into the lower part of the inner wall. We gather that none of these things has happened, for it is evident that the south front of Honeywood Grange is being severely tested and Grigblay noticed nothing wrong. How severe that test may be in an exposed situation is only fully known to architects of experience.

Rain will drive right through a 14-in. wall of London Stocks laid in lime mortar faced with the best sand-faced, hand-thrown bricks, and run from the under side of concrete lintels over window openings so as to collect in pools on the floor. It will penetrate 9-in. walls of impervious Fletton bricks laid in hydraulic mortar and cement stuccoed in two coats. It will even make a 14-in. wall, similarly stuccoed, so damp as to recommend renewal of the cement stucco with special waterproofed rendering. Stone and concrete walls present their special problems, but it will be seen that Spinlove has done well in dealing with a brick one, and in securing, under thoroughly bad conditions, that his client has a dry house.

(PERSONAL) SPINLOVE TO GRIGBLAY

Dear Mr. Grigblay,   13.3.26.

I have duly received your letter. I am aware that you always objected to the use of Riddoppo, and I also advised against it so that Sir Leslie cannot very well hold us responsible. I certainly should say nothing on the subject unless Sir Leslie himself raised it.

I note what you say of wet in the chimney, and have written instructions to-day.

Yours truly,

The tone of this letter suggests that Spinlove resents the implication that he needs guidance, so that it is a pity his attempt to show he is not such a fool as Grigblay thinks should make it clear that he is a much bigger one. The issue does not, as Spinlove implies, turn upon Brash's holding the architect and the builder accountable, but upon whether the facts make them legally responsible; and if Spinlove is going to address himself to the subject as though the point were open and debatable, he will be certain to prejudice his own and Grigblay's positions exactly as Grigblay fears, and lead Brash on to make claims which, though they may be untenable, will be likely to embroil everyone in the distresses preliminary to litigation. It will also be noticed that Spinlove brackets himself with Grigblay as though they were in the same boat. They are not. Their responsibilities are different.

SPINLOVE TO GRIGBLAY

Dear Sir,   13.3.26.
    I note that the damp in chimney-breasts is due to rain driving into the stacks, and shall be glad if you will treat the whole of the brickwork of all chimneys above roof with two coats of "Dessikex" damp-proofing, applied as directed by the manufacturers. I prefer this to treatment with soap. The work should be put in hand at once.

Yours faithfully,

A pound of soft soap in a bucket of boiling water, allowed to stand overnight and sprayed freely on to brickwork with a garden syringe, is a reliable damp-proofing which Grigblay seems to have confidence in; and soft soap is also effective in waterproofing mortar or concrete with which it is mixed. As Grigblay has had great experience of wet walls and Spinlove very little, it would be wise for Spinlove to use what Grigblay has practical experience of, rather than what recommends itself to him by report or by advertisement. There are proprietary remedies for damp walls, of proved worth; but the yearly increase in their numbers is rather a sign of the obstinacy of the complaint than of the efficacy of the cures.

SPINLOVE TO GRIGBLAY

Dear Sir,   15.3.26.

I do not understand why there has been such delay in rendering your final Statement of Account. You now send me a summary showing extras £1,500. 1 was totally unprepared for this, and can only suppose there is some mistake. Have you taken the provision for contingencies into account, and the saving on the provision for well-sinking and pump, for instance? A considerable part of the variations will come into a measured account which the quantity surveyor must deal with; and the value of that work has still to be ascertained. I shall be glad to have a rough summary of the variations account on which you base your claim. I must prepare Sir Leslie Brash for what is ahead as I am sure he has no idea that extras have mounted up in this way, and I have no knowledge of their ever having been ordered.

I enclose certificate for £2,500, which is as much as I feel entitled to certify at this time.

Yours faithfully,

We have no doubt that Grigblay's estimate of extras is right, and when Spinlove says he is totally unprepared for such a figure he only tells us what we expected to hear. It is not surprising that he should lose touch with the account, as his careful contract arrangements were upset in various ways for which he was not responsible, but he ought to have been prepared for a heavy bill, and with greater experience he would have been. He might also have found opportunities to let his client know what was happening, but it is doubtful whether experience would have prompted him to do so. When the interferences of the client, or adventitious circumstances, make hay of the careful safeguards of the Conditions of Contract and of the detailed forethought of the drawings and specification, the whole position gets out of hand for the architect; and if the building-owner, after being warned (as Spinlove warned Brash) of the results of interferences and alterations, persists in following his own devices, his architect cannot, without risk of impertinence, make any gesture of checking him.

SPINLOVE TO BRASH

Dear Sir Leslie Brash,   15.3.26.

Mr. Grigblay has asked for a further certificate on account. This was due to him, on completion of the work, in February. I find he is entitled to the sum of £2,500, and have to-day sent him a certificate for that amount. This makes the total of certificates £18,000. The contract amount, as you know, is £18,440, but there will be the cost of extra work—garage, alteration to kitchen and other variations and additions and so forth—to add, which will, I am afraid, run into several hundred pounds. I am pressing the builder for his Statement of Account giving particulars of these extras.

Yours sincerely,

P.S.—As this money was due to Mr. Grigblay more than a month ago, he will probably be glad of a cheque at once.

Spinlove's ideas of administering the gilded pill are raw, but promising. A degree of tact which may appear excessive is allowable on these painful occasions. The owner has to be informed of—and reconciled to paying—a bill of extras for which he is unprepared, and the easier the gradations by which the revolting intelligence is imparted to him, the happier for him, the happier for the builder, and the happier also for the architect, whose forethought for his employer's peace of mind is not unusually prompted by a care for his own.

Spinlove's postscript is due to Brash's habit, in the past, of holding back payments to the builder to the extreme limit allowed by the contract.

(CONFIDENTIAL) GRIGBLAY TO SPINLOVE

Dear Sir,   15.3.26.

In reply to your favour I take the liberty of writing to make clear, as there seems to be some confusion on the matter, that I painted with Riddoppo only on your statement that those were the orders of Sir Leslie Brash, and that he accepted responsibility for same; and I ask you to bear that fact in mind, as it is the position I take and hold to. I ought to have refused to touch the stuff, but I wished to oblige Sir Leslie so far as I was able; and as he would not take my advice he must settle the matter with the man whose advice he did take instead—and that, I suppose, is himself.

I write very frank and open, sir, because this is a serious matter for someone, if it isn't for me. It's not going to cost a hundred pounds, nor two hundred, nor yet three, with the cleaning of the stuff off the walls and joinery and the loss of going to a hotel—for they can't be expected to live in the house all those weeks it will be before the work is done. Therefore, I ask you, let Sir Leslie clearly understand that I have nothing more to say on this matter, as it will save a bit of trouble and be the best for everyone, including,

Yours truly,

This was evidently dictated by Grigblay.

GRIGBLAY TO SPINLOVE

Dear Sir,   16.3.26.

We have to acknowledge certificate for £2,500, which we have sent on to Sir Leslie Brash, and hope we shall receive his cheque per return, as it is a long time since we had anything on account and we were entitled to 40 per cent more than this six weeks ago, which please note and oblige.

Yours faithfully,

This letter is curt to the point of being threatening. We have already seen that although Grigblay is lavish of good offices and kindly forethought, he is impatient of sloppiness. All he says is perfectly just, and Spinlove deserves to be told it. It is the architect's duty to see that the builder, as well as the client, gets his dues. Spinlove has shown no consciousness of his remissness in holding back the certificate for so long, and has not in any adequate way apologized to Grigblay for so disoblig-

ing him. He is, further, not entitled to withhold £1,000 on the plea of his
ignorance of the state of the account. It is his duty to inform himself.

BRASH TO SPINLOVE

Dear Mr. Spinlove, 18.3.26.
I have duly received your communication anent certificate and
will arrange for cheque to be transmitted in due course. I cannot,
however, accept responsibility for Mr. Grigblay's neglect to present his claim at an earlier date. I apprehend with satisfaction that
these payments are now drawing to a final termination, but I am
considerably astonished at your off-hand—if you will pardon the
expression—intimation of additional extras running into the total
amount of *several hundreds of pounds.* I am aware that accumulated
additional extras have accrued, but the exact anticipated total of
my eventual liability is a matter of more importance to me than
you appear to divine; and though a matter of half a dozen hundred
pounds one way or the other may seem of insignificant importance
to you, it is, I may inform you, of *considerable importance to me.*

I desire that you will be so good as to ascertain the exact figure forthwith and also clearly intimate to Mr. Grigblay that the
accountancy is in your hands and that I am not prepared to acqui-
esce any inflated extortions. Surely it is not at Mr. Grigblay 's discretion to decide what additional extras he shall demand?

I have re-perused your communication to Lady Brash anent
the surveyor's certificate of sanitary efficiency, a second time. Are
you *confident* in your conviction that our sanitary provisions are
entirely without blemish? In the concluding passage terminating
your letter you surmise the possibility of a defect in the arrangements having eventuated *subsequently* to the previous tests. This I
apprehend to be a matter for further imperative investigation.

Yours sincerely,

Brash's avoidance of the low word "drain" marks a refinement that
is rare.

(PRIVATE) SPINLOVE TO GRIGBLAY

Dear Mr Grigblay,   18.3.26.

I perfectly understand the position you take and it has my approval, I shall myself most certainly refuse to accept responsibility for Riddoppo.

Yours truly,

Spinlove's assurance will further increase Grigblay's doubts. The disparity may be subtle but it is vital. The point is not what Grigblay may in future take, but what his position, in fact, now is. Spinlove's approval or disapproval cannot alter those facts, and Grigblay is in no way concerned with it. It is clear, also, that Spinlove does not appreciate his own position, and Grigblay can have little confidence that he will not allow Brash to believe he has a claim against both of them.

SPINLOVE TO BRASH

Dear Sir Leslie Brash,   20.3.26.

The delay with the certificate was not Mr. Grigblay's fault. He made his claim before the money was due, and in setting that matter aside I overlooked it. I should be obliged, therefore, if you will regard the certificate as dated 10th February, which is the day it fell due.

I cannot yet say what the total of the account is, as much detailed measuring and pricing, and checking of the daywork accounts and merchants' vouchers, etc., is necessary in order to arrive at it. Grigblay will duly render a Statement of Account which it will be necessary for me to check and certify. The actual "accountancy"—as you term it—will be done by the quantity surveyor, who ranks as auditor in ascertaining the exact sums due in respect of work which I find to be properly authenticated as extras. I shall hope, however, to be able to give you an approximate figure in the course of a week or two.

I can assure you that the drains are all right. It is inconceivable that they have developed any defects since they were tested.

I have discovered the cause of damp above the attic fireplaces, and have told Grigblay to put this right at once.

Yours sincerely,

P.S.—Will you please return the surveyor's certificate?

Spinlove has laid out the mechanism of settling builders' accounts, so that Brash will have a right idea of it, quite neatly.

He is, however, too emphatic in his pride of drain. The development of defects in Honeywood drains is not inconceivable. We heard of a clay subsoil at the time the cellars were dug, and the movements of clay in response to changes of temperature and humidity may lead to early cracking of cement pipe-joints such as would cause failure under the water test; and the heavy lorries already referred to may have done similar damage. Such defects, however, do not ordinarily lead to insanitary drainage, as the conditions of the tests, which exact perfection, do not arise in use; and if by accident they did arise, the amount of pollution of the subsoil would be insignificant.

GRIGBLAY TO SPINLOVE

Dear Sir,   22.3.26.

We note your instructions *re* waterproofing to chimneys. Our price for this work, which includes the necessary ladders and scaffolding, is £42 12s. We will use "Dessikex" if you wish, but we happen to know what this stuff is made of, and we should prefer to apply two coats of either Sorrellming or Flutate, both of which are colourless and can, in our experience, be relied on. The work, however, cannot be put in hand till the summer as, whatever we use, the brickwork must be quite dry and ought to be warm when the application is made.

Yours faithfully,

BRASH ON DRAINS

Dear Mr. Spinlove, 24.3.26.

I am gratified to know that the cause of damp in the domestics' domain has been ascertained and that immediate renovations will at once be accomplished; and I have noted your arrangements for checking Mr. Grigblay's charges.

I am however, unpleasantly disconcerted by your reference to the question of the sanitary purity of Honeywood, which is—if you will pardon me for so expressing myself—somewhat peremptory and offhand. Of course, where domestic effluents are concerned, obnoxious exhalations are in a limited degree unavoidably to be anticipated, and I should be the last person unnecessarily discriminating in such a matter; but where delicate ladies are concerned—and Lady Brash's mucous membrane is peculiarly sensitive to olfactory aggression—[*we were told something like this once before*]—it is most desirably expedient that the odoriferous emanations of which I speak—and which I need not more particularly define—should be limited to the exterior atmosphere, and not permitted to invade the interior of the domicile. Lady Brash increasingly complains that Honeywood is a stuffy house, and one of our domestic staff—the cook, to be precise—has described her sleeping quarters as "fuggy"—I use the word as reported to me, and may therefore repeat the expression without apology. I also understand that whiffs of a repul-

sive nature are from time to time encountered in various parts of
the house, but though Lady Brash has on a number of occasions
hurried me to the seat of an unsavoury effluvium newly discovered, I have not yet been so fortunate as to arrive on the scene
of offence before dissipation has eventuated; and accordingly I
am not, I regret to say, in a position to indicate a precise description of the quality of the various noxious emanations which are
proving incompatible with Lady Brash's *joie de vivre* and, I fear,
prejudicial to her good health. I anticipate, however, that I have,
in this lengthy communication, sufficiently indicated the serious-
ness of the situation, and I shall be gratified to be informed that
its prompt amelioration has your immediate attention.

Yours sincerely,

*This letter suggests that it is not the drains that require the attentions
of an expert, but Lady Brash. We must feel sorry for the poor woman, but
this need not prevent us from being far more sorry for Spinlove.*

SPINLOVE TO BRASH

Dear Sir Leslie Brash,   26.3.26.

I was naturally disturbed by the contents of your letter, but
after reading it attentively more than once I cannot help feeling
that the case is not so bad as you think, for I am convinced that the
drainage system at Honeywood, both inside the house and out,
is perfectly sound; and if it were conceivable that anything had
gone wrong it could not possibly give rise to such a state of affairs
as you describe. It is incredible that the house can be "stuffy" or
"fuggy" except for reasons which may give rise to that condition
in any house—such as overheating of radiators, accumulations of
dust, dirty carpets, lack of ventilation, etc.

I will, of course, give the matter my particular attention and
do my best to discover the reason for the complaint, but I shall
not be able to spare a day before the end of next week. In the
meantime perhaps you will be able to find the true source of the

unpleasant conditions, which certainly can have no connection with drainage.

With kind regards,

Yours sincerely,

Spinlove is not happy in the wording of the sentence in which he seeks to discredit the idea that the house can be stuffy.

SPINLOVE TO GRIGBLAY

Dear Sirs,   26.3.26.
I enclose a letter I have received from Sir Leslie Brash. I have had previous complaints of smells in the house. As I cannot go down for a fortnight, and have no time to waste, and you have work going on in the neighbourhood, I will ask Mr. Grigblay to take an early opportunity of calling at Honeywood and to let me know what he makes of it all. Perhaps he will be able to see Lady Brash and establish her peace of mind, which I have, unfortunately, not been able to do. You will remember there was the same kind of trouble over the smell of the new oak when the house was being built. They may have been overstoking and keeping the radiators too hot.

I note that waterproofing of chimneys will have to stand over till the summer.

I still have not yet received your summary of variations account.

Yours faithfully,

The stuffy, close, stale air associated with radiators is due to the hot iron causing the paint on it, and on adjoining surfaces, to smell until it has thoroughly dried up, which, in the case of oily paints, takes some time; and also to the rising currents of heated air carrying up dust particles. There is, rightly speaking, no such thing as "scorched air," though the term is sometimes used as an explanation of these unpleasant associations of radiators. Radiators, however, only in part warm by radia-

*tion; a great part of their heat is disseminated by convection, and the
repeated circulation of the same air against the heated iron dries it and
vitiates it. Many heating systems by hot-water radiators are enervating
and dispiriting to live with. These conditions are much aggravated when
the radiators are allowed to get above a certain temperature, and are
remedied by good ventilation.*

BRASH TO SPINLOVE

Dear Mr. Spinlove,   30.3.26.

Your communication encourages optimistic anticipations,
though you must allow me to intimate the suggestion that it is not
reasonably consistent with what you previously indited to Lady
Brash. You must permit me, however, to object most strongly to
the astounding suggestion that the conditions I complain of are
due to improper neglect of cleanliness at Honeywood. The house,
I must beg permission to inform you, is not unventilated, dusty
and dirty, and I am amazed that one from whom I have learnt to
anticipate polite behaviour on all occasions should so far forget
decorum as to offer any such monstrous explanatory solution of
the matter in complaint.

That the house is stuffy, and impregnated with obnoxious effluviums of some kind, there is abundant evidence to substantially
prove. The source of the annoyance, which is a danger to health,
is for you to definitely determine, and for Mr. Grigblay to cura-
tively ameliorate without delay.

Yours sincerely,

SPINLOVE TO BRASH

Dear Sir Leslie Brash,   2.4.26.

I assure you that you entirely misread my letter. I admit that
my wording was ambiguous, but I had no intention of suggesting
what you suppose. My argument was that a defect in the drains
could not possibly give rise to the conditions you describe; that

those conditions were such as would be occasioned by overheated radiators, dust, lack of ventilation and so forth and that—as you knew these conditions did not exist at Honeywood—the explanation *must lie in some other direction.* That is all I meant to say. It never entered my head that you would suppose I could mean that Honeywood was in such a condition; and *if* I had supposed it *was,* I should, of course, have been careful not to let you think I thought so. Please accept the will for the deed. [*The finishing touch!*]

I do not know what more I can say until I come down to investigate for myself. That cannot, however, be immediately, as I have to go out of town on business, but I will get in touch with you as soon as I can next week.

With kind regards,
Yours sincerely,

This letter is a wretched performance. Spinlove not only says a great deal too much, but makes it appear that his offending letter was written in the belief that his explanation of the "noxious emanations" was the true one. He then indicates that he does not consider the matter of any pressing importance, and by making plain, with characteristic tenacity, that he regards the whole thing as a mare's nest, he returns, like a fly, to the bald place from which Brash has just driven him.

GRIGBLAY ON DRAINS

Sir, 6.4.26.

I had a chance yesterday and called at the house to examine into all these effluviums and emanations and other polite stinks that are going about, but can make nothing of it. Every house in my opinion has its own smells, different in different houses, if you sit down and wait for them. There were only two real Oh Mys at Honeywood on Tuesday: one was Lysol—and the other was her Ladyship who was carrying so much scent that though I have as good a nose as most it had ought to be forty feet long to reach anything else when the lady was by. She had such a lot of things to tell me, too, that it was difficult to find out anything for myself. The plumbing everywhere is a picture to see; there never was a better job. Rumble was on it, and he's a craftsman if there ever was one: it's a pleasure to look at his wiped joints. No spigotting anywhere, you may be sure; no rubber cones.; solid lead tacks wiped on front angles and screwed and plugged; all joints between lead and iron or stoneware made with brass thimbles— beautiful; but you know all about it, sir, having ordered and saw the work being done.

All I could get at was that the bedrooms smelt funny, and the scullery—and why wouldn't that smell, I should like to know? There was an intelligent young girl there who had taught herself how to pull the cobweb grating out of the wash-up, and there she was with a bit of telegraph wire with a sharp burred end to go pushing into the trap when it gets blocked every half hour and cut a hole in the lead before anyone has time to discover what a clearing eye is for. They had hung up this grating. and the key of the back door, so that they shouldn't be wasted, to keep the clock going, because the weight had been lost plumbing the rain-water well.

There was talk that a smell came in at the window; so I told this same slut if you don't like stinks you shouldn't make them, for she had the grease-trap outside all clogged and mucked up with kitchen filth, the container not having been emptied all the time they've been there—nor never would be if I hadn't noticed. The gully by the back entrance was flooding over. They had taken the grating out and broke it with a sledge-hammer in case someone should remember what it was for, so as to make it easy to pour down the water they wash the floors with without the trouble of taking scrubbing-brushes and clouts out of the bucket first. That was what Jossling found stopping the trap when I told him get it cleared, along with a vacuum-cleaner fitting and a few other trifles that wouldn't be missed. That is all I could find wrong with the drains; but it's none of her business, says cook, and the chauffeur says it is none of his, so there you are, and we shall have more complaints before long unless Sir Leslie is told what is going on.

As for the smell in the bedrooms it is difficult to say. The cook had a lot of complaint and said it gave her asthma. It will give you measles, I told her, before ever it will give you asthma, and I think she feels more contented now; but there certainly was a close, stuffy smell in the fifth room on the second floor, in particular, though it had never been used; and my opinion is that smoky air from outside is drawn down the chimneys by the pull of other flues, or perhaps it's down-draught. These damp flues where the rain beats into them would be likely to lead to that kind of trouble.

There was a close air in three other of the maids' rooms that was not accounted for by the windows being shut, nor yet by two towels and a newspaper pushed into the chimney-throat of one of them to plug it in case of ventilation. Her Ladyship says her own room on the first floor is very stuffy; I could not notice anything, but, there you are! I am not in the perfumery myself, and a musk-rat or a civet-cat or whatever it is, spiced up with a touch of Lysol—which is about in saucers and everywhere it has no occasion to be—smells to me after half an hour pretty much like badger. Her Ladyship uses the Lysol so she won't notice the drains, and the scent so she won't notice the Lysol, which is a queer way to go to work if you ask my opinion.

However, I told the lady I could find nothing wrong except perhaps some down-draught in the chimneys, and that everything would be all right in the summer. She seemed satisfied and was very grateful and friendly and had lunch specially served to me though it was early; so I hope we shall have no more old tommy-rot about the drains.

I am sir,

Yours faithfully,

The erratic script of this letter, conjoined with Grigblay's authentic voice, indicates that he typed it himself. We may well suppose that, if persuasion of any kind could do so, Grigblay's massive resources consoled Lady Brash. Grigblay, however, here definitely oversteps the mark. He takes a great deal too much on himself: he involves Spinlove in a kind of disloyalty to his client, and the extreme intimacy of his facetiousness is subversive of discipline and, definitely, not allowable, but—as Grigblay would say—"there you are!" Spinlove has allowed himself to look to Grigblay for direction in a degree which a more substantial individuality would not tolerate.

SPINLOVE TO GRIGBLAY

Dear Sirs,   10.4.26.

I am much obliged for Mr. Grigblay's report on drains, etc. Things are very much as I supposed. I have written to Sir Leslie Brash calling attention to his servants' neglect, and have no doubt the complaint of bad smells is now disposed of. Please fix the sink grids. I do not understand how that in the scullery could be taken out.

Will you let me have your final Statement of Account without further delay? I have several times asked for this.

Yours faithfully,

SPINLOVE TO BRASH

Dear Sir Leslie Brash,   10.4.26.

I came back to the office to-day to find awaiting me there a letter from Mr. Grigblay who, in my absence and at my orders, made a thorough investigation into the cause of the smells complained of, as no doubt you may have heard. He finds the "closeness" of the bedrooms to be due to the windows being kept shut, and also, perhaps, to slight down-draught carrying smoky air down the chimneys. This is due to the stacks being damp, and will disappear when the summer comes. The chimney-throat in one of the servants' rooms was found to be stopped up. This should be discouraged, as the flues ought to be open to ventilate the rooms.

Mr. Grigblay, however, found a most insanitary state of affairs, productive of bad smells, in the scullery; due, not to any fault in the drainage arrangements or defect in the work, but to the neglect and deliberate ill-usage of the appliances provided, by your servants. The grating of the sink waste has been mischievously forced out so that the trap gets choked with filth; and this is cleared by violently ramming a steel wire down and damaging the pipe, instead of removing the screwed eye provided to make such ill-usage unnecessary. Then the grease-trap into which the sinks discharge has never been once emptied; and as a consequence the whole thing is clogged with congealed fat and stinking filth. This allows grease to get into the drain which it is the special purpose of the device to prevent. The iron receptacle in the gully should be lifted out and emptied once a week. In addition to this, the gully by the yard entrance has had its grid removed and deliberately broken, and a scrubbing brush and floor clouts and other things had been thrown into the drain, stopping the trap and flooding the yard with sewage.

I was certain, as I told you, that there could be nothing wrong with the drains, and Mr. Grigblay's report is very much what I expected. If the servants are told to use the fittings and arrangements as they are intended to be used, the smells you complain of will cease.

I am very glad to be able to give you this definite assurance. With kind regards,

Yours sincerely,

Spinlove so stresses the facts as to overweight them; and it is not tactful in him to triumph over Brash with cock-crows of "I told you so," and to remind him of his fault by rubbing his nose in it: nor is it tactful in him to appear enormously relieved in being able to give the explanation; for great relief can only be a reaction from great anxiety, and Brash will suppose Spinlove to be concerned for Honeywood's drains, when it is Honeywood's brains that are worrying him. This drain-trouble appears to be entirely of Spinlove's making. If he had written the brief, compact letters of a confident man, instead of the diffuse ones of a man anxious to appear plausible, Brash would have been fortified against his wife's complainings, and the lady, perhaps, herself assured. He is wrong in supposing that emphasis carries conviction; the opposite is true. "I saw Jones at Brighton" is more conclusive that Jones was there than: 'I am certain I saw Jones at Brighton," and much more so than: "I am absolutely positive . . ."; and it is only fatuous writers of advertisements who suppose otherwise.

BRASH TO SPINLOVE

Dear Mr. Spinlove,   13.4.26.

I am astonished to be informed of the improper neglect to observe sanitary amenities on the part of the kitchen staff, and have emphatically directed that it shall cease forthwith. it is scarcely necessary for me to signify that it is not incumbent upon me, as master, to keep myself personally acquainted with the conditions obtaining in the purlieus of the establishment; but I have now expressed my disapproval of past procedure in suitable terms to the person I hold to be responsible, and I confidently anticipate that no repetition of the previous objectionable circumstances will be repeated in the future.

You must permit me to express, however, that I fail to see how irregularities in the culinary domain can account for consequent olfactory intrusions in the sleeping quarters; nor do I comprehend in what way a down-draught in the chimneys can be applicable to the question of sanitary purity. I desire, therefore, that you will transmit Mr. Grigblay's report anent the matter of which I am speaking, so that I may be enabled to acquaint myself with the signification of your communication in more exact detail.

Yours sincerely,

If Brash saw Grigblay's letter the fat would, indeed, be in the fire!—which is proof that Spinlove should not allow such letters to be addressed to him. An architect should be able at any moment to lay all correspondence dealing with his client's business freely before him—in fact, the client has right of access to such correspondence, and also to possession of the whole of it after the work is completed. This follows necessarily from the relation of Agent and Principal which subsists between them. It is clear that Spinlove cannot do what Brash asks, and, even if there were no other reasons, Grigblay's letter, though it is not so marked, is clearly a private or confidential letter.

MORE NEWS OF EXTRAS

Dear Sir,   14.4.26.

We have been pressing on with our Statement of Account as you ask, and are arranging with Mr. Tinge to meet us for the purpose of measuring variations. We find that the total balance of extras on the variations account will be in the neighbourbood of £1,800 and shall be glad if you will pass us a further certificate for £1,000.

Yours faithfully,

Dear Sir,   16.4.26.

I am astonished to learn that your account will show extras to the amount of perhaps over £1,800. I was quite unprepared for anything of the kind, and I am sure Sir Leslie Brash will be shocked at the figure. I certainly have not authorized extras on any such scale, and have no idea how the figure is made up. I must have a summary of items, showing how the amount is arrived at, before I can consider drawing a further certificate.

Mr. Tinge has no authority to measure any work except as I may direct, and it is necessary for me to have the summary before I can do this.

Yours faithfully,

SPINLOVE TO TINGE, QUANTITY SURVEYOR

Dear Mr. Tinge,   16.4.26.
Grigblay is preparing his final Statement of Account. Will you
please note, however, that no work is to be measured except as I
may direct, as I have reasons to fear that the account is inflated
with unauthorized extras? I have asked Grigblay for particulars of
the work to be measured, and will let you know what is wanted
in due course.

Yours truly,

*Spinlove's arrangements are good, though his manners to Grigblay
are not. The measuring of work by the quantity surveyor, or even by the
architect, does not establish an authorized extra, but it certainly supports a claim for one. The quantity surveyor, also, has to be paid for the
work he does in fees that are added to the account, so that it is the architect's duty to see that no other measuring is done than the needs justify.
Extras often consist in differences between the value of work specified in
the contract and the same work as carried out, and as the only way to
arrive at this difference is to measure and value the whole of the work
replaced together with that which replaces it, and strike a balance, it
might happen that the surveyor's fees for measuring and pricing £2,500
of work twice over is tacked on to a resulting extra (or omission) of only
£50. For this reason it is sometimes expedient for an architect to agree a
figure with the builder. On the other hand, the builder will be inclined to
charge as day work (time and material) extra work which ought in the
interests of the client to be measured and priced at the contract rates, or
at rates commensurate therewith.*

FURTHER DEFECTS

Dear Mr. Spinlove,   19.4.26.

May I be permitted to remind you that you have omitted to transmit Mr. Grigblay's report on the odoriferous effusions which, I regret to say, still persist?

We continue to be delighted with the house, which will be quite perfect when sanitary amenities have been safeguarded, but we have observed various slight defective flaws in the building work. These are not so far imperatively serious, but need preliminary attention. Dripping taps can speedily be renovated, I conceive, also little cracks in the plaster ceilings which may otherwise increase. Stains in the wallpapers are, I fear, a more serious apprehension. There are openings in the woodwork, specially in the overmantels to fireplaces in the first story, and *most alarming gaping cracks* in the exterior oak window frames, particularly on the outside. Steps should at once be taken to prevent these cracks increasing in dimensions. Some are several inches in length, and in breadth wide enough for me to almost insert the terminal edge of a sixpence. I have prepared and transmit under this cover, for your convenient guidance, a scheduled list of the defects I have noticed as obtaining; but your trained eye will no doubt have no difficulty in discerning others.

With regard to the Riddoppo, this has a delightful lustrous appearance, and its variegations of different tints is charming, but it leaves stains where the under bottoms of doors rub over the carpets, which will only imperfectly brush out; and it has failed, I am informed, near the range in the kitchen. Mr. Grigblay should be notified

Yours sincerely,

Brash's "scheduled list" is missing from the file, but if it is fairly represented in the above letter, the "defective flaws" are nothing to complain about (so far) except, of course, Riddoppo. Brash has not realized what is happening to his new novelty super-paint.

(PERSONAL) SPINLOVE TO GRIGBLAY

Dear Mr. Grigblay,   20.4.26.
I reported to Sir Leslie the substance of your letter describing your investigation of supposed smells, and he has since twice asked for a verbatim copy of your letter. I cannot possibly send it him—besides, it is a private letter—so will you let me have a version suitable for sending to Sir Leslie? I enclose the original in case you should not have kept a copy.

Yours truly,

Spinlove is unwise in allowing Grigblay to write to him confidentially, but more unwise in his method of disguising the fact. He has a frank, straightforward nature; slyness is foreign to him, and must be distasteful. He could perfectly well have replied to Brash: "Grigblay reports as follows. He says . . ." and completed an accurate paraphrase in that form. If Brash were so obtuse as to press for the original, he could be told it was a private letter.

SPINLOVE TO BRASH

Dear Sir Leslie Brash,   20.4.26.
The blemishes of which you send me a list are only what appear in all new houses, and do not point to serious defects.

Grigblay will do all necessary restoration, but this will be in six months' time when such defects as there may be have fully developed. Of course, if anything goes wrong he will send down and put it right, but it appears that nothing has. Certain sulphates or other exudations appearing on the face of new plaster kill the colour in wall-papers, which is why I recommended only tinted lining papers designed to serve as a foundation for the better papers you may afterwards decide to hang. The cracks in the oak frames are of no consequence. They are characteristic of English oak.

Yours sincerely,

P.S.—I will send you copy of Mr. Grigblay's letter tomorrow.

This pretence of an afterthought in order to gain time is regrettable: thus does one deceit involve others. Spinlove's comments are well-informed, but by omitting all reference to Riddoppo and thus including its failure with defects that are "not serious," he may be applying Grigblay's advice to "take no notice" too drastically.

GRIGBLAY TO SPINLOVE

Dear Sir,   22.4.26.
     We enclose report for Sir Leslie Brash, and return original of Mr. Grigblay's letter.

Yours faithfully,

(HOLOGRAPH) GRIGBLAY TO SPINLOVE

Dear Sir,   6.4.26.
     I called at Honeywood on the 5th instant to examine into the effluviums and emanations complained of, but I could not ascertain any olfactory aggressions indicating blemishes in the sanitary provisions.
     There was a bit of odoriferous exhalation in the scullery, and a whiff of noxious emanation in the yard, because the domestic staff

had removed the grating out of the scullery sink instead of emptying the grease-trap. Unsavoury effluviums from the yard gully are due to the grating being missing and the drain being too small to pass the size of scrubbing brushes used.

The obnoxious exhalation in the bedrooms is due to windows being kept shut and chimney-throats stopped; but it is likely that there is down-draught in some of the flues owing to them being damp as yet.

Yours faithfully,

Spinlove asked for a report so worded as to be suitable for sending to Sir Leslie Brash, and it is probable that Grigblay supposed it was intended he should adopt Brash's euphemisms, and that his inveterate habit of irony, his lack of literary accomplishment and his impatience of nonsense, did the rest: he did not understand what was wanted and resented the folly of what he was doing. Grigblay's habit of veiling his irritation by irony is so ingrained that he is likely to be in great part unaware of the gorgeous effects he sometimes gets. Some such explanation seems necessary. We can imagine that Grigblay is unaware here, as elsewhere, of the vividness with which his letters reveal his state of mind.

SPINLOVE TO GRIGBLAY

Dear Sir,   23.4.26.

I am much obliged for Mr. Grigblay's report on drains, but I think that Sir Leslie Brash might misinterpret certain passages. I have, therefore, altered some of the terms and return the report. If Mr. Grigblay will copy it as amended and sign, I will send it to Sir Leslie.

I am still awaiting your summary of variations account.

Yours faithfully,

GRIGBLAY TO SPINLOVE

Dear Sir,   24.4.26.
We have rewritten report as you suggest and enclose same. We
hope that this now ends the matter.

Yours faithfully,

(ENCLOSURE) GRIGBLAY TO SPINLOVE

Dear Sir,   6.4.26.
I called at Honeywood Grange on the 5th instant to investigate complaints of smells, but could find nothing wrong with the
drains.

A smell in the scullery was due to the removal of the grating
of the sink, and to the container of the grease-trap not being emptied. The flooding of the yard gully is due to the grating being
missing and scrubbing brushes getting into the trap.

The stuffy smell in the bedrooms is partly due to windows
being kept shut and chimney-throats stopped up, but it is likely
there is down-draught in the flues owing to their being damp as
yet.

Yours faithfully,

*A very colourless version! Spinlove has ventured, it will be noticed, to
touch up Grigblay's grammar.*

BRASH TO SPINLOVE

Dear Mr. Spinlove,   24.4.26.
I note your comment anent the subject of blemishes. So long
as we are not inconveniently incommoded I am quite willing to
permit matters to stand over for the present, on the understanding that Mr. Grigblay is previously advised beforehand and com-
prehends that the increase in defects due to the remissness of his

attentions is a matter for which he solely is responsible. I certainly consider, however, that it would be advantageously to his interests to intervene before the increase in blemishes becomes more aggravated, as I apprehend that a small defect is more readily ameliorated than one of greater magnitude, and that the anticipated augmentation of cracks, for example, is better prevented than cured. That, however, is a matter for your and Mr Grigblay's eventual decision.

Since I wrote, a new defect has appeared, which needs immediate attention, as it is causing the establishment considerable unnecessary inconvenience. On Thursday afternoon last, at about 4.25—so far as I can precisely ascertain—it was observed that when the push in the drawing-room was depressed the front door bell rang; and it subsequently transpired that all the other pushes rang the front door bell , and that the bell-pull at the front door rang the bell in the lady's maid's room on the second floor instead of its own. As the indicator has also ceased to appropriately function, the consequent inconvenience can be imagined, and is not—may I be permitted to say?—what I feel is compatible with a house designed by a qualified architect and erected by an expensive builder. I shall be gratified if you will ring up the house to-morrow and instruct us in what it is desirable to do.

Your communication omits to intimate anything regarding Riddoppo super-paint. My apprehensions on this question are commencing to engender considerable doubts, as a small narrow strip was yesterday observed to have detached itself away from the wall above the skirting of the inner lavatory compartment adjoining the front entrance, and investigation indicates that similar disasters threaten to immediately eventuate in various other different positions. Inspection also substantiates that serious ridges and rims of paint, which break away from the surface in little crumbs and flakes that adhere to the carpets, are accruing in diverse localities, which conclusively demonstrates that *Riddoppo is beginning to commence to disintegrate*. Immediate attention is most desirably expedient, and I request that Mr. Grigblay shall be informed that I expect immediate remedial precautions to be embarked upon at once.

May I intimate the due reminder that you have not yet transmitted Mr. Grigblay's report on the sanitary anomalies? These cause me increasing apprehension. Also the damp places over the chimneys continue, although the promised remedy was intimated to be on the point of eventuating several weeks ago. Other evidences of damp places are now ocularly discernible in the corners of some of the first-floor sleeping apartments.

I have transmitted cheque to Mr. Grigblay but still await promised figure of total sum of extra cost.

Yours sincerely,

We have seen Brash making heavy weather of "blemishes" which do not amount to defects, or are of no importance. He has yielded to the weakness, common with owners of new houses, of crawling over every part with the minute scrutiny of an ant, instead of enjoying his well-planned and soundly-built house. The Riddoppo failure is, however, a serious matter.

SPINLOVE TO BRASH

Dear Sir Leslie Brash,   27.4.26.

I do not know in the least what has gone wrong with the bells, but, as I telephoned to-day, I have arranged for Grigblay to send an electrician to the house to-morrow.

I enclose copy of Grigblay's report on drains. I am sorry I omitted to send this before.

The necessary work in preventing damp appearing in chimney-breasts will have to be put off till the summer when the brickwork has dried out. I will inquire into the cause of the other damp places you speak of. The house has hollow walls, and there cannot be much wrong.

I assure you that your fear of faulty drains is without foundation. I really do not know what more can be done.

I am sorry to hear that the Riddoppo paint is proving unsatisfactory. As you know, I never had confidence in it, and Mr. Grigblay objected to its use.

Yours sincerely,

*There is a directness and brevity in this letter which, though per-
fectly appropriate to the occasion, indicates that Spinlove is busy in
other directions and is getting tired of Honeywood. He has not followed
Grigblay's advice of repudiating responsibility for Riddoppo, but he perhaps does better at this juncture in implying that the matter is Brash's
concern, only.*

SPINLOVE'S SELF-LOCKING DOOR

Dear Jazz,   30.4.26.

This is to warn you to form a solid British Square and prepare to receive cavalry, as Dad is on his high horse. You are a mutt. Dad even suspects a practical joke. This is what happened; no guy, honest indian.

We had a big house-warming dinner-party to-night, very swell and solemn, all the poshest of the posh, no one under about seventy, all good Gargantuans with digestions treasured by leading physicians—Dad simply wallows in that sort of occasion—when the writing wobbles it is because I am laughing.

Mum and I were out with the car, and didn't get to home sweet home till nearly seven, to find the kitchen staff—as Dad calls them—waiting *outside* the kitchen door, which was open just wide enough to allow a choking smell of burning glue and feathers to be nosed. They could not get in to finish cooking the dinner, nor to stop its cooking. The back entrance was bolted, the windows all fastened—except the little top ones—and the door jammed; it would not open nor shut. I pushed my arm through and found the door of the cupboard, just inside, pressing against the knob of the kitchen door. The knob of the cupboard was against the other, so that the door would not move either way. How it got fixed no one knows. The servants found it so at half-past five, after they had run to see an aeroplane stunting at the front. The gardeners had all gone, not a man was about, and so the loonies just waited, with sauces burning and everything going wrong inside, and nothing being done to get the dinner ready. The chauffeur fetched a ladder and reached through one of the little top windows with a golf club and undid a lower window, and, by heaving himself up against the door, freed it. You can imagine the to-do with all the arrangements knocked sideways. Of course, it would not have mattered if it had not been such a swanky occasion; but not a word was said, and the seventeen seventies sat solemnly marking time in the drawing-room with cocktails and caviare sandwiches, while the servants struggled and sweated in the kitchen and the hired men gloomed in the hall, till nearly a quarter to nine. It is a thousand pities you were not invited—as you should have been—as the triumphant architect of the arrangements.

Ever yours,
PUD.

Spinlove appears to have a friend in the enemy's camp.

This accident is extraordinary. Spinlove ought to have been more wary than to allow any door to open against another in such a way as to block its swing: such a chance is always in mind for the planner. It happened, however, that the kitchen arrangements at Honeywood were altered after the trenches had been dug and the foundations begun, and this unlucky fouling of doors may be the bequest of that revision. Afterthoughts and alterations are frequent cause of such mishaps. When the plan is originally made the whole scheme is subject to minute concentration; but when alterations are devised there is great danger that all consequences of the changes will not be foreseen.

Fantastic as this misadventure may appear, it will seem so to the experienced architect or builder only for the grotesque catastrophe associated with it. It is, in fact, typical of the kind of accidents that frequently happen. Pud's description makes pretty clear what occurred. It is a thing that the most exact detailing by the designer and anxious care of the builder could scarcely accomplish, so that had the thing been—as Brash's irritation led him to suggest—a practical joke, it would have done honour to the ingenuity and assiduity of its perpetrators.

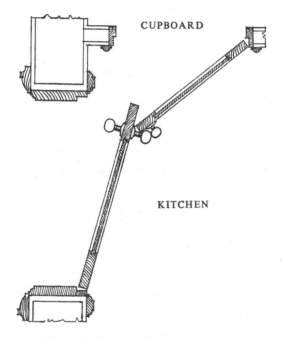

SPINLOVE'S AUTOMATIC SELF-LOCKING DOOR.

The sketch shows what apparently happened. The title I have given it seems justified; for if anyone hereafter discovers a right use for the device, Spinlove ought most certainly to have credit for the invention.

BRASH TO SPINLOVE

Dear Mr. Spinlove,   30.4.26.

It was with considerable astonishment—will you permit me to say?—that I read the copy of Mr. Grigblay's report on the sanitary abnormalities obtaining at Honeywood; as this, so far from elucidating the circumstances elaborated in your letter on the subject, intimates no reference whatever to many of them. This is a matter I will take an early convenient opportunity of investigating in oral conversation with you as, also, other important matters somewhat lightly—if you will pardon me—touched on by you.

Yours sincerely,

Oh, what a tangled skein we weave
When first we practise to deceive!

SPINLOVE TO GRIGBLAY

Dear Sirs,   1.5.26.

Sir Leslie Brash rang up to-day and told me that the kitchen door in some way jams against the handle of the cupboard, and the servants were not able to get into the kitchen. Will you please send someone over to put things right? The cupboard door had better be hung the other way round and a spring catch fixed so that it remains fast when closed.

Sir Leslie Brash also spoke of the Riddoppo paint as developing serious defects. He had previously referred to this matter in a letter. I reminded him that it was used by his orders and against my wishes and your advice. Could Mr. Grigblay call or send over a painter to see what can be done?

Yours faithfully,

Spinlove seems to have suffered puncture! There is a note of moral deflation in this letter. Our young friend makes no attempt to put the blame on the builder, as he has taught us to expect, but actually accepts responsibility for the kitchen door fiasco. He seems also to have given ground deplorably in the matter of Riddoppo. Apparently Grigblay's urgent representations have made no impression on him. Is Mr. Spinlove losing heart? If so, he had better give up practice at once. The letter that follows offers some explanation.

RIDDOPPO BOILS UP

Dear Sir Leslie Brash,   1.5.26.

I write to confirm telephone conversation this morning.

I still think that the explanation of the stuffy smell complained of is that given in Mr. Grigblay's report. As I explained, my own report to you was partly based on private messages from Mr. Grigblay. In any case the condition is not, I am quite sure, due to faulty drains or to any defect in the building work.

I am unable to say to what the defects in the Riddoppo paint are due. You will remember that I never recommended it, and Mr. Grigblay also objected to using it. As arranged, I have asked Mr. Grigblay to see what can be done.

I am very sorry indeed for the accident of the kitchen door. I have to-day written to Grigblay with instructions for alterations that will prevent anything of the kind happening again.

I have this morning inquired by telephone, and find that the breakdown of the bells was caused by a large nail driven into the wall of the pantry by one of your servants.

Yours sincerely,

Brash, we may judge, has been truculent over the telephone. The bell-wiring does not seem to have been done as well as it should. Presumably, the electric light wiring was drawn in through tubes, and the bell wires ought to have been run in the same way.

GRIGBLAY TO SPINLOVE

Dear Sir,   3.5.26.

We shall be obliged if you will inform Sir Leslie Brash that we cannot advise him *re* Riddoppo, as the paint is composed of ingredients which are a trade secret, and we know nothing of it. He will remember that we refused to take responsibility for painting with same and only did so by his orders on the understanding that he took responsibility for the results.

Yours faithfully,

If, as Grigblay claims, he is not responsible for the defects in Riddoppo, it would be a grave error in judgment for him to offer any opinion on the nature or cause of them, and much more unwise for him to have anything to do with reparation.

SPINLOVE TO BRASH

Dear Sir Leslie Brash,   4.5.26.

I wrote to Mr. Grigblay asking him to see what could be done to make good defects in the paint, and I enclose copy of his letter in reply.

Yours sincerely,

Spinlove has no business to pass on Grigblay's disclaimer without comment or explanation. His duty, as architect and arbiter under the contract, is to master the facts, to balance the scales between owner and builder, and to uphold the rights of each.

BRASH TO SPINLOVE

Dear Mr. Spinlove,   7.5.26.

Although I have in the past had no occasion to form a particularly favourable opinion of Mr. Grigblay's good manners, I confess that I was completely taken aback with surprise at the high-handed style in which he has indited his communication to you intimating his refusal to make himself amenable to my desire that he should apply himself to the reparation of the failure of the paint; but you must permit me to say that I was even more astonished at the detached aloofness of your communication covering its transmission. What the man intends to signify by saying that I, *I* of all people, who have had nothing to do with it, am responsible for the disintegration of Riddoppo—unless he is going off his head, which is precisely what I should anticipate of the fellow—I entirely fail to comprehend. What have I to do with the "results" of his work? This, you must permit me to intimate, is a most preposterously impudent suggestion for a builder to propound, and I take strong objection to your affirmative acquiescence in such a monstrous proposition. I desire that you will at once require Mr. Grigblay to perform his duties, for I divine that the reserve held back by me as security for the reparation of defects is to reimburse me for losses due to unjustifiable refusals. I am not, I apprehend, to be at the mercy of the contractor!

Yours sincerely,

Brash is precipitating disaster, for he has evidently forgotten the circumstances in which he ordered Grigblay to paint with Riddoppo.

SPINLOVE TO GRIGBLAY

Dear Sirs, 8.5.26.

I sent Sir Leslie Brash a copy of your letter on the subject of Riddoppo, and I have received one from him in which he disclaims responsibility for the failure of the paint, as he has had nothing to do with it, and renews his request that you will give immediate attention to the matter.

Yours faithfully,

This letter strengthens the earlier impression that Spinlove is held by other activities and is tired of Honeywood. He has, however, adopted an untenable position in standing aside while builder and owner fight the matter out for themselves.

GRIGBLAY TO SPINLOVE

Dear Sir,   10.5.26.

We will thank you to kindly note and to politely inform Sir Leslie Brash that Riddoppo paint is his own concern and no sort of business of ours, as he knows well enough without being told. We used the stuff by his orders on the undertaking he gave to accept full responsibility for results of same, after we objected and refused to take responsibility, which please note and see correspondence.

We also will thank you to respectfully point out to your client that we called attention to the defects he has just discovered for himself, nearly six months ago, and warned him before the painting was finished what would happen, and he ordered us to go on and finish in spite; and also politely inform him with our respectful compliments that it will save him a bit of unnecessary trouble if he gives up trying to put the blame for his own obstinacy on to us, and kindly note that we politely refuse to have anything further to do with his mistakes, having completed our contract to instructions; and decline to pickle off, burn off, scrape off, hack off or touch up or have any further hand with new novelty super or other painting at Honeywood of any kind whatever or for any consideration whatever; and if Sir Leslie Brash wants our advice, the advice we respectfully send him is to leave off trying to put the blame where it does not belong, and ask those to set him right who set him wrong, and that is the people who manufactured the paint and supplied to us at his orders.

                                                Yours faithfully,

Grigblay is warming up, and no wonder! This "respectful" and "polite" message is evidently dictated by him. The general run of letters from his firm is apparently the work of a secretary.

SPINLOVE TO BRASH

Dear Sir Leslie Brash,   11.5.26.
I sent Mr. Grigblay your message, and his reply is much what
I expected. He disclaims all responsibility for Riddoppo on the
ground that you accepted responsibility when you ordered him to
use it. He recommends that you should apply to the manufacturers, or to the suppliers, for advice on the matter.

I do not know what more I can do for I know nothing of the
composition of the paint, which is a secret. As you will remember,
I always advised against its use and disclaimed responsibility for
the result.

Yours sincerely,

It is ridiculous for Spinlove to suppose that he can stand aside as
though he were the disinterested spectator of a dog fight. At the same
time, it must be admitted that the line he takes is strictly consistent with
his disclaimer of responsibility, so that, except that he is precipitating a
break with his employer, he has not prejudiced his own nor Grigblay's
position as we had good reason to fear he might.

BRASH TO SPINLOVE

Dear Mr. Spinlove,   12.5.26.
I was astonished to peruse your communication transmitting
Mr. Grigblay's impertinent asseverations of refusal and denials of
responsibility. Am I to understand that you are desirous of taking
sides with the preposterous attack of the builder upon me? Have
I to remind you that, as my accredited architect, it is incumbent
upon you to protect my interests and enforce on the contractor
the due observance of his obligatory duties? If so, I apprehend I
have been seriously mistaken in the character of the gentleman
to whom I have entrusted the management of my building operations. The paint in the house is displaying disastrous signs of ocu-

lar disintegration which develop increasingly, and my architect refuses to stir a finger in the matter because he objected to the paint and is "not responsible" forsooth!

The whole matter is perfectly unendurable and beyond bearing, and I desire that you will intimate to Mr. Grigblay, with necessary emphasis, that unless he forthwith immediately agrees to restore and renew the defective paint in a properly permanent and workmanlike manner, I shall engage the service of some other building contractor to do the work, and subtract the amount of the cost as a deduction from the next payment I am asked to make to him, for I divine that the security retained by me is designed to be applicable to this purpose.

Yours sincerely,

In the event of a builder refusing, or failing to satisfy his covenant, to make good defects, the retention money may be applied as Brash proposes; but it can only be so applied after formal warning and notification to the builder, and only if the defect in question is due to improper workmanship or materials for which the builder is responsible.

SPINLOVE TO BRASH

Dear Sir Leslie Brash,   14.5.26.

I think you must have forgotten what occurred at the time you directed me to order Grigblay to paint with Riddoppo, and I therefore enclose copies of various letters that passed, including—in case you may not have kept copies of them—your letters to me.

It seems clear that Grigblay cannot be held responsible for the failure of the paint. He also asks you to excuse him from expressing an opinion of the cause of the defects or from having anything to do with renovations, and for the reason I gave, namely, that he knows nothing of the paint, the ingredients of which are a trade secret. When you read the letters you will see that Grigblay called attention to defects before the painting was finished, but that you ordered him to complete; and you will also see that

I always strongly objected to the use of Riddoppo and disclaimed responsibility for the results of using it.

Yours sincerely,

Spinlove is certainly keeping on safe ground, but his detachment seems chiefly due to his being sick of Honeywood. The proper action for him to take would be to study the case exhaustively and give the best advice he can, and—instead of leaving his client to find his own way—guide him to the wisest course and, possibly, contrive a compromise. However, Grigblay is too wary ever to have anything more to do with Riddoppo either on the walls of Honeywood Grange or in the tin.

LADY BRASH TO SPINLOVE

Dear Mr. Spinlove,

We have a small party here on Friday and hope you will come to tennis in the afternoon and stay the night.

It is all getting into the carpets and I shall have to take them up if it goes on and they do not stop it and so *dreadfully* noisy to walk on!! I hope they will do it soon and have finished with once for ever. It is all so very trying isn't it and so stuffy, it seems as if we should never be able to settle down but Mr. Grigblay says wait for the summer so I suppose we must it will not be long now I am thankful to say.

How beautiful all the blossom has been lately.

Yours sincerely,

Monday.

BRASH TO SPINLOVE

Dear Mr. Spinlove,   17.5.26.

I have re-perused your communication and the transmitted copies of enclosed correspondence a second time. My previous recollection of the matter had, as you correctly divine, escaped my memory, but Mr. Grigblay's proposition that by intimating willingness to take responsibility for ordering I made myself liable for the eventual default of persons other than myself is—you must permit me to point out—most excessively preposterous, as I shall get an early opportunity of requesting my legal advisers to authoritatively confirm. If, as Mr. Grigblay impudently contends, the liability for defective blemishes is not his responsibility, then it is the responsibility of the manufacturer, and they must decide the dispute between themselves. My precise directions to yourself are that the progressive disintegration shall be immediately arrested and necessary reparations proceeded with without delay. The matter is now *imperatively urgent*, as the little flakes of paint cannot be removed by brushing the carpet, and have to be individually picked off with the thumb and finger, a duty so laboriously irksome to the domestic staff that it is performed in a perfunctory manner, and particles of Riddoppo are, for this cause, on all sides being *trodden into the carpets* with resultant consequences you may conjecture.

As I do not apprehend that I have at any time intimated that I regard you as responsible for the disintegration, your disclaimer of responsibility appears to me—if you will permit me to be perfectly frank—somewhat unnecessarily premature; nor do I perceive, as you intimate, that you disclaimed liability for any prognosticated eventual results.

Yours faithfully,

Brash's gracious intimation of his "willingness to take responsibility for ordering" was in these words: "I do not know what the man [Grigblay] means by 'responsibility' and—if I may be permitted to be perfectly frank—I do not care. I give the order and the responsibility for giving the order is mine. Mr. Grigblay's responsibility is to do what he is told at once."

The history of the matter as recorded in The Honeywood File *is briefly as follows:*

Brash writes to Spinlove giving glowing advertisement accounts of a wonderful New Novelty Super-Paint called Riddoppo, and directing

Spinlove to use it. Spinlove objects that he knows nothing of Riddoppo and that the well-tried paint specified by him gives the best possible results. Brash grows peppery, and retorts that for Spinlove "to asseverate condemnation of a paint of which he admits he knows nothing, is a little wanting in logical reasoning," and insists on Riddoppo being used. Spinlove gives the order to Grigblay, who replies that he knows nothing of Riddoppo and has failed to obtain any satisfactory accounts of it, and that he "cannot accept responsibility for same." Brash, on hearing this, objects, angrily, at being "dictated to"; and delivers himself as first above quoted. Spinlove thereupon writes to Grigblay: "I am instructed by Sir Leslie Brash to order you to paint with Riddoppo. Sir Leslie Brash accepts all responsibility."

Those are the facts; and if, as they appear to show, Brash is responsible for the paint having been ordered, then, in that case, Grigblay is responsible to Brash for properly applying the paint; Brash is responsible to Grigblay for the integrity of the paint; the manufacturers are responsible to Brash, Brash is responsible to Spinlove, Spinlove to Brash, Spinlove to Grigblay, and Grigblay to Spinlove—all in different degrees and on different issues—so that when Grigblay described the approaching disaster as a "mix up" his term was not inappropriate. If Brash had not interfered there is no doubt that Spinlove, with Grigblay's experience and integrity to back him, would have completed the house with sound paintwork, but had things by any chance gone wrong, Brash would then have been secured under the contract, and his remedy would have been the simple one of requiring Grigblay to repaint. He has brought all this trouble on his own head.

SPINLOVE TO BRASH

Dear Sir Leslie Brash,   18.5.26.

I have told Mr. Grigblay the position you are taking. I will not reply to your letter as we shall be able to talk matters over during the week-end.

With kind regards,

Yours sincerely,

SPINLOVE TO GRIGBLAY

Dear Sirs,   19.5.26.

I communicated the contents of your letter to Sir Leslie Brash and sent him copies of the earlier correspondence. He says that in ordering Riddoppo he did not make himself responsible for defects due to improper materials or workmanship. He calls on you to make good at once as the carpets are being spoilt; and holds that the matter is for you and the paint manufacturer to settle between you. He is consulting his solicitors to decide what action to take in the event of your refusing to make good.

Yours faithfully,

Spinlove is not content to stand aside and watch the dog fight; he must, it seems, throw the animals one at the other.

GRIGBLAY TO SPINLOVE

Dear Sir,   20.5.26.

We note Sir Leslie Brash's views on responsibility for the failure of the paint, and have nothing to add to our last re same.

Yours faithfully,

GRIGBLAY IS CONFIDENTIAL

Sir,   24.5.26.

I happened along Honeywood way and looked in, as Jossling is clearing up after finishing road which I hope is to your approval, and I just write to drop you a hint that the old gentleman is still worrying over his defective drains, as I gather you have nothing to do with a sanitary expert he has called in. There was a very young gentleman, with two handy-men to help him, had been putting the water test on the vertical soil and filling the pans to the brims, and so on up to the second floor servants', like a piano-tuner at work, till he had near 30 foot head of water above the first man-hole—so Jossling told me—and enough to burst the pipes. I found him down at the disconnecting chamber with a parcel of rockets and boxes of matches to find out with smoke how much damage he had done with water.

The drains don't ventilate Mr. Grigblay he says, I've put three rockets in and been waiting half an hour and I can't see any smoke out at top yet. You're in too great a hurry I told him; you keep at it another hour or two with all the rockets you've got there, and you'll see a bit of smoke right enough. This sucking expert had wetted all the pipes right up, and made them stone cold, and then expected to find a nice draught! However, a fashionable gentleman drove up in a saloon and rang the front bell; Jarrad, of Quince and Jarrad, patronized by Royalty—I've seen something of their

67

doings before now. Jarrad didn't get asked in to tea, it seems, for he soon came round to find out how his young hopeful's drain-bursting experiments were getting on; and then they brought a pressure pump and other gear from the saloon and so I left him to go running his nose round the joints like a terrier dog, and rub the skin off same as he does at his Royal Palace, to try and catch a whiff of smoke after he's pumped up the ten pounds or whatever the pressure is they keep on their mercury gauges and contraptions. I hope no harm will come, Sir, but his kind are very mischievous fellows that get their living finding fault with other people's work, and the more faults they find the bigger man they hold themselves out to be. I thought best to let you know what was going forward, and if you hear any complaints perhaps our good friend Mr. Potch will have a kind word or two to say to Mr. Jarrad or to anyone else who claims he knows better ways of find-ing fault with other people's drains than what Potch does.

Apologizing for troubling you but thought you better know what is afoot.

Yours truly,

Brash, as we have noticed, commonly does not know the right thing to do; or, when he knows, frequently does not do it. He ought to have told Spinlove he wanted the drains tested by an independent authority, and either left Spinlove to nominate someone or directed him to employ Quince and Jarrad. To go to the firm behind his architect's back is, if not a definitely hostile step, a sharp reminder to Spinlove that he has lost his employer's confidence. Brash's insensitiveness, however, probably exonerates him from any intention of wronging Spinlove; and Spinlove has invited this treatment by his unaccommodating attitude and his impatience at the suggestion that all is not as it should be. Grigblay's apprehensions are justified, though his contempt for Messrs. Quince and Jarrad is not at all likely to be. Mr. Potch is the District Surveyor who brought Spinlove much trouble while the house was being built.

(PERSONAL) SPINLOVE TO GRIGBLAY

Dear Mr. Grigblay,   26.5.26.

Yes, you are correct—I have heard nothing of any drain-testing; but as I am sure everything is right no amount of testing can find anything wrong.

I am obliged to you for writing.

Yours truly,

Spinlove is in a fool's paradise indeed, if he can welcome the approach of the sworn tormentor of drains—for to that dire body I divine Quince and Jarrad to belong.

SUMMARY OF VARIATIONS

Dear Sir,   29.5.26.

As requested, we send you herewith summary of variations and shall be glad to receive certificate for £1,300 further on account. We have heavy commitments just at this time, and as the amount fell due in the middle of February last we shall be glad to receive your certificate and Sir Leslie Brash's cheque without further delay. The account, we may point out, now stands as follows:

	£	s.	d.
Contract....................	18,440	0	0
By variations account.........	1,892	14	7
	20,332	14	7
Less 5 per cent retention........	1,016	11	6
	19,316	3	1
Already certified.............	18,000	0	0
Due February 10th	1,316	3	1

This is the third or fourth application Grigblay has made for payment on account of extras in respect of which Spinlove has previously certified only for £500.

70

(ENCLOSURE) GRIGBLAY TO SPINLOVE
INTERIM SUMMARY OF VARIATIONS

[*I have numbered the items and added in italics the thoughts likely to
be awakened in Spinlove.*]

AMOUNT OF CONTRACT £18,440   0   0

1. Alteration to kitchen . . . . say 400   0   0
   (*"My goodness! It cannot possibly amount to as
   much as that! I told Brash 'about 2100'—but
   that was before I had made the working drawings. Tinge must measure carefully, Damn!"*)
2. Piping ditch (Day-work account) 114   5   6
   (*"Damn! I told Brash £20. They must have in-
   cluded other work on the time-sheets. I ought to
   have insisted on the day-work vouchers being
   sent in regularly. Tinge must check carefully."*)
3. Pulling down and altering partitions and re-
   storing (Day-work). 137   9   0
   (*"Pity it is not more. Serves B. right for letting
   Lady B. interfere."*)
4. Extension and alteration of drains (day-work). 84   17   6
   (*"That must be the fish-tank extension. No
   business of mine, thank goodness!"*)
5. Extra price picked facings (Hoochkoft) 92   0   0
   (*'What the . . . ! Why, they agreed to send
   picked after I refused to allow extra! No go, my
   friends!"*)
6. Cutting out defective and making good (Day
   work). 8   14   0
   (*"Hoochkoft and Grigblay can settle that be-
   tween them. I told H. I would not have the soft
   under-burnt bricks, and G. that he was not to
   use them."*)

7. Raking and pointing to order in lieu of plain
struck joint (Day-work) 49   6   3
(*"Frost got at the joints. That's all right—Act
of God. Tinge had better fix rate and measure.
No justification for day work—besides, how
could they separate the time when the joint was
struck as the bricks were laid?"*)

8. 795 yds. sup. pointing to order in lieu of plain
struck joint at 4½d. per ft. 134   3   0
(*"Oh, I see! So the last item was for raking
and pointing joints damaged. Oh! Right!—but
Tinge must check the measure and rates."*)

9. Work in draining cellar (Day-work) 84 17   9
(*"Oh, Lor! Twice what I expected! All that tun-
nelling through walls, I suppose! Wish I had
checked day-work vouchers at the time."*)

10. Extra foundations to order (Day-work) 66   3   9
(*"What's this? 'To order'? Not mine. There was
a little give and take, certainly. Tinge would
have measured the whole if there had been talk
of any extra. No go, my lad!"*)

11. Timber garage outhouse (as estimated) 372 10   0
(*"Very cheap too and a clinking design I will
say. Old B. very pleased. A decent old boy."*)

12. Extension of washing-place (Day-work). 54   9   0
(*"Why couldn't B. take my advice and include
it with the building? He was sure to want it.
Would have saved him money. Must be measured, anyhow. Day-work is all nonsense."*)

13. Terrace steps (special charge as notified) 11   6   3
(*"Don't know anything of this. Lady B. per-
haps."*)

14. Alterations to back stairs to order (Day-work). 41 12   0
(*"That mistake of mine! They've charged far
too much. Must question it."*)

15. Alterations to ground-floor window heads
    (Daywork)................................65 10 0
    *("I won't allow it. It was Grigblay's mistake, not
    mine. Anyhow I never sanctioned an extra.")*
16. Repairs and new bottoming to Entrance Road
    (as estimated)...........................62   0 0
    *("A low charge. Wish I had got estimates for
    everything, but how the deuce can one, with all
    the interferences and hurry?")*
17. Renewing two broken catch pits (Day-work)........4 13 0
    *("They ought to have included for these when
    they estintated for the road repair. Out it
    goes!")*
18. Oak floor to kitchen passage (To order)...........14 12 0
    *("Lady B. I forgot this. They never had order
    for extra.")*
19. Waterproofing chimneys (estimate)..............42 10 0
    ("Not done yet.")
20. Various minor works and attendances...........192   6 8
    *("Ridiculous! I must have particulars. They
    must show the orders for all extras.")*

    ────────────────

                                        2,033   5 8

EXTRAS ON PROVISIONS
("Expected this. Not altogether my fault.")

21. Grates and range (Chiddle, etc.) 22   0 0
22. Electric wiring (Poggle) 21   5 0
    *("I couldn't know they would want
    so many points.")*
23. Electric light fittings 48   4 6
    *("Well, I told Brash what was al-
    lowed.")*
24. Sanitary fittings (Wide)........... 53 17 0
    ("He did it with his eyes open.")

25. Radiators (additions and alterations) . . 28   0   0
26. Locks and furniture. 32   4   9
    ("I cut this too fine.")
27. Casements and glazing (Watkins). . . . 13 10   6
28. Special opening gear (do.) 27   7   0
    ("This was absolutely necessary.")
29. Extra journey money *re* do. 11 13   3
    *("When Lady B. sent the man away,
    I suppose.")*
30. Balance of small variations 21 13   8
    ("What does this refer to?")

    Total 279 15   8   2,033   5   8
    Profit. 48   3   0
    *("What a nuisance! Tinge must
    check the profit charge carefully.")*

                      327 18   8   327 18   8

    Total additions 2,361   4   4
    ("Oh, I say!")

OMISSIONS

31. General contingencies 100   0   0
    *("I thought it was £300—but now I
    remember I cut off £200 when I was
    trying to get down the contract price.
    By Jove, that's unlucky! Damn!")*
32. Well (omitted) 135   8   0
    *("I wish I had not cut down that
    provision so much.")*
33. Saving on ram and piping, etc., in
    lieu of pump 21   0   0
    *("I expected a much larger saving.
    Oh, dear! This must include the spe-
    cial pipe and tank linings the ana-*

lyst recommended. That is not my
fault, anyway.')
34. Omission of return terrace wall, say . . 100   0 0
35. Entrance gates 4   2 4
("Every little helps.")
36. Omission of sun dial 59   1 0
37. Various credits and allowances 32   4 5
('What does that mean?")

Total	451	15	9	2,361	4	4
Profit	16	14	0			

('Why have they allowed such small
profit?")

Total omissions	468	9	9	468	9	9

Total extra cost		1,892	14	7

("Oh, Lor! There will be an awful row about
this! Brash has no idea of how things are. Any-
how, it's not my fault. I saved him the cost of
the well, too. Let's see! How much of all this am
I actually responsible for?")

So far as may be judged, the cost of making good omissions and defects due to oversights and mistakes of the architect is just about £400; and if Spinlove had provided in the contract against water driving into the chimneys and rising in the cellar, and so forth, the contract price would have been increased, so that his guilt in inflating costs is represented by an even smaller sum. In fact, having regard to the unavoidable small accidents and unforeseeable contingencies and interferences that attend all building operations, a man of far more experience than Spinlove would be well satisfied to have no larger sum to account for. Spinlove has unfortunately misled Brash with inadequate estimates given offhand but it did not appear that Brash attached importance to those estimates, nor that he would have abandoned the work had he been given exact ones. Spinlove has also let the account get out of hand! He has not kept himself informed of the state of affairs; he has neglected to enforce the contract condition that extras shall be formally authorized, as such, at the time the work is done, and he has not enforced the condition requiring that day-work vouchers, showing the time and materials expended on additional work which from its nature cannot be estimated by measurement, shall be rendered week by week. This is bad; but so many alterations were made by Brash, and there were so many interferences with the contract arrangements, that some excuse may be made for Spinlove. He did, in fact, warn Brash at the beginning of the building operations that, if the contract arrangements were interfered with, it would be impossible to safeguard extras.

The most indigestible part of the account is, however, the large excess of expenditure over the sums provided in the contract as "provisions" to meet the cost of work done by specialists, and of fittings subject to choice. These appear under the subheading "Extras on Provisions." The provision for general contingencies (item 31) was reduced by Spinlove from three to one hundred pounds, when he was trying to bring down the amount of the tender to a figure commensurate with Brash's swallow; and it seems likely that he pared down the provisional sums originally allowed by him at the same time, and with the same object. It is a great temptation to an architect to let his hopes for the best overrule his judgment, in this way; but it is a counsel of weakness and folly, or even worse; for his client supposes the contract sum covers the equipment he needs, and for the architect knowingly to mislead him for the purpose of committing him to the undertaking is dishonest. We cannot, however, take Spinlove to task, for we do not know the facts. What we do know, however, is that in the course of a year or two extras mount up, all unbeknown, in a most embarrassing way; and that building-owners, after they are habituated to the contract price and warmed with enthusiasm for the undertaking, are prone to indulge their ambitions, and sometimes even try to forget past extravagances lest they shall discourage new ones.

It will be noticed that in imagining Spinlove's reflections on the summary so obligingly drawn by Grigblay in a form that analyses the account and saves Spinlove the trouble of analysing it for himself, I have represented him as accepting Grigblay's charge for pointing to make good damage by frost. This is a peep ahead on my part.

SPINLOVE TO GRIGBLAY

Dear Sir,   31.5.26.

I have duly received your Interim Summary of Variations, for which I am obliged, but I am concerned to notice that the total is even higher than you led me to expect. There are a number of charges that want explaining and others I certainly cannot allow, and I should like Mr. Grigblay to make an appointment to meet me here to go into the account, as soon as ready; bringing with him orders for extras, day-work vouchers, etc., supporting your charges. Also particulars of "Various minor works £192," and reasons why the charge for picked bricks is made. I expressly arranged with Hoochkoft to supply at their original quoted price, as I informed you at the time.

When I have been into matters with Mr. Grigblay I will arrange for Mr. Tinge to take up the account. Some of the items charged day-work will have to go into a measured account.

Yours faithfully,

I cannot see Grigblay spending hours unravelling day-work sheets to Spinlove's satisfaction, but perhaps he will temper the wind to the shorn lamb and send round the estimating clerk who has charge of the account. This clerk, however, would not be able to explain or justify the charges. The proper course will be for Spinlove to push his head into the papers; get explanations from the builder on obscure points; settle contentious matters with him, and then refer the account for Tinge to arrive at the exact figures.

SPINLOVE TO BRASH

Dear Sir Leslie Brash,   31.5.26.

I have at last received an "Interim Summary" of the account from Grigblay; the exact figure has still, I am afraid, to be determined by the quantity surveyor, and there are certain charges which I cannot agree to—at least not without explanations—but I am very sorry indeed to say that the total is a good deal more than I expected. I am afraid the extras have mounted very much, although you were perhaps prepared for this. I enclose a brief summary showing how the account stands, but is not the final figure which, I hope and trust, will be substantially less. If I can give you more information will you please let me know? The final account will not be ready for several weeks, I am afraid.

I enclose note of my own charges in respect of the last two certificates, which I omitted to send at the time. Will you please accept my apologies for my forgetfulness?

Yours sincerely,

This is not, I fancy, the best of all possible occasions for Spinlove to apply for payment of his fees, even though he apologizes for not having done so before; and our young friend's amiable characteristic of identifying himself with the torment his client suffers in parting with his money, is here particularly inappropriate. We see Spinlove crouching before a lash he in no way deserves, and which he would have no reason to fear if he did not show he expected it. He invites Brash to be dissatisfied with his architect, who tells him he had no idea the total would be so large and apologizes for the amount, thereby avowing that he was neglectful in not keeping himself informed; and who takes responsibility for matters which do not lie at his door at all. He is "very sorry indeed" for the total of the account; he is "afraid" the extras have mounted up, although he supposes Brash expected they would; he does not know how it has all happened, and he is "afraid" the account will not be ready for several weeks, although the delay is an unavoidable circumstance with which he has nothing to do and only Brash's undisciplined impatience will suffer from it. If Spinlove's purpose had been to represent himself in the worst light he could scarcely have devised a neater or more complete way of doing so.

His letter is the more absurd for the finished tact he displays in the document that accompanies it—the "brief summary" which is to inform Brash how the account stands. Spinlove, it will be seen below, lumps the whole of the total balance of extras on to Brash by the adroit device of appropriating the whole of the credit items, totalling £468 9s. 9d., to himself, and cancelling them out against the extra expenditure for which he is personally responsible. The document is, in fact, not so much a statement of account between Brash and Grigblay as an apportionment of guilt between Brash and Spinlove. We may, I think, admire his ingenuity without being positively noisy in our applause. The facts set forth, however, are true: the figures are exact; the information is what Brash asked for. Brash undoubtedly ordered the extras laid to his charge, and is responsible for the inflation of the account by the total of them, precisely as stated. At the same time. . . . However, the point for astonishment is that Spinlove should cover a document so conclusive of his innocence by a letter so eloquent of guilt.

(ENCLOSURE) SPINLOVE TO BRASH
SUMMARY OF EXTRAS ORDERED BY SIR LESLIE BRASH

	£	s.	d.
Approximate cost, alterations to kitchen	400	0	0
Piping Ditch	114	5	6
Pulling down and restoring partitions by Lady Brash's orders	137	9	0
Extension and alterations of drains (for Aquarium)	84	17	6
New garage and washing-place	426	19	0
Time lost on Terrace steps by Sir Leslie Brash's orders	11	6	3
Repairs, new entrance road	66	13	0
Oak floor to kitchen passage (Lady Brash)	14	12	0
Various minor alterations	192	6	8
Grates and Ranges (excess as ordered)	22	0	0
Electric wiring (additional points as ordered)	21	5	0
Electric fittings (excess as ordered)	48	4	6
Sanitary fittings (excess as ordered)	53	17	0
Radiators (additions and alterations)	28	0	0
Special opening gear to Casements (as desired)	27	7	0

Extra journey money (men dismissed
by Lady Brash)............................. 11 13 3
Various small items........................... 21 13 8

OTHER EXTRAS

Restoring brickwork damaged by frost.............183 9 3
Various small extras 26 16 0
                                              ─────────────
                                         £11,892 14 7

BRASH ON EXTRAS

Mr. Spinlove,   2.6.26.

Eighteen hundred and ninety-two pounds! Is *eighteen* hundred the sum you intended to intimate when you informed me anticipated additional extras accruing to "several" hundreds? So you did not anticipate so largely augmented a figure, but supposed that I was prepared for it; and the final amount is still to be eventually ascertained, and you *hope* it will be a substantially reduced figure, and you will not agree to these monstrously extortionate inflations without "explanations"! Explanations, indeed! Permit me to emphatically indicate that I will certainly require something more than mere *explanations* of this scoundrelly attempt to victimize me. Is this the gentleman of high professional attainments who undertook to safeguard his employer's interests and protect him from the inordinate rapacity of building contractors—whom I was always well aware to be no better than packs of thieves and robbers? Is this the Associate of the Royal Institute of British Architects of impeccable credentials, specially recommended to my favourable attention for his distinguished achievements, who allows himself to be cajoled and humbugged and swindled as long as "explanations" are given? The matter has taken a most serious magnification of aspect, and you may inform Mr. Grigblay that, explanations or no explanations, I will not so much as condescend to consider his preposterous account unless he cuts it down by *at least one half.*

£400 for alterations to kitchen! The claim is perfectly monstrous. The kitchen arrangements, may I remind you, were not
increased in dimensions by the corrective emendations. I certainly anticipated a small extra cost to reimburse the builder for
his trouble in adapting the work he had previously performed;
but four hundred pounds! and as "approximate cost"! Does this
intimation signify that, if I consent to the additional charge, the
fellow is to be at liberty to further augment the amount?

Then, "piping ditch—£114." Will you permit me to ask leave
to remind you that you quoted me £20 for that work—and that
I hold your letter tendering the offer? *That* item of cost of £114,
at any rate, will not, I warn you in anticipation, be amenable to
any "explanations"; for I definitely repudiate any intention of paying more than the previously stipulated sum. "Time lost by Sir
Leslie Brash's orders!" When did I order time to be lost? Preposterous! "Various minor alterations—two hundred pounds!" Does
my architect seriously propound the suggestion that I should dis-
burse any sums this saucy fellow demands without even being
previously informed under what pretence the exaction is extorted?
"Extra journey money"—what does that portend, may I be permitted to ask? I was prepared for an additional extra in respect
of various grates and fittings, but what conceivable excuse is pro-
pounded why I should be mulcted for electric wiring and casement
gear and heating radiators and drains and water-pipes; and why,
may I venture to inquire, has the fellow made no deductions for
the saving on the well and pump which you previously held out
as an inducement to me to sanction the alternative arrangement?
And why has the £300 saving disappeared, which you informed
me had been included in the contract to reimburse expenditure
for additional extra work which might eventually become need-
ful, and which you asseverated must be reserved for that express
purpose? Am I to understand that Mr. Grigblay has appropriated
these credits, and that you have failed to detect the fraud?

It is necessary that I should take an early opportunity of con-
ferring verbally with you without delay, as the whole matter has

attained most serious proportions. Nineteen hundred pounds! It is the most monstrous and unheard-of imposition that ever was attempted; and if Mr. Grigblay or my architect supposes that I am a gentleman who will meekly submit to such barefaced robbery and extortion, he will regretfully find himself very greatly mistaken.

Yours truly,

Poor old Brash! He has let himself go with a vengeance, and it is to be hoped he felt better afterwards.

SPINLOVE SEEKS ADVICE

Dear Uncle Harold,   5.6.26.

I do not know who to turn to for advice. I have just finished a house for a certain Sir Leslie Brash, and the enclosed is a copy of a letter I have received from him in reply to one of mine covering a summary of the builder's Statement of Account. There is rather a heavy bill of extras, but that is not altogether my fault; and, whether it is or not, how can I allow anyone to write to me as he does? I want to do the right thing and to avoid quarrelling with him, but how is it to be done? Can you tell me what you think I ought to do? and can you write at once, please? My love to Auntie and yourself.

Your affectionate nephew,

Apparently, Brash has aroused unrighteous impulses in Spinlove, who feels the need of a little spiritual guidance to ginger up his humility, console his wounded pride, and enable him to swallow the affront without doing violence to his self-respect.

Dear Fred,   5.6.26.

Look what your friend Brash has written to me! How can I answer such a letter without hopelessly quarrelling with him? The whole bother about the extras is really his fault and not mine—or most of it is, anyway. Did you ever read such disgraceful abuse? As it was you who introduced me to Brash I feel you might be able to help smooth things over. Hurry up with your reply.

Yours,
JIM.

Spinlove's position is made difficult by the fact that he is so much younger a man than Brash; but, if he were not, Brash would scarcely have written as he did.

DALBET TO SPINLOVE

Dear Jim,   6.6.26.

I don't see what I can do. Tell the old bounder to go to blazes. I warned you he was peppery, and he has gone in off the deep end this time, that is all. He has always been nice to me—but then I am not his architect. Cheer up!

Yours,
FRED

THE VICAR OF RUNCHESTER TO SPINLOVE

My dear James,   7.6.26.

We were all most pleased to hear from you again, as it seems a very long time since you wrote either to your Aunt or to myself.

Patience, my dear boy, patience! Nothing is to be gained by hasty action of any kind. As you have often heard, no doubt, to forgive all is to understand and—or rather the other way about; and your wish not to quarrel with your employer, but to do the right thing, is highly commendable and just what your aunt and I would expect of you. Be not cast down; fight the good fight, and above all, as Hamlet says, "To your own self be true, and it must follow as the night the day that thou canst not then be false to any man."

I think if I were you I should be inclined to send Sir Lindsay Brosh a small token of esteem—a brace of trout if you happen to be fishing, or a souvenir of your recent travels; or failing these, possibly a copy of my *Pensées from Parnassus*, which I shall be glad to autograph and send you for this purpose. The fact that the author is a near relative would give the gift the character of a spontaneous expression of goodwill.

We gather from your letter that you are unaware that your aunt was seriously indisposed for several weeks during the winter.

Your affectionate uncle,

With all respect to the Vicar, Hamlet does not speak the words quoted and, though the maxim is admirable of its kind, it is not the kind of maxim Spinlove wants.

However valuable advice on technical points and on questions of principle may be, it is worse than useless for Spinlove to ask for direction in matters touching his personal relations with others. He must brace himself to draw the decision from his own inwards, where alone it is to be found. To turn to friends, as he here does, is to turn tail and to confirm the indecision he seeks to escape. He expects others to understand conflicting reactions of his own soul which he cannot himself interpret.

Neither Dalbet nor Uncle Harold the Vicar has made any attempt to put himself in the supplicant's shoes, but—as can only be expected—they show themselves much more concerned to adopt a pose flattering to their own self-esteem than to solve Spinlove's difficulty. Even if they were in possession of the whole history, and succeeded in identifying themselves with Spinlove's plight, the quarrel would be theirs and not his, for their individualities are different; and, for the same reason, their advice, however sound for themselves, would be valueless for him. The boisterous, good-humoured resentment of Dalbet, and the ingratiating affability of the Vicar, might meet their respective cases excellently had Brash become involved with them; but it would be wildly inappropriate for Spinlove either to tell Brash to go to blazes or to present him with a copy of uncle's new book.

No one can help Spinlove. So far from getting help from his friends, their letters can only increase his perplexity and aggravate his indecision. By yielding to the impulse to ask advice at all, he surrendered not only his belief in himself, but his power to decide; and he has allowed a shrinking admission of defeat to fill days which should have been applied to arriving at a decision.

BRASH TO SPINLOVE

Dear Mr. Spinlove   9.6.26.

May I be permitted to apprise you that I have received no communication from you anent my urgent request for an immediate appointment.

Yours sincerely,

GRIGBLAY TO SPINLOVE

Dear Sir,   7.6.26.

Our Mr. Tobias, chief prime-costing, will call at your office with vouchers, etc., at 11 on Wednesday, for the purpose of going into the account with you, as arranged over phone.

Yours faithfully,

Their Mr. Tobias will not be able to give Spinlove the sort of information he chiefly needs. A builder's prime-costing clerk deals only with the pricing and collection into the account of workmen's time-sheets and merchants', storekeeper's, carters', and other vouchers allocated to it by the foreman and others. What Spinlove chiefly wants is the authority, or justification, for the various extra charges. Bloggs, the foreman, could give him the facts; but Bloggs, of course, is now in charge of other work, and perhaps far afield.

SPINLOVE TO BRASH

Dear Sir Leslie Brash,   10.6.26.

I have not replied to your letter as I have expected that on reflection you would wish to withdraw it.

Yours sincerely,

This is a capital move. The evasion is neatly managed and Brash is warned, and in such a way as to encourage him to reconsider his position.

BRASH TO SPINLOVE

Dear Mr. Spinlove,   11.6.26.

I was taken aback with natural surprise on receipt of your communication. I indited my protest in terms which the circumstances suitably warranted, and you must permit me to remind you that it is yourself I have to thank for the necessity of doing so. I consider that the suggestion of withdrawal—though it might meet the very natural desires of a professional gentleman in your situation—is not one that is properly appropriate to the occasion, and I must request an adequately complete reply without further delay.

Yours sincerely,

P.S.—I shall be obliged if you will transmit a copy of my letter as I omitted to make a transcription of it.

Brash has had eight days in which to calm down. He seems to have written his offending letter in an hour of liver-inspired fury, and has quite forgotten what he said. Spinlove ought to be able to find his cue here. It is unfortunate Brash kept no copy of his letter or he would probably have accepted Spinlove's invitation to withdraw.

SPINLOVE ON EXTRAS

Dear Sir Leslie Brash,   12.6.26.

As you ask, I enclose copy of your letter, and in accordance with your instructions reply to it as completely as I can.

In disparaging my concern for the large total of the extras, you forget that that concern was not on my own account but on yours, and also that it is not I who am responsible for the figure, but yourself. I warned you at the beginning that if you interfered with the work the extras would mount up, and that it would be impossible for me to keep control of the cost if you gave orders direct to the builders. You paid no attention to the warning, and now wish to saddle me with the consequences of having ignored my advice.

The value of the kitchen alteration is a question of fact to be ascertained by the quantity surveyors, and I am no more responsible for the cost of the work than I am for the ordering of it, as a moment's reflection will surely show you. The amount is an approximate figure, because the exact figure has still to be ascertained.

I regret that I misjudged the probable cost of piping the ditch, and I think that, on examination, Grigblay's figure will be found to be in error; but I did not "quote" for the work. What I did was all that any architect can offer to do, namely, to give his opinion of probable cost. Only the builder quotes (i.e. estimates or tenders), and in this case Mr. Grigblay was not called on to do so, as you did

89

not ask for an estimate. The exact cost will be proved by vouchers recording the time and materials expended on the work, which the quantity surveyor will embody in the account when I have examined and certified them as properly to be included in it.

It is such vouchers as these, furnished by the builder, that I referred to when I spoke of "explanations." Your assumption that I used the word in a sense that made it idiotic, instead of in an exact technical sense, can only be explained by an intention to affront me.

Other items you mention it will be necessary for me to see you about, for, as the works they refer to were ordered without my knowledge, I have naturally little knowledge of them.

The £300 contingencies was cut down to £100 in order to reduce the tender to a reasonable figure; and this sum and the saving on the well, and certain other credits, have been set off, in the brief summary I sent you, against the cost of other works that became necessary. [*Ahem!*] The final Statement of Account will be laid before you when I receive it. I am not responsible for the delay, which is due to intricacies arising from the many extras and variations ordered by yourself.

The extras on wiring, radiators, water supply and drains are due to extensions and alterations of completed work ordered by you or by Lady Brash, or made necessary by interferences with other work, and they have nothing whatever to do with me. The extras on fittings is the excess of the cost of goods you yourself chose after I had informed you of the provisional amounts included in the contract to cover them.

Your aspersions on Mr. Grigblay are, so far as I know, without any kind of justification; and you have, I think, had abundant opportunities during the past two years of forming a very different opinion of him.

I think, Sir Leslie, that you wrote in haste and in anger, and. that you will wish to make amends for references to myself which seem to me openly contemptuous and intended for no other purpose than to affront me. In that confidence I will here merely say that, however mean an opinion you may hold of my capacities, I think I am entitled to a chance of explaining technical matters before being abused because you yourself do not happen to understand them.

Yours sincerely,

This is a remarkable letter for Spinlove to have written; but although some of his explanations are thin, we have before noticed that he always comes out strongest when his indignation is involved. We have also observed Mr. Spinlove to be a temperamental person, torn by conflicting impulses of vanity and prudence, in whom self-control is schooled by terror. Here, however, we find him expressing himself forcibly, as the circumstances require, but with restraint and cool purpose, and enough of courtesy—in presuming good intentions in his opponent—as to rob the frankness of his retort of offensiveness. This letter of Spinlove's, however, as well as that to which it replies, has a colour foreign to professional correspondence: they suggest a quarrel between men whose relations are proof against frank interchanges.

BRASH TO SPINLOVE

My dear Mr. Spinlove,   13.6.26.

I certainly was not aware of the asperity of language into which my natural rancour at the very inflated extortions of Mr. Grigblay betrayed me, and I desire to entirely withdraw my disparaging inferences anent yourself, which I greatly regret and for which I offer you my profuse apologies. They certainly are such as I had no intention of intimating, nor do they represent my opinion; in fact, I have to regretfully admit that I wrote hastily and in a moment of heated indignation, and I hope you will entirely eliminate from your mind all memory of my accidental and quite unpremeditated lapse from discreet language.

As regards the various matters expounded in your communication, I still consider that your elucidation is—if you will permit me to say so—very far from completely satisfactory, and it is imperatively desirable that I should discuss the whole aspect of the situation with you.

I enclose cheque for £270 further on account of your fees. You will comprehend that until some explanation of the inflated sum upon which the percentage is computed was forthcoming, this disbursement was not one I could reasonably contemplate.

Yours sincerely,

It is to be noticed that by putting himself in the wrong in one matter, and having to make a withdrawal, Brash has disorganized his whole line, and is even reduced to paying up as a step towards re-establishing his fortifications. This, however, is not the first occasion when Brash has justfied Dalbet's original description of him as a "real good sort." He here again reveals himself as a man whose foibles overlie generous instincts.

SPINLOVE TO BRASH

Dear Sir Leslie Brash,   15.6.26.

Many thanks indeed for your extremely kind letter. I need not tell you what very great pleasure it gave me. Of course, I am delighted to accept your apology and withdrawal, and will now forget all about the matter—in fact, I have already put it entirely out of my mind, and I am only sorry I felt obliged to make the protest, although I feel sure you will realize I could scarcely avoid doing so or I should not, I need hardly say, have put you to so much trouble.

I confirm appointment with your clerk by telephone to-day to see you here on Wednesday morning next. I shall before then have discussed matters with the builder.

I enclose form of receipt for cheque, for which I am much obliged.

Yours sincerely,

This is much more like the Spinlove of old acquaintance.

A SANITARY CONSULTANT

Dear Mr. Spinlove,   14.6.26.

I write to intimate that some weeks ago a medical practitioner, called in to attend a member of the domestic staff who had developed asthmatic symptoms, informed Lady Brash that attacks of this disorder may be provoked by *defective sanitary provisions*. This practitioner is not our own medical adviser, but is employed by me to minister to the domestic staff, and since his responsibilities are small his fees are, of course, low; but I understand he has good credentials and is well thought of by the local population, among whom—and this is of special import— he *must have gained exceptional experience of the effect of obnoxious effluviums*. His statement to Lady Brash has, therefore—you will not be surprised to hear—definitely established my most unfavourable prognostications.

As you had previously intimated inability to determine what curative measures to adopt, and Mr. Grigblay had no recommendations to propose, I communicated with Messrs. Quince and Jarrad, Consulting Sanitary Specialists. These gentlemen are employed by certain of my acquaintances, and also by Royalty and by members of the aristocracy, and *any* opinion of theirs is accordingly conclusively final. Mr. Jarrad attended to the matter himself personally, and made exhaustively thorough explorations and tests, and I enclose his report. I make no comment of any kind whatever. The report is exactly what I expected; the sanitary work has been disgracefully badly done, and will have to be drastically renovated—however, I will make no comment. My architect has failed me, the builder, instructed and supervised by him, has defrauded me, and it is a providential mercy that we are all alive and in relatively good health to-day; but, as I say, I make no comment, but confine myself to requesting you to *read* the report (enclosed)—simply to read what these authoritative experts say of our sanitary provisions, and then to favour me with explicit assurances that the necessary renovations will be put in hand at once, and of the date when they will be completed, as it will be necessary to vacate the house while the work is being performed. No doubt you may wish also to offer some observations justly appropriate to the occasion.

As the necessity for employing the services of Messrs. Quince and Jarrad was due to remission of care on the part of Mr. Grigblay in performing his duties, and his refusal to give attention to the emendation of defects, I shall most certainly deduct their fee of twenty guineas from the next payment due to Mr. Grigblay.

Yours sincerely,

We may conclude that under pressure from Lady Brash the doctor yielded the admission that defective drains may precipitate attacks of asthma in a person subject to them.

(ENCLOSURE) QUINCE AND JARRAD TO BRASH

Sir,   12.6.26.

We have the honour to say that in accordance with your instructions we visited Honeywood Grange on the 3rd of this month and made an exhaustive examination of the sanitary works, and now have the pleasure to enclose our Report.

We have the honour to be, Sir,

Your obedient servants,

At first glance, this letter might be a command to attend a State function at Buckingham Palace. It is beautifully typed in green on an exquisite linen paper self-edged like a bank note, and is headed in embossed gold lettering with an address adjoining Cavendish Square and with the statement that Messrs. Godolphin Quince and Hartington Jarrad are Consulting Sanitary Specialists, Patronized by Royalty and by the Nobility and Gentry.

The report covered by the letter extends to seven typed foolscap sheets, with a printed heading reproducing the intelligence gilded on the letter, and stating, in italics, that passages typed in red are so rendered in order to call attention to them. A glance shows that these red letterings all refer to points to which Messrs. Quince and Jarrad take exception; that there are a considerable number of such passages; and that, for greater emphasis, they are all typed in capitals.

The report is evidently based on an exhaustive survey and is the skilled work of men of highly specialized knowledge and wide experience in a restricted field, but while Spinlove's task was to provide Honeywood with a well-devised and soundly executed drainage system that was in no way unnecessarily costly, Quince and Jarrad pursue a fantastic ideal of theoretic perfection in which expense has no consideration. With that qualification, and except that it makes no allowance for those differences of opinion which exist in the theory and practice of sanitation, as in everything else, and confines itself to adverse criticism, the report is fair. It does not, however, except by implication, say what should be done to meet the objections raised; for the reason, no doubt, that Messrs Quince and Jarrad were not asked to reconstruct Honeywood's drains, but only to report on them.

There would be no purpose in here reproducing the report, which describes, first, the system Spinlove has adopted; second, the layout of the drains; and third, every detail of the work. It is the passages typed in red which have scared Brash and will trouble his architect and which alone concern us, and as Spinlove has to meet these criticisms, we may expect to learn all we want to know of them from future letters.

(PERSONAL) SPINLOVE TO GRIGBLAY

Dear Mr. Grigblay,   15.6.26.

I am much disturbed to receive the enclosed letter and report of Quince and Jarrad from Sir Leslie Brash. They make out that everything is wrong. Will you read and let me know what you make of it all?

Yours truly,

As usual, when in difficulties Spinlove looks about for advice—a bad habit, for it is only by settling things for himself that he will learn to make decisions. At the same time, he is right to confer with the builder on this matter, before acting.

(PERSONAL) GRIGBLAY TO SPINLOVE

Sir,   17.6.26.

I return herewith Quince and Jarrad's latest. It is their usual pack of nonsense, but it may be an awkward job to get the old gentleman to agree. I think, Sir, I had better have a talk over. I can make convenient on Saturday at 11.30 if you will kindly confirm by phone, and oblige,

Yours truly,

We may suppose that Spinlove gained great advantage from his talk with Grigblay.

SPINLOVE TO QUINCE AND JARRAD

Dear Sir,   21.6.26,

I have received from Sir Leslie Brash your report on the drains at Honeywood Grange, of which house I happen to be the architect. I must protest that it is most unfair of you to give mere differences of opinion the appearance of condemnations. You find no actual fault in the arrangements anywhere, and yet you have led my client to believe the drainage of his house is insanitary.

You even tell him that the joint of lead waste to gully has not been made, without troubling to look to see whether it has been or not.

Yours faithfully,

It was undignified of Spinlove to write this letter, and also not worth while, for Messrs. Q. and J. probably receive a good many like it, and some that are more violent.

QUINCE AND JARRAD TO SPINLOVE

Sir,   22.6.26.

We have the honour to acknowledge your letter informing us that you do not agree with our views *re* drains Honeywood Grange, and which we may say we are not surprised to hear as we happen to know our own business.

The differences of opinion you refer to are quite common and have no signification whatever, being quite usual with architects.

We have the honour to be, Sir,

Your obedient servants,

Spinlove asked for something of this sort. Q. and J. have not used their gold-embossed bank-note stationery for this letter.

SPINLOVE TO BRASH

Dear Sir Leslie Brash,   22.6.26.

I could not write to you on the subject of Messrs. Quince and Jarrad's report until I had thoroughly investigated the points raised.

I do not think that you yourself read the report closely, or you would not have formed the opinion that the drains are insanitary. Although the report is drawn in such a way as to lead you to a contrary impression, no fault is anywhere found, as you will see, either with the system or with the work; and attention is called to only *two* "*defects.*" One of those defects is not a defect in the drains at all, but a defect in Mr. Jarrad who tells you that a joint has been left unmade without troubling himself to see whether it has been or not; the second so-called "defect" is not an actual defect as, if it exists, it refers only to tests applied by Mr. Jarrad, and not to the normal use of the drains.

I am aware, Sir Leslie, that you will consider that I am on my defence, and will be reluctant to accept my views; but I am glad to say that I am not called upon to defend myself, and for your own peace of mind I ask you to hear me out with patience for I shall confine myself to showing what the report does actually say. Before I do this I should like to point out that the whole of the matters stressed by red lettering, except the two above mentioned, are mere expressions of *opinion*, and do not involve the question of sanitary soundness in any way whatever; and also that this difference of opinion is in all cases due to the fact that, while I designed the system so as to avoid unnecessary expense, Messrs. Quince and Jarrad's ideas are of the most extravagant and costly kind. I enclose the report and take the red-lettered points in their order.

"The aerobic filter might well be bigger and the tipper set 9 ins. higher. Gun metal bushes and trunnions are desirable, as in course of time rust will interfere with action of tipper."

The filter and tipper are the standard device of Wreek & Co., who are leading specialists in the work. I cut out the bronze bushes, etc., as being needlessly costly.

"We prefer detritus chambers and manholes to be lined with glazed brick. Also the effluent channels would be better in glazed ware. We recommend tallow for sealing manhole covers."

Glazed brick is expensive, and here quite unnecessary for sanitary efficacy. The rims are sealed with axle grease, which is usual. The sealing, in any case, is a counsel of perfection.

"The glazed channel discharging waste from scullery sinks over grease trap is unnecessary and objectionable."

As this channel is required by the local Sanitary Authority it *is* necessary, and the Local Government Board does not agree that the arrangement is objectionable or it would not describe it in its Model Bye-laws.

"The ventilation of the drains is sluggish. We recommend the up-and-down-cast system in preference to the up-cast here employed."

Messrs. Quince and Jarrad are in a minority among sanitary engineers if they hold this opinion; the up-cast is almost universally employed. The sluggishness was due to Messrs Q. and J.'s representative having wetted and thoroughly chilled the pipes before he tested for ventilation. Mr. Grigblay will at any time demonstrate to you that the system ventilates properly.

"That lavatory wastes discharge over open rainwater heads near to windows. This arrangment is most objectionable as, when the down pipe and head get fouled, air passing up the pipe will smell offensively. We recommend lead waste pipes properly ventilated and discharging through inlets under grids of gullies as employed near the front entrance."

This condition *may* arise in the future. When it does, it can be readily cured by cleansing the pipes. It does *not exist to-day*. The arrangement I have adopted has much to recommend it, in addition to effecting great saving in cost. As nearly all the bedrooms have lavatory basins, Messrs. Quince and Jarrad's device would cover the elevations with a network of pipes with ventilating branches standing up above eaves.

"We much prefer and always recommend cast-iron waste and soil pipes in place of the lead used at Honeywood."

As in an hotel or workhouse! The associations of domestic architecture favour lead, and Messrs. Quince and Jarrad do not say—and cannot say—that lead pipes are not at least as sound as any other.

"The lead bath and lavatory waste by front entrance has been merely pushed through the gully inlet and not jointed to it."

This is not the case. A flanged ring has been wiped to the lead and jointed to the stoneware in cement, as anyone could discover who wanted to know.

"The plate on clearing eye at the junction of the soil pipe vent by north-east gable has not been properly bedded, and allows foul air to escape from the drain."

I will have this plate taken off and re-bedded, but as there is, for all practical purposes, *never more pressure inside the open vent than outside,* leakage cannot take place; if there were any leakage it would be of no consequence as the whole purpose of ventilation is to prevent the air in the drain from getting poisonous, and if it became foul the position of the plate at the side of the gable and above the main eaves gutter would still make the matter of no consequence. The leak can only exist when the ends of ventilating pipes are stopped and air pumped into the drains under pressure.

I have written at some length, Sir Leslie, but at not, I hope, too great a length. If any doubts still remain of the soundness of the drains, I hope you will let me know what they are.

Yours sincerely,

This letter would have been more dignified if Spinlove had denied himself backhanders at Messrs. Quince and Jarrad, whose destruction would also have been more complete if Spinlove had made his points coolly instead of with warmth. The tone of the letter is unprofessional; but Spinlove's relations with Brash—who long ago made fervour, rather than decorum, the characteristic note of their interchanges—excuse it. Except for this he seems to have done extremely well and has given Brash grounds to be most grateful to him. With Grigblay's help and guidance (the "defect in Mr. Jarrad" obviously originated with Grigblay) he has thoroughly mastered the facts, and applied himself to make a most effective display of them; and he accomplishes a difficult task with a tact which even touches on charm—a most unusual achievement for him. It has been apparent that Spinlove is decently educated, and here we particularly see his advantage in this respect. The position is an awkward one, for Brash has been led by Spinlove's own lack of gumption to doubt his architect's capacity in matters of sanitation and, as we know, has a high opinion of Quince and Jarrad which is rooted in snobbery and therefore almost indestructible. Brash has no technical knowledge of drains, yet it is for him to decide between the conflicting opinions of architect and expert, whether his drainage arrange ments are perfectly sanitary, or not; and if Spinlove cannot re-establish himself with his client and persuade him to his views, it is difficult to say what may not happen.

GRIGBLAY TO SPINLOVE

Dear Sir,   21.6.26.

You directed us to let you know if we were asked to make any structural alterations at Honeywood. Her Ladyship lately asked us to fix a grate she has bought, in the boxroom, and this we have done with a bit of pipe carried well up into the flue serving the small servants' bedroom (No. 5) on the second floor, by her Ladyship's orders. We do not know whether this is what you mean by structural work, but think well to mention the matter. Her Ladyship says the fireplace in No. 5 will never be used.

Yours faithfully,

A fireplace in a boxroom is scarcely to be found in the most lavishly equipped house, and it is a mystery how anyone could imagine any kind of use for one there. Two fireplaces connected to one flue are likely to give complete satisfaction only while neither of them is in use.

BRASH TO SPINLOVE

My dear Mr. Spinlove,   24.6.26.

I have to confess that I read your communication anent sanitation with some impatience, but after carefully reperusing your arguments I am inclined to regard Messrs. Quince and Jarrad's proposals as unnecessarily redundant. Although I make no pretence of being a sanitary expert myself, I certainly agree with you that excessive costliness of refinements are inappropriate when not visually evident. There are certain aspects of the matter I desire to discuss with you, but so far as I can judge you have demonstrably answered Messrs. Quince and Jarrad's criticisms, and you will be glad to know that the odoriferous conditions are now rapidly ameliorating; in fact, they appear to have eventually dissipated, for though Lady Brash has been expectantly apprehensive no undesirable olfactory evidences have, I understand, been lately detected.

In view of the fact that the sanitary provisions are not—as Messrs. Quince and Jarrad led me to suppose—defective, I shall expect those gentlemen to allow me a substantial discount off the heavy fee of twenty guineas they have the effrontery to ask for their superfluous services.

Lady Brash informs me that we are to anticipate the pleasure of your company during the week-end. I shall then have an opportunity of discussing various matters with you.

With kindest regards,
Yours sincerely,

This is a triumph for Spinlove. It is to be hoped that Brash is grateful to him. He certainly seems to be, but his unusual good humour may be chiefly due to his having got this tormenting question of the drains settled, and Lady Brash appeased. Why these troublesome smells should so suddenly disappear is a mystery; but then it is also a mystery why they should ever have existed—if they ever did exist outside Lady Brash's imagination.

Messrs. Quince and Jarrad, by Spinlove's showing, here cut a sorry figure; but in point of fact they belong to an order of men to whom society has been in the past greatly indebted. It has to be remembered that what are now commonplaces of sanitary decency were, sixty years ago, only taking shape in the minds of scientific inquirers; and that forty years ago the general application of modern principles of sanitation was an innovation bolstered by public panic. In those days doctors, faced with the complicated symptoms of patients who had nothing wrong with them, had only to say, "Are you sure there is nothing wrong with the drains?" to escape with honour from the field. The nobility and gentry—who, we noticed, are patrons of Quince and Jarrad—were obsessed with drains, which thereupon became fashionable just as appendicitis did a few years later. Country gentlemen talked drains over the wine after dinner, compared drains on their way home from church, and rivalled one another in the renown of their sanitary adventures. There was scarcely a house in the country which was not, according to present ideas, poisonous; and none that was what we would consider sanitary. Throughout the country, people who would spend nothing on anything else were eager to celebrate themselves with drains, and this work was in great measure done—and thoroughly well done—by the forerunners of Quince and Jarrad.

The firm's fantastic test-exactions and extravagant ideas are also, for them, unavoidable, for if after they have approved the sanitation of a house the drains are surveyed by another expert in order to satisfy the covenant of a lease or conveyance, or because of a suspicious case of illness, and this rival expert, by more exacting refinements of test or stringency of standards, reports a defect or imperfection, Quince and Jarrad might be liable for damages, and in any case the reputation upon which their very existence depends would suffer. This danger is so imminent that firms of the standing of Quince and Jarrad will apologize for the stringency of their tests and the triviality of their objections even while making them. This is perfectly understandable. The expert tells the owner exactly what sort of drains he has got; that is the expert's responsibility: the owner decides whether to risk living in the house or not; that is the owner's responsibility, and the expert's comment, "I should not hesitate to live there myself, " and so forth, does not shift those responsibilities. If Spinlove is ever called upon to re-drain a house he would benefit by knowing this—however, it is not likely he will be, for old houses have nearly all now been re-drained, and new ones do not need it.

A DISPUTE

Dear Sir,   24.6.26.

As arranged in your interview with Mr. Grigblay on the 10th, we have been in correspondence with Messrs. Hoochkoft on the subject of refund of their charge for picking facings. We enclose copies of letters and wait your further instructions *re* same.

As Mr. Grigblay reminded you, the bricks were selected by you and ordered by us to your instructions without our seeing samples, and were inspected by you on delivery. You afterwards informed us you had arranged with Hoochkoft to send their picked quality, and we paid them for picked as per their quotation to you.

We must again press for certificate for £1,316 3s. 1d. Mr. Grigblay understood from you that certificate would follow, and we expected it would be received before now as it is a long time overdue.

Yours faithfully,

(ENCLOSURE 1) GRIGBLAY TO HOOCHKOFT

Dear Sirs,   16.6.26.

The architect objects to your charge of 28s. extra for picked facings over your original quotation of 147s. per thou. He states you agreed to pick over free of charge, as the bright-reds objected

104

to were not according to approved sample. We will thank you accordingly for refund of £92 overcharge paid you by us in error.

Yours faithfully,

(ENCLOSURE 2) HOOCHKOFT TO GRIGBLAY

Dear Sirs,   21.6.26.

Mr. James Spinlove gave us order for picked as per our special quote to him of 175s. per thou. as duly invoiced by us which please note is correct and oblige.

Yours faithfully,

Spinlove handled this matter badly. Instead of getting samples and quotations through the builder, he dealt direct with Hoochkoft and told Grigblay to order a certain broken-colour brick at a certain price without sending him the approved samples or otherwise letting him know what bricks he was to expect. He also did not definitely rule out a bright-red under-burnt sample to which he objected, and Hoochkoft accepted the order, perceiving that they could contend that their bright-reds had not been excluded. The bright-reds, to the amount of about 15 percent of the whole, were delivered, and were used by Grigblay until Spinlove stopped him. Spinlove then had a wrangle with Hoochkoft, who asked 35s. a thousand bricks extra for picking out the bright-reds, which charge Spinlove refused to allow on the grounds that Hoochkoft had agreed to exclude the bright-reds. Hoochkoft then reduced their claim for extra price to 28s. and, by manipulating an ambiguity, led Spinlove to write them a letter that might be interpreted as agreeing to the extra price, although the opposite was intended by him.

SPINLOVE TO HOOCHKOFT

Dear Sirs,   26.6.26.

Mr. Grigblay has sent me copy of your letter to him stating that I agreed an extra price for picked facings.

I did nothing of the kind. As you are well aware, I refused to countenance the extra. I cannot pass your account for more than the rate of 147s. a thousand originally quoted, and accepted, and I have so informed Mr. Grigblay.

Yours faithfully,

By yielding to impatience and showing bad manners Spinlove throws away the advantage he has in knowing better than to do so. If it comes to a slanging match he will have no chance against Hoochkoft. He also makes a great mistake in asserting himself before he knows what position Hoochkoft takes, for if he is forced later on to withdraw, he will lose ground that he might otherwise hold. The vehemence of his letter, too, is a sign of weakness. If he were sure of his case he would not be so noisy in proclaiming it.

SPINLOVE TO GRIGBLAY

Dear Sirs, 26.6.26.

As I reminded Mr. Grigblay, I did *not* agree Hoochkoft's price for picking. I gave you no authority to pay the extra, and I cannot pass the account for more than the originally quoted price of 147s.

I enclose certificate for £1,000 further on account. I should explain that Sir Leslie Brash raised great objection to the total of the account, and I could not very well draw the certificate until I had had an opportunity of explaining matters to him. Even so I am afraid he may make difficulties about honouring the certificate, and as there are various matters in dispute I do not feel able to certify for more than £1,000 at this time.

Yours faithfully,

It will be noticed that Spinlove has, by sloppy organization and lack of precision in expressing himself, not only given Hoochkoft an opening for setting up an unfair claim, but has also misled Grigblay who could have no other reason for paying Hoochkoft's extra charge than the belief that Spinlove had told him to pay it.

If Spinlove is satisfied that Grigblay is entitled to a certificate, he is
bound to draw it; and the reluctance of the owner to accept the account or
honour the certificate is no justification for Spinlove's holding it back.

SPINLOVE TO BRASH

Dear Sir Leslie Brash,   26.6.26.
Grigblay has been pressing for a further certificate on account.
I held this up until I should have had an opportunity of going into
the account with him and with you, although the amount—£1,316
3s. 1d.—has, in fact, been due to him since *early last February.* As
some items in the account are still in dispute I have certified for
£1,000 only. This leaves £1,332 14s. 7d. as security in your hands
for the making good of defects, and to cover any deductions which
may hereafter be made from the account.

Yours sincerely,

HOOCHKOFT TO SPINLOVE

Dear Sir,   28.6.26.
We were naturally surprised at the contents of your letter. We
may say that we regret the confusion that has unfortunately arisen,
but you have evidently overlooked that you ordered picked as per
our special quotation to you of 175s. and that we duly acknowledged same. This you will see is quite correct if you will refer to
previous correspondence at the time. Trusting the above explanation will be quite satisfactory to you,

We remain, dear Sir,
Yours faithfully,

Hoochkoft are plausible rogues. They seem likely to get the better of
Spinlove, who will find it difficult to believe this letter to be part of a
deeply laid scheme to deceive him.

GRIGBLAY TO SPINLOVE

Dear Sir,   28.6.26.
We have to acknowledge certificate for £1,000.
As you sent us copy of Messrs. Hoochkoft's letter quoting 175s.
for picked facings, and afterwards wrote us you had arranged
with Hoochkoft to supply picked, we naturally paid their invoices
in accordance and do not see how we could be expected to do otherwise. We do not see what more we can do in the matter.

                                        Yours faithfully,

*Spinlove is getting the worst of this. He has put himself into the same
kind of difficulty as that in which Brash finds himself over the Riddoppo
paint; that is to say, he has made two parties who should be accountable to one another each accountable to him. Experienced architects are
careful to avoid dividing responsibility, and are particularly wary of
sandwiching themselves between conflicting parties as Spinlove has here
sandwiched himself. This, in fact, is a first principle of good organization as understood by architects.*

SPINLOVE TO HOOCHKOFT

Dear Sirs,   30.6.26.
Our early correspondence makes it perfectly clear that I
objected to the bright-red samples when I accepted your tender,
and that you accepted the order on the understanding that they
were not to be included. When I found the bright-reds were being
included in deliveries I at once told you consignments containing
them would not be allowed on the site. When you then proposed
an extra charge for picking over, I refused to agree, but called
upon you to supply to approved samples and pointed out that it
was no concern of mine whether this was effected by picking or
otherwise. I made myself perfectly clear and I will not allow the
extra charge.

                                        Yours faithfully,

Spinlove evidently feels the need of justifying himself, or he would not enter upon a florid recapitulation of facts which he twice states are "perfectly clear." If they were perfectly clear it would not enter his head to elaborate the point. Hoochkoft will be quick to notice this, and also to notice Spinlove's naive admission in his last sentence, that if he had failed to make himself perfectly clear he would not contest the charge.

SPINLOVE TO GRIGBLAY

Dear Sirs,   30.6.26.

I did *not* say I had "arranged with Hoochkoft." My words were "Hoochkoft has now agreed to pick out the soft bright-red bricks," which, in view of previous letters on the subject, is a perfectly clear statement that no charge for picking was to be made, and I therefore cannot pass the account.

It is for you to inform Messrs. Hoochkoft of my decision and require them to refund. If I had said *I* had agreed for Hoochkoft to pick, it would have been a different matter, but I did not say so.

Yours faithfully,

It is a pity Spinlove did not shorten his letter by the length of its last sentence. As usual, in his doubt of himself and anxiety to be plausible, he says too much. Although he omitted to state in so many words that the picking was being done free of charge, Grigblay was, nevertheless, at fault in assuming the contrary; but Spinlove surrenders all possibility of making good his claim by gratuitously admitting that its justice depends on niceties of syntax the exploration of which causes—in me at least—sensations of vertigo. He also reveals that he is now out of his depth in his own muddle. The only ground on which Grigblay can ask a refund from Hoochkoft is that he misunderstood the architect's instructions when he paid, and the only reply which he can expect from Hoochkoft is: "We are sorry for you."

HOOCHKOFT TO SPINLOVE

Dear Sir,   2.7.26.

We were naturally astonished to receive your letter. After our definite refusal to supply picked at the price we quoted for unpicked, and your acceptance of our special rate to you of 175s., we are surprised you should consider it worth while to press this unreasonable claim against us after we have reminded you of the facts which we supposed you had overlooked, and must now consider the matter at an end so far as we are concerned.

Yours faithfully,

SPINLOVE TO HOOCHKOFT

Dear Sir,   3.7.26.

It is perfectly clear from the correspondence that facings were to be picked free of cost. You had no right to make the extra charge and Mr. Grigblay had no authority to pay it. As I shall not pass the account, it will be for you and Mr. Grigblay to settle it between you. You will hear from him.

Yours faithfully,

As has been said, there is nothing for Hoochkoft and Grigblay to settle between them. Spinlove, as agent for Brash, has either to force Hoochkoft to refund on the ground that the charge should not have been made, or compel Grigblay to stand the loss on the ground that he had no authority to pay it. Failing that, Brash will have to meet the charge, unless he can prove it to be set up by the culpable negligence of his architect; in which case Spinlove would be liable to Brash for the amount.

HOOCHKOFT TO SPINLOVE

Dear Sir,   5.7.26.

We certainly have no intention of settling with Mr. Grigblay. So far as we are concerned the matter was long ago settled, and the only reason we have corresponded with you was to explain your mistake. In view of your hostile attitude the matter is now closed.

Yours faithfully,

Hoochkoft evidently realize that they cannot persuade Spinlove they have not cheated him, nor hope to retain his esteemed favours.

GRIGBLAY TO SPINLOVE

Dear Sir,   5.7.26.
We can only repeat that we acted in accordance with your instructions in paying Messrs. Hoochkoft's charge for picked. As you have kept this matter in your hands throughout we are not in a position to approach Messrs. Hoochkoft further *re* same. We have already told them your views on the matter.

Yours faithfully,

This letter, and Hoochkoft's, seem to signalize the final discomfiture of Mr. James Spinlove, A.R.I.B.A.

BRASH FORGETS HIMSELF

My dear Mr. Spinlove,   5.7.26.
I duly received your communication anent certificate, which
document has been transmitted to me by Mr. Grigblay, and have
been for some days contemplating inditing a communication to
intimate my apprehensions that, in disbursing this very substantial sum, I shall appear to acknowledge the justice of claims which
still await eventual elucidation when the detailed account is produced.

Your own attitude in this matter continues to impress me as
being—if you will permit me to say so—extremely inexplicable.
It must be obvious to you—although natural reserve makes me
hesitate to say so—that I am a gentleman of not altogether neg-
ligible weight and importance in the business world, who has
attained a certain degree of social eminence and monetary afflu-
ence; and I assume that young gentlemen embarking upon professional careers with ambitions for success in their elective sphere,
are aware of the directions in which advantageous opportunities
are to be anticipated and final prosperity likely to eventuate; to be
precise, they comprehend—if you will excuse a vernacular collo-
quialism—upon which side their bread is buttered.

You have on several occasions taken the opportunity to remind
me that the contract allows you a very wide and free discretion
in deciding points in dispute, and I am naturally surprised to

notice that you consistently favour Mr. Grigblay's claims against me and urge—with considerable stiffness, you must permit me to remark—his views of contentious matters in preference to supporting my interests. I feel it my duty to a much younger gentleman who has not, I apprehend, enjoyed the opportunity of such wide experience of affairs as has been my providential good fortune, to intimate the illogical aspect of the position in which you put yourself, and the difficulty in which you place me. I meet one of my wealthy and influential acquaintances—let us suppose—who naturally refers to my building operations and asks: "How do you find your young architect, does he safeguard your interests and does he protect you from the rapacity of builders and contractors; is he a pliable and conciliatory gentleman?" How am I to answer that question in such a way as to encourage my influential friend's confidence in your professional capacities, while you keep me in serious doubts of the matter? This you will, I apprehend, regard as a subject deserving your thoughtful consideration, as it is obviously apparent that it has escaped your attention.

Believe me, my dear Mr. Spinlove,

Yours very sincerely,

The greasy affability of Brash's protestation—which so far as I can recall is without precedent—is evidently employed to give a gloss of magnanimity to a dirty purpose. The thing, however, is not quite what one would have expected of old Brash, and it is only fair to put the best interpretation upon it that circumstances allow. If Spinlove made clear to Brash that under the terms of a building contract the architect is constituted final arbiter of technical matters, and that his discretion is also decisive in many that are not technical, then it is perfidy of a detestable kind for Brash to use the power his years and station give him to subvert the honesty of the younger man; but we do not know that Spinlove made this clear to Brash, and the spectacle we have had of Brash's many flounderings makes it quite possible that he did not know what the obligations of an architect are. Brash may, perhaps, have regarded Spinlove as his agent in the ordinary sense of one whose services are remunerated by a commission, and did not understand that his architect's obligations to the builder were as binding, in fact and in honour, as his obligations to his client. At the same time, it is clear that Brash was conscious of meanness in tempting Spinlove to favour his interests.

SPINLOVE TO BRASH

Dear Sir Leslie Brash,   9.7.26.

As I explained in my last letter, I held back the certificate until Grigblay should have proved that he was entitled to it. Your honouring the certificate does not prejudice your right to challenge Grigblay's charges; but, in any case, responsibility for drawing the certificate is mine. Under the terms of the contract Grigblay can claim payment of all sums certified, and as he has been kept waiting a long time I hope you will make it convenient to send him a cheque at once.

I have some difficulty in understanding the drift of your letter. I do not think you need assurances that I am watching your interests closely to the best of my ability. It is also my duty to see that you are not called upon to pay any charge which is not properly substantiated. You cannot mean to suggest that I should unfairly interpret the contract against the builder in your interests, and disallow his just claims, in order to win your favour; yet that is the impression your letter gives. Will you, therefore, be so good as to explain what it is you have in mind?

Yours sincerely,

Here, again, what are we to understand? Has Spinlove failed to see the purpose of Brash's letter, or has he perfectly understood it and framed such a reply that Brash can make a graceful retreat? As Spinlove does not respond to, but rather repulses Brash's pose of cordiality, the latter explanation is probable; but it may be that, without knowing exactly what Brash intended, Spinlove so dislikes the implication of the letter that he yields to a healthy impulse and asks Brash what the devil he does mean.

BRASH TO SPINLOVE

Dear Mr. Spinlove, 10.7.26.

It is scarcely necessary for me to intimate that nothing was farther from my intentions when I indited my last communication than to suggest that you should "unfairly interpret the contract" or "disallow the builder's just claims." As you very naturally divine, I certainly have no such desires and would be the last person to consent to any such nefarious proposition. I am a gentleman who has always disbursed his just liabilities without demur and *up to the hilt* as it is sufficiently self-evident I shall be required to do on this occasion by Mr. Grigblay with the due approbation of my architect. At the same time I apprehend that it is within the prerogatives of the employer to indicate an aspect of the situation which it is clearly advantageous for his architect to comprehend. A judicial deportment is obviously an appropriate desideratum for a young gentleman engaging in the sphere of professional activities.

It will, I anticipate, signalize to you that I am pliably amenable to appeals of logical reason when I intimate that I have to-day transmitted cheque for one thousand pounds to Mr. Grigblay. I also enclose cheque for £60 in satisfaction of your own fees in respect of that disbursement.

Yours sincerely,

Brash appears to be sulky, and even a little embittered, at being taken up by Spinlove. His letter is a clever one: although it disclaims the sinister implications of its predecessor it, in fact, stresses them.

BRICK DISPUTE RENEWED

Sir,   10.7.26.

I have been looking into this matter of Hoochkoft's facings. You will understand it is no business of mine what understanding you came to with them, but as you cannot agree the matter I venture to drop you a hint that you have no occasion to argue it as those reds you objected to were under-burnt bricks that the fire hadn't properly reached and, as you know, some that got built in began to go almost at once. Hoochkoft cannot hold out that those soft reds were fit for what they sold them for, which is high-class facings—and which was their warranty or I am much mistaken. I enclose just a little statement that perhaps you may be interested to see and to have a word with Messrs. Hoochkoft about; but as I say it is no business of mine. It is lucky for them you had the softs thrown out or where would they be now!

Apologizing for troubling you but thought you might like the information.

Yours truly,

SIR LESLIE BRASH
DR. TO JOHN GRIGBLAY, BUILDER

EXTRAS ON FACINGS
SUPPLIED BY MESSRS. HOOCHKOFT AND CO., LTD.

	£	s.	d.
Paid Messrs. Hoochkoft for picking out defective under-burnt bricks	92	0	0
Paid Messrs. Hoochkoft for 1,050 defective bricks delivered and not used, at 147s.	7	14	4
Picking over 7,000 bricks for throw-out at 28s.	9	16	0
No. 87 cutting out defective under-burnt bricks built into wall-face and making good, at 2s.	8	14	0
	£118	4	4

It is a pity that this view of the matter did not occur to Spinlove before, but it has to be remembered that his objection to the wider-burnt bricks was that he did not like the colour of them. Defects only appeared in a small number which were, by oversight or misunderstanding, built into the walls; and as Spinlove held Grigblay responsible for this, and required him to cut out and replace, Hoochkoft's liability did not obtrude itself.

SPINLOVE TO GRIGBLAY

Dear Mr. Grigblay, 9.7.26.

Thank you for your letter and enclosure. I will write to Hoochkoft, but at the same time I cannot agree that you had instructions from me to pay their extra charge, and I do not depart from my decision that you are responsible for cutting out and making good defective facings, for they were built in contrary to my orders.

Yours truly,

We may suppose that Spinlove does not want to relinquish his claim against Grigblay, but this is not a happy occasion upon which to insist on it. Bloggs, the foreman, did his best to interpret Spinlove's instructions in throwing out the red bricks, and it was his misfortune, and not his fault, that some of those he built in began to decay.

SPINLOVE TO HOOCHKOFT

Dear Sirs,   12.7.26.

I have just received from the builder the enclosed account of his claim against my client in respect of defective facing bricks supplied by you, and shall be glad to receive your cheque drawn in favour of Sir Leslie Brash for the sum of £118 4s. 4d. forthwith, as the matter is of long standing and the account is now being closed.

Yours faithfully,

Appearances are that Spinlove took an opportunity to consult some longer head than his own on the drafting of this letter—perhaps that of Mr. Tinge, the quantity surveyor. The words he commonly wastes are conspicuously absent, and some good influence has also restrained him from his characteristic digressions in self-justification.

HOOCHKOFT TO SPINLOVE

Dear Sir,   13.7.26.

We do not understand why Mr. Grigblay's account with Sir Leslie Brash has been sent to us, and return it herewith as we can only suppose your suggestion of a cheque in settlement is intended as a joke. The matter is ended so far as we are concerned.

Yours faithfully,

SPINLOVE TO HOOCHKOFT

Dear Sirs,   16.7.26.

I have to point out that the matter of the defective facing bricks supplied by you is by no means ended, and is very far from being a joke so far as you are concerned.

The facts are that some of the soft, bright-red under-burnt facings included by you in the early consignments, and built into the walls, almost immediately began to decay and, to the number of eighty-seven, had to be cut out and replaced.

As you neglected to pick out the under-burnt bricks from early consignments totalling 7,000, this work had to be done on the site by the builder.

The under-burnt throw-outs were unusable and had to be replaced by sound bricks to the number of 1,050.

The charge you made for picking is not allowable as the bright-red under-burnt bricks were unsuitable for facings.

Mr. Grigblay's charge is the sum he paid you for picking, together with the cost of picking over in your default. The other charges are based on time and materials, and the amount paid you for defective bricks that could not be used.

The bricks offered by you, ordered by me and invoiced, are "facings"; you were under warranty to supply facings, and Sir Leslie Brash claims from you £118 to reimburse him for losses directly due to your breach of warranty. I return the account and have to repeat my request for cheque in settlement forthwith.

Yours faithfully,

It is difficult to believe that Spinlove settled the draft of this letter. The probability is that some architect friend of wide experience, or a lawyer, gave him guidance. It is to his credit that he realized he was on delicate ground, for it is most difficult in positions such as this to be lucid, and to keep to the essential facts, and to avoid prejudicing the position, or actually making it untenable, by accidental admissions or inconsistencies.

SPINLOVE TO BRASH

Dear Sir Leslie Brash,   16.7.26.

Thank you for cheque. I enclose formal receipt. I am glad you have sent Mr. Grigblay a cheque as he had grounds for feeling aggrieved at the delay.

I am obliged for your reply to my letter, but I still do not completely understand what it is that you expect of me. You seem to express dissatisfaction with my conduct of the business of settling

Grigblay's account. I can only assure you that I will spare no pains to see that no improper charge is included.

Yours sincerely,

HOOCHKOFT TO SPINLOVE

Mr. Spinlove,   17.7.26.

We now understand your new move to make us refund in order to cover your own liability to your client by now saying bright-reds were defective; but unfortunately you *told us nothing of this at the time*, but waited till your other trick failed, knowing that nothing was wrong with the bricks; and if you did have a few cut out they were sound ones and only done to bolster up a false claim against us by holding out they were defective when they were not; but very likely *none were cut out at all*, and this is just a dirty job to put responsibility on to us and get a refund because your other trick of saying you never ordered picked has gone wrong.

We return you Grigblay's account and suggest try again as this has not come off and something better is needed to humbug us.

Your most obliged humble servants,

Such contemptible devices as Hoochkoft, by return of post, here ascribes to Spinlove, could scarcely enter their heads if they did not themselves practise them. Its abusive diction and general likeness to the barking of a dog is not uncommon in some fields of business correspondence. Hoochkoft for the first time honours Spinlove by meeting him as man to man, and Spinlove should take heart.

SPINLOVE TO HOOCHKOFT

Gentlemen,   19.7.26.

I do not know whether you intend your letter as a final disclaimer, but as there is the testimony of the builder, foreman, bricklayers and others to support me, perhaps you will prefer to reconsider your position before I advise Sir Leslie Brash to take action to enforce his claim; in which case I do not think such letters as that you last sent me will help you. I enclose the account and await your reply.

I am, Gentlemen
Your humble servant,

This diplomatic answer was certainly not drafted by Spinlove. It is clear he had guidance.

HOOCHKOFT REMEMBERS HIMSELF

Dear Sir,   22.7.26.

Your favour of the 19th inst. with enclosure and previous correspondence has been laid before our chairman and managing director, Mr. Eli Hoochkoft, who proposes to wait on you at any time convenient to your good self for the purpose of amicably settling the matter to your satisfaction in a personal interview.

We may say that we were naturally taken aback at the contents of your previous letters, as the matters referred to were quite new to us and the official who dealt with the correspondence was under a misapprehension. Mr. Hoochkoft tenders you his apologies for same, although our suggested explanations were not intended in any way as a criticism of your good self.

We are, dear Sir,
Yours faithfully,

Delicacy of touch is not a strong point with Hoochkoft; in fact, one of the few disadvantages of having a hide like a rhinoceros is that you assume everyone to be sheathed with an insensibility equal to your own. Hoochkoft are quite unaware that their ingratiating affability presents the picture of deceits spurred by funk. The trick by which, after one bluff has failed, they approach the subject de novo from a new angle, by a pretence of referring it to higher authority, is a very old one.

SPINLOVE TO HOOCHKOFT

Gentlemen, 28.7.26.

I confirm arrangement by telephone that Mr. Hoochkoft will call to see me here at noon on Wednesday.

I am, yours faithfully,

(HOLOGRAPH) MR. ELI HOOCHKOFT TO SPINLOVE

Dear Mr. Spinlove, 5.8.26.

As promised I have carefully considered the position of my firm in the light of our friendly talk and now respond to your kind offer to entertain a payment in settlement by enclosing Treasury notes to the value of £25 in the belief that this will meet your favourable ideas. Will you kindly initial for receipt of this letter to the bearer who has been instructed to deliver it into your hands?

I trust that in the future I may be honoured by your esteemed favours, when I will make it a personal pleasure to see you receive complete satisfaction in any orders you may entrust to us and that no irregularity as that complained of occurs.

Believe me, dear Mr. Spinlove,

Yours truly,

Eli is trying to bribe Spinlove; a bribe being the giving to, and acceptance by, an agent of any gift or consideration, as an inducement to the agent to do, or forbear from doing, any act in relation to his principal's affairs. Although it is a thing the slightest hint of which all right-minded men shrink from as intolerable to their self-respect, and a violation of the rudiments of personal honour, yet bribery, in one form and another, is a common usage for greasing the wheels of business, and all architects sooner or later become aware of its detestable implications Many men whose fields of activity involve them in the practice, excuse it by the cynical sophistry that all human actions are swayed by a coveted reward, and that in essence there is no dif-

ference between actions framed in ambition for social and political advancement or the favour of powerful men, and those where the goal is more directly money—just as it has been argued that all motives are at bottom selfish or that there is no such thing as a bald man because it is impossible to say at what point, when single hairs are plucked from the head, it becomes bald.

We lately saw Brash holding out inducements to Spinlove to betray his trust which, though morally bribery, would scarcely have made him guilty at law, but this attempt by Hoochkoft is a particularly flagrant example of the crime—for crime it is. To take or give a bribe is an offence punishable by a fine not exceeding £500, with or without imprisonment not exceeding two years. If Eli were brought before me, I should award him a fine of one hundred pounds with nine months in the second division for undisturbed meditations on bricks. He is, however, unlikely to be brought before anyone; for such nefarious understandings as he here seeks to establish are reached by each party advancing towards the proposal by hints and innuendoes to which either can readily give an innocent meaning if his overture wins no response, and it is thus usual for the illicit agreement to be reached tacitly and by implication, without anything being said that would entitle either party to affirm that a bribe had been offered or asked by the other.

Thus we find Hoochkoft sending money to Brash's agent in fulfilment of an apparently honest agreement for settlement of Brash's claim, he could—although it is a question whether any jury would agree—hold out that he had no intention of bribing. He also, it will be noticed, makes it safe for Spinlove to pocket the money and decide, for any reason he chooses to give, that Brash's claim is untenable. There is the evidence of no third person; and there is no record, such as a cheque or bank notes would set up, that the money has changed hands. There is nothing but Hoochkoft's oath that he sent Spinlove the money against Spinlove's that he never received it, and vice versa, to establish the fact; and as both would be equally guilty and the arrangement meets the desires of each, there would be no likely need for either of them to thus add perjury to their conspiracy to plunder Brash.

(REGISTERED POST) SPINLOVE TO MR. ELI HOOCHKOFT

Sir,   7.8.26.

I am not prepared to recommend Sir Leslie Brash to accept any such disproportionate sum as the £25 you sent me in settlement of his claim against you.

As your offer is in no way adequate to your professions at our interview, I have to say that the sum I am prepared to recommend my client to accept in full settlement is the amount paid to you in error by Mr. Grigblay for picking out defective bricks, namely £92; and I shall be glad to receive, *not cash*, but your *cheque* for this amount *drawn in favour of Mr. Grigblay*, on receipt of which I will return your Treasury notes value £25. In the event of your not accepting this offer the matter will go out of my hands.

I am, Sir,
Yours faithfully,

The reason Spinlove did not send back Eli's Treasury notes by the messenger who brought them is, probably, that he could not at the moment make up his mind how to handle the matter. It is just as well he did not so return them, for it would have been a gesture of wiping out the interchange, and left things as though Hoochkoft had never offered the affront. As it is, Hoochkoft is likely to have an uneasy feeling as to what may have been happening in the enemy camp in the three days' interval between his sending the notes and Spinlove's letter, and this uneasiness will be increased by Spinlove's action in holding the notes for return, instead of putting them to Hoochkoft's credit in his account with Brash. Spinlove clearly has someone guiding him in this ticklish business, and perhaps the awkwardness of dealing with the cash, and a wish to enforce decorum on Hoochkoft and hold the whip hand over him, decided his action.

It still remains unexplained why such a practised rogue as Hoochkoft should have concluded that Spinlove was open to bribery. It is clear that he was misled by Spinlove at their interview; and it is also clear that Spinlove had no intention of so misleading him. We may suppose, therefore, that it never entered Spinlove's head that Hoochkoft's aim was to find out whether he was corruptible and, if so, his price; and thus Spinlove neither encouraged Hoochkofit to show his hand nor, in his complete unconsciousness, warned him by word or look that his task was hopeless. It is easy, on this supposition, to understand that Hoochkoft's offer of a money payment to Spinlove as "a sum in friendly settlement"—or however else he disguised his true meaning—was accepted in all good faith by Spinlove as a proposal for settlement to Brash, while Hoochkoft supposed Spinlove was veiling his acceptance in the same way that he himself was veiling the proposal. The extreme innocence of Spinlove, in fact, gave Hoochkoft, who is clearly a lumbering, obtuse fellow, the idea of excessive subtlety and wariness.

It is to be noted that no sum was named at the interview. The position was threshed out, and Hoochkoft went off to consider the sum he would offer in settlement.

HOOCHKOFT TO SPINLOVE

Dear Sir,   10.8.26.

With reference to Mr. Hoochkoft's interview with you on 4th August, we now enclose cheque drawn in favour of Mr. Grigblay for the sum of £92 as refund of disputed charge for picked facings, which you state was paid in error. The acceptance of this sum to be understood to be in full settlement of Sir Leslie Brash's claim against us as per enclosed account and which is in dispute.

Yours faithfully,

And so Spinlove has won! He has made a fight in which his native tenacity and his vanity have probably served him better than his devotion to his client's interests.

There is no doubt that Hoochkoft's false step in attempting to bribe Spinlove has precipitated his decision to pay up and so avoid any chance of litigation and exposure. It is to be noticed that Hoochkoft ignores Spinlove's letter and sends the cheque as though in fulfilment of an understanding come to at Hoochkoft's interview with Spinlove. His object in this is to cover his tracks, so far as may be, and avoid any official record of the illicit project.

A FALSE STEP

Dear Sir Leslie Brash,   11.8.26.
I think you will like to know that after considerable trouble I
have at last succeeded in securing refund of ninety-two pounds
which was overpaid to the manufacturer of the facing bricks by
mistake.

With kind regards,
Yours sincerely,

*Spinlove's guardian angel seems to be resting after the heavy task of
seeing him safely through his struggle with Hoochkoft; for though we have
had many examples of Spinlove's impetuous folly, he has never surpassed
the adroit idiocy of this letter.*

*It is obviously desirable to avoid pushing poor old Brash's dislocated
nose down into the extras account, yet Spinlove here goes out of his way to
do so. Not only is any letter at all quite unnecessary, but Spinlove entirely
discredits himself by vaunting his achievement. His childish impulse was
evidently to court Brash's esteem; but to do this it was important for
him to put that strange face on his own perfections which Shakespeare
tells us is the witness of excellency. His noisy acclaim of his own scanty
merit, which he represents in the worst possible light, can only make
his client sick with distrust. If Spinlove had merely allowed the fact to
emerge without any exhibition of complacency, his client would have
been favourably impressed with his capacity and vigilance, but what is*

Brash to think of an agent who writes—with kind regards—applauding himself for making a merchant give back money that ought never to have been paid; and who breaks the news with "I think you will like to know . . ." as though such glad tidings were beyond all imagining?

The explanation no doubt is that Spinlove, in the exhilarating moment of victory, is moved to demolish the adverse criticism of Brash's last letters, and writes, as he so often does, without pausing to consider what effect he will produce.

BRASH TO SPINLOVE

Dear Mr Spinlove,   13.8.26.

I was, of course, gratified to receive the intimation communicated by your missive, but you must permit me to convey the comment that the considerable difficulty you experienced in exacting repayment of an erroneous disbursement does not favourably impress me with the expeditious conclusion of negotiations for settlement. May the interrogation be permitted 1, *why* the excess amount was paid to these grasping manufacturers; 2, *how many more* of these irregular disbursements have been allowed; and 3, when—may I ask again—shall I eventually receive the detailed Statement of Account so often promised? This account, it is now obviously clear, will have to be carefully audited by qualified accountants.

My lengthy negotiations with the Riddoppo Company anent the failure of the paint are now approaching termination, and I shall shortly have further communications to make.

Yours sincerely,

Brash's auditing accountants will not be able to deal with Grigblay's statement of account, and are likely to raise many more questions than they will understand the answers to, so that the resulting turmoil will bring Brash more suffering than consolation. The proposal itself is, however, futile: Grigblay would refuse to allow interferences, and Spinlove and Tinge (the quantity surveyor) would support Grigblay; for under the contract Brash has agreed that the architect shall decide all technical matters and questions of fact, and that the quantity surveyor shall measure and value all variations, so that Brash's auditors would have no standing.

SPINLOVE TO BRASH

Dear Sir Leslie Brash, 14.8.26.

In reply to your questions:

(1) The manufacturer supplied bricks some of which I condemned as not up to sample. He then supplied a better quality for which he charged the builder a higher, unauthorized, price. In order to secure a refund I had to make good my contention that he was not entitled to a higher rate than that first quoted.

(2) None.

(3) Directly I receive it.

Yours sincerely,

Spinlove's hackles were erect when he wrote this.

DRY ROT APPEARS

Dear Jazz,   14.8.26.

Mum is away so what about a beano on Saturday sans all paren-
tal tennis crocks; just Snooty, Biff, Woggles, Boojum, you and
me—a whole afternoon of fast and furious? Boojum wants Snooty
for keeps, but don't let on as it's most *frightfully serious*. Boo served
hatfulls of doubles last Thursday and poor Snooty dunno where
she are. Buzz in early and bring tuxedos and pys as the caboodle
flits to Bingham's at nine. Only the usual old rampage but Porky B
with two snotties out of his old bum-boat are there on a week-end
binge and we shant go home till the Hullaballoo-bala-balay. I'm
perfectly potty but YOU know what I mean.

Now don't scream, but:

> There's suthin' funny amiss, Miss;
> Along by the pantery sink.

Thus our Judith cussically obsairve (see Art. Ward) jerking poetry
in your honour. Seriously, the suthin' funny is decidedly dud. Dad
is having the paintwork scrubbed to keep it from flaking off, and
to-day the fairy hand of Judith burst the wood thingy that runs
along under the sink. It is evident suthin' is amiss, for the wood is
bulged, and cracked and woolly, and seems to be crumbling and
it is very much rather all along under the windows in the kitchen.
No one dares tell Dad except Mum, and it is a shrieking necess to

130

have suthin' done before they come back in three weeks' time. Dad joins her on rest cure next week.

Meet the posh cubby hole and patent pocket nest Mum has made of the boxroom! You really never! It's *too* dilly! Twice as good as a caravan! Copied from the "converted attic" at the Ideal Homes Exy but *ever so much nicer* as the window is simply microscopic and it is all dim and penurious, and the roof slopes so that you can only stand up near the middle but, of course, when its a case of sits there is tons of room. The windey stairs are absolutely thrilling and there is the most dinky furniture you ever, and Mum and I simple *cuddle ourselves* there. Mum bought an old dud grate she saw lying in a cottage garden for *one and ninepence*, which was a bargain as the man asked two at first; and Grig's people made a fireplace with it. Mum is trying to find some old oak beams so that it will all be posher; and old panelling for the sloping part where the white comes off. We will have tea up there on Saturday.

Yours,
PUD.

Mum is going to be psychoed.

This letter has probably been preserved to us because of its intimation of dry rot; for that fell disease, which is a more fierce enemy of new houses than of old ones, is here clearly indicated.

We now learn why Lady Brash asked Grigblay to arrange a fireplace in the boxroom.

SPINLOVE TO GRIGBLAY

Dear Sir,   17.8.26.

I was at Honeywood during the week-end and it was pointed out to me that the skirting under the pantry sink is crumbling away like touch-wood. I imagined that water from the sink had rotted it, but there is no sign of wet, and the skirting along the outer wall of the kitchen is going in the same way. It is clear that the wood was not properly seasoned and it will be necessary to renew these skirtings at once.

Yours faithfully,

It seems that Spinlove has never seen, or smelt, dry rot, but one would think that he might have guessed what the extraordinary condition was due to. To attempt to cure the trouble by fixing new skirtings would be like trying to extinguish a fire by throwing fuel on it. The only remedy is to remove the whole of the rotted wood, to thoroughly sterilize surroundings, and to discover and end the cause of the outbreak.

GRIGBLAY TO SPINLOVE

Dear Sir,   20.8.26.

We gathered from your letter that dry rot is the trouble, and yesterday sent over our shop foreman, Hassoks, who says no great harm done but it has got into the back of the china cupboard. He pulled the vertical scotia off and there it was five feet up, but does not seem to have taken any hold. He says it has started on the edge of wood-block flooring but not gone far he thinks. The kitchen is not so bad, but there is a soft place in the skirting at foot of stairs and it sounds dead all along, Hassoks says. So it has got a hold there too. We do not know cause as Hassoks reports walls seem dry as a bone. Perhaps you would like to meet Mr. Grigblay at the house and decide what best to be done, and if you will appoint a day we will send over to take out the cupboard and open up for your inspection.

Yours faithfully,

This is a bad business, but how bad, remains to be seen.

Dry rot is a disease of timber caused by various species of fungi which feed on wood, penetrate it, and destroy it. Infection is by contact with diseased wood, or by spores latent in it, borne on the air or conveyed by dirt. If conditions favour its growth, dry rot may be regarded as inevitable; if they are unfavourable there is no danger. Favourable conditions are the coincidence of damp with warmth and lack of ventilation; and it is particularly the responsibility of architects and builders, as the law. decrees, to so design and build that those conditions shall not anywhere arise. As warmth is always present in a building, and it is impossible to ventilate every cranny of it, damp is regarded as the prime cause of dry rot. The need for entire prevention of damp is, therefore, always in the mind of the architect, the builder, the clerk of works and the foreman in charge. Ventilation, by carrying away evaporation, is a safeguard against "damp."

The beauty of dry rot—in the opinion of its admirers—is that when it once gets going it sends out, with devastating rapidity, thread-like tendrils which carry moisture, yards from the source, over the surface of walls and even through them, and which multiply to form mats of dense, cobwebby filament that collect moisture from the air and so set up and maintain new centres of growth from which new foraging tendrils spread. Thus the good work continues, so that one solitary brick carelessly thrown into the broken rubbish under the concrete foundation of a wood-block floor, and disposed in such a way as to conduct damp from the ground to the concrete, may set up in the wood blocks dry rot which in a few weeks will have travelled to the space behind skirtings, invaded the back of the door linings, passed into the staircase and involved the first floor before its presence is anywhere noticed.

The circumstances that give rise to dry rot are innumerable, and are a continued source of interest and pleasure to irresponsible observers; but the conditions of damp combined with warmth and lack of ventilation, are always present. A few days after a radiator is installed below a sliding sash window in an unfinished house, dry rot has started inside one of the jamb casings and involved the whole of it; eighteen months after a roof is finished by pointing the tiles without ventilating the roof-space, sagging outlines lead to the discovery that the whole of the inside surface is a mass of cobwebby fungus, and that the timbers are perished to the point of collapse, and—as made famous in the Courts half a century ago—the floors and joinery of a hospital have to be renewed at a cost of several thousand pounds because the wooden pegs, driven into the ground to fix the screeding-level of concrete floor-foundations, were not

*taken out. What exactly has happened at Honeywood we do not know;
but some source of continuous dampness in contact with the skirting,
with other woodwork near to it, is indicated.*

SPINLOVE TO MISS PHYLLIS BRASH

21.8.26.

I am coming down on Thursday to meet Grig about the pantry
do. Am arranging to get all done before the two P's return, but
there will be carpenters to take out the china cupboard so will
you get the crockery cleared?

*Apparently Spinlove has some sensitiveness about typing his super-
scription and subscription to this lady. It is, of course, inadvisable to
delay the work, for the harm is growing, and it will occasion less upset—
both physical and moral—if all is completed before "the two Ps" return.*

*Spinlove's light-hearted assumption that the trouble can be readily
cured, while he does not know the cause of it, is lamentable. It is clear
that not only has he had no experience of dry rot, but that he has no
knowledge of it at second hand, or he would view this manifestation of it
with consternation. The rot in the pantry and kitchen may be only first
evidences of an outbreak involving the whole of the ground-floor skirtings, which may itself be but the first visible flicker of flames that are rag-
ing out of sight in the floors, and which have already secretly invaded the
cavities at the back of panelling and of door and window linings and of
fireplace surrounds. Even this does not measure the full dimensions of the
possible catastrophe, for not only has the damaged work to be restored
and all parts near it to be doctored to destroy the infecting spores of the
fungus, but the cause of the outbreak must be fully proved and, when
proved, then entirely eradicated; and as this cause may be fundamental
in the design of the structure or inherent in the materials employed, the
little pieces of decayed skirting, as every experienced architect knows,
may, as likely as not, signal a great calamity.*

SPINLOVE TO WILLIAM WYCHETE, ESQ., P.P.R.I.B.A.

Dear Mr. Wychete,   24.8.26.

You have been so extremely kind in the past in advising me, that I hope you will not mind my troubling you, but I have a case of dry rot which I do not know how to deal with. I enclose prints of ⅛ in. scale plan, and ½ in. section of the outer

The house has been occupied now for six months, and the skirting along the outside north wall of the kitchen, pantry and hall up to the stairs, is rotted, and the under edge of the Columbian pine wood-block flooring has begun to go in places. The larders, scullery and cloaks along the same front are tiled and have tiled skirtings. I should mention we pulled up some of the wood blocks, but there was no sign of rot except just at the outer edges, and no evidence of rot anywhere else; and though the growth had run up behind the china cupboard the wood was sound.

The walls behind the skirting were "bone dry," the builder said; but he was doubtful of the concrete under the block floor. We cut this away where it lies against the wall, and the builder then said he understood the cause.

If you look at the half-inch detail you will see that the damp-course lies just below the concrete foundation of the floor; but the floor was lowered 1½ inches after the damp-course was built, and the bottom of the concrete comes an inch *below* the damp-course. The brickwork below the damp-course is full of water, and the builder says that damp is drawn into the concrete where its lower edge lies against the wet bricks, and that this has started the dry rot. Can this be possible? He also says that moisture creeps up between the bricks and the concrete, and gets into the brickwork above the damp-course, but I could not see any evidence of this. Do you think he is right? I could see no sign of damp myself. Before we cut away the concrete the builder thought the trouble might be due to the rain, which beats through the outer 4½ ins. of the hollow wall, collecting on the damp-course and getting into the inner wall, but he forgot that the hollow goes down *below* the damp-course.

The main question is—If the builder is right, what is to be done? He says he cannot advise me; that he built as I directed and cannot accept responsibility. I pointed out that *he* suggested lowering the floor so that the threshold of front entrance would line up with the brick joint and make a neat finish; but he says that the decision was mine and that he followed my directions in lowering the floor.

The north wall of the billiard-room is panelled in oak and the floor is of oak boards nailed to fillets let into concrete. The panelling is ventilated behind by openings in the skirting and in the top of the capping. There is no sign of dry rot here, and the builder says he thinks there is no danger.

I should be so very much obliged if you will tell me what you think I had better do, if it is not troubling you.

Yours sincerely,

The sketch below illustrates the positions of the floor and dampcourse described.

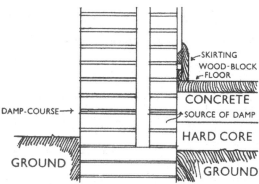

The eminent Wychete must be a good friend, indeed, to lay himself open to the fatigue of solving posers of this kind: and Spinlove must have great confidence in his opinion or he would consult a friend closer at hand instead of writing to Manchester, where, as his address indicates, Wychete operates. We know from earlier letters that the site of Honeywood slopes towards the south, and that it is only the floors on the north side that are laid directly on concrete. The others are carried on joists supported on steeper walls.

WYCHETE ADVISES

My dear Spinlove, 26.8.26.

This is an awkward business, and if you cannot deal with it yourself you ought to get the advice of someone on the spot; but, of course, *you* alone are responsible to your client, and no one but yourself can decide what course to take. The question between you and the builder is a difficult one. If I were you I should not press your point of view to the extent of making him antagonistic. He may be willing to do what is necessary without any charge, but, quite naturally, he will take no action that will involve him in responsibility. This is the reason he refuses to advise you, and he will not, you will find, handle the matter as a "defect" under the terms of the contract. If he did this, he would admit liability for the whole extent of the damage. This may, of course, become extensive.

I do not, however, think that it will extend. In my opinion the builder's view of the cause of the outbreak is likely to be right, but as the growth appears not to be vigorous, I think that the amount of damp is probably very small, and that the use of infected wood may have led to trouble which otherwise might not have occurred.

To make the house perfectly safe it would be necessary to cut away the concrete floor-foundation against internal walls as well as external, wherever there are "solid" wood floors—that is, over nearly half the area of the house—and make good clear of the dampcourse; but I think the case will be met if you replace all affected skirtings and blocks on top of an impervious bituminous coating made continuous with the mastic in which the wood blocks are laid, and covering walls behind skirtings. Bellflower and Snooter Ltd. manufacture coatings for various purposes and would advise what best to use. You should also treat the back parts of the cupboard, and all contaminated work, as well as the back of the new, with a solution of sulphate of iron. There is nothing better for killing dry rot and it does not smell as creosote does.

If this fails, you will have to cut away the concrete. If it succeeds, you can treat any other similar outbreaks in the same way, but let us hope that there will be none. I have no doubt the ventilation of the panelling in the billiard-room will prevent any trouble there.

Ever, my dear Spinlove,

Yours sincerely,

Wychete's tactful reminder that Spinlove is responsible to his client, and that whatever action he takes must be his own decision, is much to the point. Wychete's advice—whatever it is worth—cannot lead Spinlove astray; for the reparation, if experimental, is simple, and should it be without effect, little time and money will have been wasted. There is, however, the risk that while Spinlove is dealing tentatively with this small outbreak, far-reaching growths, which immediate drastic action would prevent, may be establishing themselves secretly in other parts of the house. The decision whether to take this risk or not and, if not, what measures to adopt, devolves on Spinlove; and no one can relieve him from the need to rely on his own discretion, for that discretion is linked to a responsibility which belongs to no one but himself. It is the exercise of discretion hampered by considerations of cost, of risk, of exact justice, of conflicting interests, of uncertainty as to facts, of misunderstandings and of diverse individualities and dishonest or incapable agents, which is the chief care and preoccupation of architectural practice. To design a building, to draw and specify every part of it, and to direct its construction and see it completed with no other anxieties and dilemmas than belong to the exercise of those duties, is unknown.

SPINLOVE TO WYCHETE

My dear Mr. Wychete,   27.8.26.
Thank you extremely for your most kind letter. I am enormously obliged for your advice. I will act on it at once. Surely, as the dry rot is due to the builder's use of infected wood, the outbreak is *his* fault and he can be held responsible for making good?

                                    With kind regards,
                                    Ever yours sincerely,

Spinlove's impetuosity here again prevails to his discredit. He plainly tells Wychete that he has not troubled to read his letter.

WYCHETE TO SPINLOVE

Dear Spinlove,   28.8.26.
I give no advice but merely make suggestions. There is no means of knowing that the wood was infected; and the "cause" of the outbreak is, in any case, *damp.*

                                    Yours sincerely,

Exactly! Wychete was particular in warning Spinlove that he must use his own judgment: by replying "I am taking your advice at once," Spinlove announces that he is relying on Wychete's. Wychete, naturally, will allow no such interpretation of his letter. Wychete was also particular in exculpating the builder; and if Spinlove had reflected, he would not have requited his benefactor by plaguing him to say once again what he has already been at pains to make clear.

SPINLOVE TO GRIGBLAY

Dear Sirs,   27.8.26.
I enclose specification of work in making good where dry rot has appeared. If you see any objections to the proposals will you let me know? The work should be completed if possible before the end of next week when Sir Leslie and Lady Brash, who are away, return.

                                    Yours faithfully,

GRIGBLAY TO SPINLOVE

Dear Sir,   28.8.26.

We have to acknowledge your instructions for making good where dry rot has appeared, and will do our best to complete same before the end of next week, as requested.

Yours faithfully,

Grigblay has no intention of committing himself in any way, it will be noticed. Spinlove will realize how much support and guidance he has had in the past, now that he can get neither.

BLOGGS ON EXTRAS

Dear Sir, 30.8.26.

As promised you by Mr. Grigblay, we have referred to our foreman Bloggs for explanations of certain extras under "Various minor works" and other matters queried by you, and enclose sheets with his answers to same which we hope will give the information you want.

Yours faithfully,

(ENCLOSURE) GRIGBLAY TO MR. F. BLOGGS
C/O JOHN GRIGBLAY, BUILDER,
BY PORTENWALSH MEAD, BAGGERFOSS, HUNTS

Dear Fred, 7.8.26.

The architect queries extras as attached sheets. The governor wants your answers in blank spaces. No doubt you have your diary along. Enclosed is copy of Statement lettered so you can pick up easy. The jim crow was put on passenger last night. The governor says if you can't manage take along to Potters, Nottington, who will straighten while lorry waits. To be charged up against Ry.

Yours,
T. P.

Hear with OK. F. Bloggs, Aug. 28th.

*This letter must have been sent to Spinlove pinned to the other papers,
by an oversight. It shows Grigblay's business to be conducted in the old-
fashioned style that still lingers, with the best intentions of the building crafts, in the provinces, where son follows father to the bench or the
scaffold, and the master calls his men by their Christian names, knows
the domestic circumstances of each, and distributes joints and poultry
among them at Christmas. There may be somewhere in this world happier men than these, associated in more delightful work, but it is a hard
thing to imagine. The tail of the letter indicates that Bloggs is in difficulties with a steel joist delivered bent from the railway.*

*Bloggs, it will be noted, is businesslike. He answers the letter concisely
and dates his signature. The attached sheets proclaim a most studious
devotion on his part, handicapped by a very gritty pencil and by india-
rubber deeply involved with butter. The papers are greatly fatigued at the
folds, and Bloggs has evidently lost the saucer of his teacup, but—with the
help of stamp-edging—they survive, and Bloggs, as he might be trusted to
do, has done the job, although it has taken him three weeks to finish it.*

HONEYWOOD

The Architect queries the following. The letters in margin refer
to Statement items.

A. EXTRA IN FOUNDATIONS, ETC.? ARCHITECT SAYS HE NEVER
ORDERED ANY.

Sep. 20th. 24. Architect bring along drawings of terrace, put
out acause she wants steps moved further up kitchen end. It were
the day her little nurse dog made to bite him so he will know it.
First I must lower bench of terrace he says; then after I peg out
that wont suit, so then it was three steps he ordered and that wont
do neither, it got to be two he says, wich where 9⅝ and brought
bench down to 7" or thereabouts above top of footings, and no
harm as I could see, but I must put foundation down four courses
along front and jump up with extra stepping on return he says. I

put Rumbler on it and after dinner found he got mixt and rekoned four courses has 13¼ instead of 11⅛ gauge we was on, but architect passed all on 13tht see dairy hearwith for measurs has per weekly return.

Bloggs's identification of Lady Brash with "she," after an interval of six months, is eloquent of the place the lady had won for herself in his regard.

Oc. 13tht. Archtect come on to pass trenches, dont like bit of slop down drawing room end (S). He drop his pipe and I send Joe Perks for a bit of waist I add in the window of my office, so he will know all about it. He wont have me to scrape up but I must dig out 4" to satisfy, and I level up with concrete to save jumping footings has he agreed to measure I give (see dairy) and marked with the toe of my boot for architects approval the oner see me do it and can say.

Nov 11tht. Syd broke his hand, architect was there so will know he ordered me to lower excavation for cellar floor one course, reason acause headroom to thight at door under stairs reason of lowering ground floor 1 ½."

Nov. 23tht. I had bench pegs set for screed of cellar floor and he came on afternoon latish about Hoochkofs facings and left a letter on my table I sent after. He dont like top course of footings standing above screed acause of bottom being dug 3" lower, and I must knock off to level. I says suppose inspector see what were at dam Mr. Potch he says, but after he left he came back and I haerd him shouting wehn I was in my office and put my head out to see who was and he had come back to gate and called I was to put floor back as it was and headroom were good enough, so there was that bit extra digging and hard core to level up again after, as per my weekly and see dairy.

As the due offset of footings is defined in the bye-laws, the local surveyor would object if he found a course being cut away.

B. EAVES SPROCKETS AND TILT TO RIDGE? ARCHITECT REMEM-
BERS GIVING DIRECTIONS BUT SAYS NO EXTRA.

June 6tht 1925. Architect come on roof an add me to fake a bit
of eaves has per No. 41 but that dont suit, must be bigger projectn.
and tilt. Well gage wehre 3½" so he says better make it one course,
so I botched it to get what he wanted but the rafter feet was all
lined and cut and no tilts would carry over that far, and what finish would he have an so I says it mean cutting back feet and fix
sprockets to make a job; and he says yes do it and make a job so
I done it D.W. as per weekly and all stuff cut out in shop which
proves it see dairy.

14 Juy tht. Tilers add left. Architect says must put more tilt to
gable ends of ridges. It come on raining pretty sharp and he tore
is mac standing in the door of my office wehre staple was jagged
after I had to burst the door along of the boy losing the key, so he
will remember. I say all I can, but it got to be done to satisfy and a
nice job pulling off the ridges and all that fancy filling on face and
breaking of the verges with there double undercloaks an pointing
and filleting in cement, it could not only be a botch but he would
have it and pleased when it were done he told me Jan 3 tht.

*As the verges of the roof, where the tiling ends at gables, are slightly
tilted so as to throw the water back on to the roof and prevent its being
blown to run down face of gables, it is natural that the end ridge tile at
gables should be given a corresponding tilt. This tilt at the end of ridge is
conspicuous, and is exaggerated in the designs of some architects apparently because an upward curve of the ridge to apex of gable—the result
of settlement of the roof timbers—is often seen in old houses, and has the
deadly sentiment of the "dear old." The same exaggerated effect is given by
artists who make drawings of houses for Christmas cards and kindred des-
tinies. Spinlove had various fanciful notions for the roof at Honeywood,
most of which were wrecked by the obstructive inertia of the British craftsman when asked to vary from accustomed usage; and one cannot help
regretting that he was not similarly baulked of his extravagantly belled
eaves and "old moated grange" gable ends. The devices of the building*

crafts, which have served the skilful and efficient use of humble material for centuries, are a pure delight to everyone who has studied them, and have come to be loved as a tradition of beautiful building; but it is the perfection with which they serve their purposes, and not the forms they present, which delight us; and to give those forms an emphasis beyond what their purpose demands, is fatuous. It is the thing that, in the main, makes the modern villa a monstrosity; and as it has no part in architecture, and as Spinlove is evidently a man of educated taste, we must suppose that his preoccupations with his ridges and eaves was to get them to look right, and did not result in making them look wrong. Strong associations are aroused when we view any building and, if the style or tradition of its design awakens a certain group of associations, it is important that every detail of the design shall accord with that tradition and strengthen the association. In a house with eaves, no feature is more expressive than the degree of projection of them. As the rafter feet had been cut to agree with the drawing (No. 41) they could not properly be used to carry the increased stand-over of the tiles. They had to be cut back close up to the plate, and false rafter feet, set at a slightly flatter slope to give the required tilt, spiked to them. These are the "sprockets" spoken of.

C. TAKING DOWN AND REBUILDING RETURN DIES OF TERRACE WALL. ARCHITECT STATES IT WAS YOUR MISTAKE.

Feb. 23tht. Architect come on in white trousers he left his bat against flooring stacked in kitchen an a long job to find so he will know wehn it were. He says break back at side of dies had ought not to be battered same as face but plumbded, but I reckon his drawing No. 22 showed it other way same as I had it, and so I told him and charged D.W. has per weekly.

P.S.—There were a line on that drawing you could not tell waht was meant for and he dont know neither so that makes sure for if he cant say how were it my fault not to.

Privet. He says I don't know a good drawing when I see one, an I says may be has I dont but I knows a bad one when I sees hit I says. Privit.

Spinlove seems to have had words with Bloggs on this matter and not to have got the best of the exchange.

Bloggs's microscopic memory is clearly an immovable barrier to all argument or question, and indicates resources of a kind that will infallibly repulse any attempts at cross-examination. His acumen in forestalling a denial of the circumstances he adduces can only be the result of tried experience in similar contests. What foothold can Spinlove find for protesting "I remember nothing about it," when he is told the event occurred on the day he dropped his pipe in the trench, or mislaid his tennis racquet? Demonstrably, Bloggs knows exactly all that happened, and Spinlove, who can remember nothing—even of the muddied pipe and the bit of cotton waste fetched from the foreman's office to cleanse it—clearly has not a leg to stand on.

This proof of the evidence of Frederick Bloggs covers five and a half laborious foolscap sheets, and I will make no further exerpts. Pinned up with these sheets are certain pages from his "dairy"; and the ungrudging liberality with which he has gutted it in the good cause is almost touching. "Leaves from a Diary" has a new meaning for me since I have seen Bloggs's. The entries are hieroglyphic and also cryptic; and if I describe the pages as having been "torn" from the book, I only do so because no more destructive-sounding word occurs to me. "Captured in Battle" best describes their appearance.

SPINLOVE TO GRIGBLAY

Dear Sir,   1.9.26.

I am obliged for your letter covering your foreman's replies to questions. I have, however to point out that in no case is the fact substantiated that work, stated to have been authorized by me, *was ordered as an extra.* As you are aware, unless work is definitely authorized as an extra *at the time it is done,* the assumption is that there was no understanding that it was to be an extra. I should be glad if Mr. Grigblay would make an appointment here to go with me into the various points raised.

I saw Mr. Tinge two days ago, who called my attention to the fact that you have charged for repointing work damaged by frost; but under the terms of the contract the responsibility for making good damage by frost is *yours*. I overlooked this, or I should have objected to the item before. I have told Mr. Tinge that it must be struck out.

Will you ring up to-morrow and let me know whether the work in making good dry rot has been completed as promised?

Yours faithfully,

Spinlove is right on the point of authorization of extras, but, actually, the terms of the contract are more rigid, for they require that, in order to rank as an extra, work must be authorized as an extra in writing.

Tinge is right, too, in the matter of damage by frost. Grigblay contracted to "protect from damage by frost," and is therefore responsible for making good damage due to failure to protect.

GRIGBLAY TO SPINLOVE

Dear Sir,   3.9.26.

Mr. Grigblay will call to settle account on the 7th at 2 o'clock, as arranged over phone.

We will ask you to note that we have on many occasions carried out work, charged as extra in Statement and accepted by you, on your verbal order alone; and have always accepted your word and put in hand as desired without delaying for written order or where should we be with all the variations there have been ever since the work was begun, waiting for written orders and not getting same. There are not above half a dozen written orders from first to last, and in general the only orders we have had have been verbal, which we have acted on at your request and to your approval. Now that this does not appear to please you, we shall be glad to have written authority for extra making good dry rot as per your instructions and oblige. The men cleared up yesterday.

If you will look at the Interim Statement we sent you, you will find we have charged only difference in value between plain struck joint and special pointing to your instructions and approval.

Yours faithfully,

Grigblay, in his own way, presents his view of the authorization of extras with clearness—if for "verbal" we read oral—and the position he takes is just. The contract stipulation that all work that is to rank as extra shall be authorized as an extra in writing at the time the work is done, is a good one; but like many excellent rules it can, in practice, not be always exactly followed; and in cases such as Honeywood—which are the rule rather than the exception—where there are a large number of small variations, its strict enforcement would entail delays and consequent losses which no builder could be expected to tolerate. We know that Spinlove was lax in enforcing the rule and, in the circumstances, it is hard to see how it could have been enforced; but as he has accepted as extras a number of items in the account which were not formally authorized, he cannot object to other claims on the grounds that they were not formally authorized, and accordingly each case will have to be settled by wranglings to decide what the facts giving rise to the work actually were. In that wrangle Grigblay will have the advantage of holding records which he can use as may best serve his ends; while Spinlove will have little but his memory with which to oppose them.

LADY B.'S CONVERTED ATTIC

Dear Lady Brash,   6.9.26.

As I understand you are now home again, I think I ought to write and just let you know about the new "converted attic" your daughter showed me—in fact, we all had tea up there. It is delightful, I know; so snug and cottagy with the low sloped ceiling and dingy light and the warming pans and the jolly little boxed-out chimney corner—all most ingenious, I have never seen anything at all like it before; but perhaps you do not know that it is not a *habitable room* as defined by the Regulations of the Local Government Board and required by the bye-laws. The roof space arrangement, you see, was only allowed by the District Council on my undertaking that it was to be used as a boxroom or store, *only*, so that you are violating the local building regulations—breaking the law, in fact—by using the place as a habitable room. If I had not promised that the place would *not* be used as a habitable room, the District Council would have refused to allow the house to be built. You see, in order to comply with the minimum requirements of the Model Bye-laws, the ceiling would have to be much higher, the roof-tops much less, the window much larger and the walls, all the way down to the ground, thicker. Of course, if it were an old house built before the bye-laws were adopted, you could do as you liked; but, unfortunately, Honeywood is a new house, and if the District Council gets to hear of what has been done I am afraid there will be serious trouble. I feel I ought to write and let you know this, so that you may be prepared.

I hope you enjoyed your visits, but I'm afraid you had wretched weather during the last week.

Yours sincerely,

As Spinlove is evidently afraid of Lady Brash, and is tremulous with anxiety lest he should be misunderstood, it is clear that he only wrote in the belief that it was his duty to give the warning. What poor Lady Brash will make of the Local Government Board, the Local Building Regulations, the Requirements of the Model Bye-laws, the thundercloud imminence of the District Council and the awful admonition "Prepare for Trouble," it is hard to imagine, but the whole thing is a mare's nest—a figment of Spinlove's imperfect knowledge. If it appears that spaces allocated in the plans to boxrooms, stores, and so forth, are usable as habitable rooms, the Local Authority can require them to comply with the dimensions, lighting and ventilation ordained for habitable rooms; but it cannot prevent owners from screwing up and shuttering windows, or blocking the vent flues. The plans of Honeywood were duly approved, and the house completed and certified as conforming to the building regulations; and if Lady Brash prefers to entertain her friends in the boxroom, or to dine in the bath, or to sleep in the cupboard under the stairs, it is no business of Spinlove's, nor of the District Council's, nor of anyone—except possibly of a commissioner in lunacy.

If people are found living in conditions inimical to public health and sanitation, the Health Officer can intervene, but that is another matter.

LADY BRASH TO SPINLOVE

Dear Mr. Spinlove,   7.9.26.

I knew you would admire my Ideal Homes converted attic. I meant it to be a great surprise, but Phyllis has told you so now it will not be. You cannot think what a comfort it is to get away from the servants! I just slip upstairs and know nothing of anything that is going on. Leslie prefers the lounge or the den so we do not sit there in the evenings, I think it is because of all the stairs! ! Would it be very expensive to put in a lift for the coals as well because there will have to be coals in the winter although it is a delightfully *warm* room, in fact in hot weather it is *too* warm and I cannot sit there so it will be delightfully cosy in the winter. Can anything be done about the noise the water makes; and is it quite *safe* when it whistles all the time and roars and rushes as though it was going to run over the side, particularly when Leslie comes home and is having his bath; and then noises like a man hammering to get in and people choking and dreadful sighs and groans and sometimes cries for help, so *alarming* if anyone was able to get up there without being noticed, but I am sure you would not allow such a thing for one moment.

Your letter is so very clever I could not follow it, but I should certainly object most strongly if the District Counsel tried to interfere; he is only a greengrocer with a *quite* small shop and a nursery garden, and he would not *dare* go against Leslie; such a *common* little man too, though always most civil and obliging, but if Mr. Bunseer says *one single word* I shall go to the Stores *instantly.* They send out here twice a week as he knows *perfectly well,* and the idea of this insignificant little man interfering in *my house* is a most unheard of state of things and I would never for one moment allow it. Really I do not know what things are coming to nowadays.

What delightful weather we are having again.

Yours very sincerely,

P.S.—Can you get me some old oak beams for it do you think?

Lady Brash does not appear to have been "psychoed" yet, but she knows well how to stand at bay and, ridiculous as is her view of the matter, she is nearer the truth than Spinlove. Mr. Bunseer is presumably the Chairman of the District Council, or possibly a notorious member of it; at any rate local authority is, for some reason, identified with him in the lady's mind.

The boxroom is evidently cheek by jowl with the tankroom, and the noises complained of are merely manifestations of the healthy, joyous life of cisterns and of ball cocks that are out of knowledge to all who do not seek community with them. Lady Brash's realization of the Ideal Home presents a charming domestic interior: the fond wife sitting secluded and remote and lulled by the murmuring song of the cisterns, suddenly warned, by their glad outburst into full triumphant symphony, that her Leslie has returned to her and is having a bath.

Flush tanks are the source of other water-noises. The full-toned, reverberating flush tank or "water waste preventer," which is offered in great variety and at most reasonable prices by a large number of manufacturers, appears, however, to be popular, and those in search of a powerful instrument will like to know of Gladdener's "Orchestral" in D flat major with domed resonator and piccolo cadenza as finale.

Lady Brash is, of course, quite astray in supposing that warmth is inherent in her snuggery. The cause of the room's being hot in summer is that its outer fabric is ineffective as an insulator. This will also make it cold in winter, because the wide expanse of roof which allows outside warmth to pass readily in will equally readily allow interior warmth to pass out. We know that Spinlove hung his files to battens nailed direct to the rafters without any intervening boarding and felt, and, although the place is plastered, Lady Brash's snuggery is unlikely to bring perfect content to anyone not previously acclimatized to Arctic exploration as well as to the stoking of battleships in the Persian Gulf.

Experienced architects will recognize in this episode a trait of human nature which leads certain clients who are discerning in requiring the nicest efficiency in the arrangements made for them, to rejoice in make-shifts and discomforts of their own devising. We may be sure that Lady Brash will continue to broil or shiver in her posh cubby-hole up among the cisterns to the limits of her endurance, and, when the stimulus of novelty no longer supports her resolution, will find some other reason than the true one for her defection.

SPINLOVE TO LADY BRASH

Dear Lady Brash,   9.9.26.

Of course there is no harm unless the Authorities find out about the use being made of the boxroom, but I thought you would like to know how things were.

The noises you describe are quite usual. There is no danger of any kind and you will be glad to hear there is no access to the tankroom, except by the door, so that if you lock it and keep the key yourself you can be certain no one is in there.

I expect you will find you will want quite a good fire in the winter. There will not be much sun to warm the place then, will there?

A lift would no doubt be a great convenience, as you say; but I am afraid it could only be accessible from the kitchen or the dining-room, and that would not be very convenient, would it? Then, of course, it would mean taking square bits out of the dining-room and the bedrooms on the first and second floor; have you thought of that, I wonder?

Yes, the weather has been delightful, but I am sorry to see in to-day's paper that a change is coming.

Yours sincerely,

P.S.—If I come across any old oak beams for sale that will fit I will let you know, but I fear that is not very likely.

If Spinlove had any sense of humour he could not write such a letter as this; but we know he has none, and perhaps he is, on this occasion, lucky, for his nervous solicitude is the result of experience that has taught him never to appear to oppose the lady's wishes, and that any indication of decisive contrary opinion will have the effect of opposition. Spinlove writes as though the poor woman were only half-witted, but in doing so he seems—if I may obtrude the opinion—on the safe side.

LADY BRASH TO SPINLOVE

Mr. Spinlove,   10.9.26.

I was so much relieved to get your nice letter as Mr. Bunseer never comes to the house and I have now given strict orders that *no one* is allowed further than the passage and keep the cisterns locked up although I am sure he would never *dream* of doing such a thing, and I am bound to say that he is always *fresh* though the Stores is *not* but of course we rely on the garden for most of them.

They all tell me there is dry rot Mr. Grigsby has been seeing about, but I always wanted a dry one [*?house*] so I suppose now it is finished it cannot be helped if it is too dry, but that is better than a damp one for my dear mother was a martyr and a cousin as well and I take after *both*.

We are giving a small dance on the 27th as the 26th is Sunday and hope to have the pleasure of seeing you and staying the night. We dine at seven.

How quickly the evenings are drawing in though still quite light in the morning!!

Yours sincerely,

We are not, I think, to understand that the lady has any fear of Mr. Bunseer hiding in the tankroom. What she means to say is that as Bunseer never comes to the house he can learn nothing of the converted box-room, that to make things quite safe she has forbidden any tradesman to come into the house at all, and that she has ordered the tankroom to be kept locked, but not—she is careful to let Spinlove understand—from any fear of Bunseer, whose vegetables are always fresh although those supplied by the Stores are not.

SPINLOVE TO GRIGBLAY

Dear Sir,   10.9.26.

Will you send cheque for £6 to Borter as extra on bird-bath. He came to see me some time ago and called again yesterday bringing his correspondence with the quarry company. It seems that he sent them my sketch and depended on their measures in making out his tender, but they carelessly took the scale to be 1 in. instead of ½ in., and gave him a wrong figure so that he is out of pocket. He is in quite a small way of business, working himself with the help of two or three journeymen, and I have decided he ought to be allowed the cost of the stone he used.

I am expecting to receive Mr. Grigblay's promised proposal for settlement of items still in dispute.

Yours faithfully,

Spinlove has no right to do this. It is to be hoped that neither Brash nor anyone else would wish to profit by the misfortunes of an artist who has made a beautiful thing for him with his own hands, or to take advantage of a technicality which enables him to force an individual craftsman to bear the cost of the work instead of paying for it himself; but it is not for the architect to usurp his employer's discretion and, on an impulse of vicarious generosity, make a present of his client's money as Spinlove here does. His duty, as Brash's architect (or agent) was to give Borter exact particulars; examine the tender so as to assure himself that Borter understood what was wanted and was not opening his mouth too widely; then set up an exact contract, And see that it was exactly completed. All Spinlove was entitled to do when Borter made his appeal was to master the facts and lay them before Brash with any representations he thought fit to make. If Brash then elected to pay, payment would more appropriately be made by Brash's cheque drawn in favour of Barter and transmitted by Spinlove, than by making it an extra under the contract, for it is not an extra, but a free gift by Brash; and as a gift was all Borter was entitled to ask for it is right he should understand that what he has received is a gift and nothing but a gift. I have assumed Borter's to be a genuine case; but though we may sympathize with him we need not condone his inability to take care of himself. After all, business is business. Borter and his kind bring discredit on the calling of individual craftsman which, above all others, deserves well of architects; and if Spinlove feels as I do, he will not employ Borter next time he wants a bird-bath or a sundial.

RIDDOPPO AGAIN

Dear Mr. Spinlove, 18.9.26.

My protracted absence on an unexpected prolonged round of visits to yachting and other sporting acquaintances has postponed the earlier transmission of my correspondence with Messrs. Russ and the Riddoppo Company anent the failure of the paint, which I now enclose herewith for your perusal previous to our anticipated meeting on the 25th. It would be advantageous if you would be so obliging as to allocate the forenoon of the 26th to a discussion of the proposition which will then be assisted by the convenient presence of the defective paintwork.

I am considerably astonished at the attitude now adopted by my friend Mr. Ziegfeld Swatmug, under whose personal recommendation I eventually arrived at the final decision to utilize Riddoppo; but you will see that the failure of the paint is demonstrably due to the remission of Mr. Grigblay to apply Riddoppo by methods sufficiently workmanlike to procure desirable results. This—may I be permitted to remind you—is precisely what I have all along prognosticated.

As you are aware, I have caused the disastrous consequence of the disintegration of the paint to be mitigated by the application of frequent scrubbings, and it is desirable that I should intimate for your information that this arduous duty has made it imperatively necessary to *further augment the domestic staff*, and that I am keeping an exact account of the extra disbursement occasioned. The dilapidated aspect of Riddoppo is, as you must have discerned, a perfect disgrace to *any* gentleman's house, and I desire that Mr. Grigblay should be finally informed that remedial action without further protracted delay is at once imperatively necessary.

Yours sincerely,

It will be remembered that, four months before, a deadlock was produced by Grigblay's flatly refusing to accept responsibility for, or have any hand in the restoration of, the defective Riddoppo paint, and that Brash then said he was going to take the advice of his solicitors.

(ENCLOSURE 1) RUSS AND CO., SOLICITORS, TO BRASH

Dear Sir,   28.5.26.

in accordance with instructions you gave to Mr. Russ in interview on 7th May to take Counsel's opinion, we referred the case for the opinion of Mr. Geoffrey Chawlegger, K.C., and this opinion we have now received.

We do not enclose the opinion as it is of considerable length and highly technical, but Mr. Chawlegger holds the same view of the facts as Mr. Russ expressed to you in conversation, and which may be stated as follows:

1. Your letter to your architect of 24th September 1925, instructing him to order Grigblay, the builder, to use Riddoppo paint, and stating that you accepted responsibility for so ordering after Grigblay had previously, in his letter of 22nd September 1925, objected to the paint and refused to take responsibility for the results of using it, absolves Grigblay from any liability for defects which subsequently manifested themselves, except defects which can be shown to be due to his neglect to use reasonable care in applying the paint.

2. The Riddoppo Company is responsible to you for breach of warranty if it can be shown that the paint was not suitable for the purpose for which it was supplied.

3. The Riddoppo Company is not responsible to Grigblay for breach of warranty in supplying, and Grigblay is not responsible to the Riddoppo Company for negligence in applying the paint.

4. Your right of action is against the Riddoppo Company for breach of warranty, or against Grigblay for negligence, or you may cite both and make them jointly defendants to an action for damages.

5. The architect is not responsible to you for breach of warranty by the Riddoppo Company, but action may lie against him for negligence in not seeing that the paint was properly applied, and he may be joined as defendant in any action you may bring against the builder.

In view of this opinion we think it desirable to settle the matter by getting the parties each to agree to bear a portion of the cost of renovation; failing which we think your only course will be to make all three joint defendants of an action for damages.

Yours faithfully,

(ENCLOSURE 2) BRASH TO RUSS AND CO.

Dear Mr. Russ,   2.6.26.

I have perused your communication with some consternation as it intimates, I apprehend, that a considerable period of time must elapse before the desired renovation will be eventually completed. Is there any prohibited reason why I should not employ some person to carry out the necessary restoration of the paintwork as a preliminary to suing the defendants for the amount of my consequent disbursement?

Yours sincerely,

(ENCLOSURE 3) RUSS AND CO. TO BRASH

Dear Sirs,   5.6.26.

In the event of both Grigblay and the Riddoppo Company refusing to restore, you are entitled to have the renovations carried out and to include the cost of the work in your statement of claim in any action you may take. It is, however, imperative that the work done should be confined to putting the paintwork into the condition in which it would be if the defendants had fulfilled their obligations. It will also be advisable to have technical evidence that nothing more was done than was necessary to this end.

Yours faithfully,

(ENCLOSURE 4) BRASH TO SWATMUG

My dear Mr. Swatmug,   9.6.26.

I anticipate you will remember that some twelve months ago you were so very obliging as to interest yourself anent a certain small domestic building-adventure of mine, and to strongly recommend a new novelty super-paint manufactured by Riddoppo, Ltd., of which you are, I think, chairman; and that you also most kindly introduced me to an official of the Riddoppo Company who gave me most invaluable advice upon the appropriately suitable variegation of tints to be selected, and for which kind assistance I had occasion to offer you my very sincere appreciation and thanks.

I regret, however, to communicate that a very brief period of time after the completion of the interior painting of my house, Riddoppo commenced to disintegrate and peel off in a most alarming manner, and it is now demonstrably evident, I am pained to intimate, that the whole work will have to be again renewed as it is in a deplorable condition and a disgrace to *any* gentleman's domicile, as you would, I am confident in thinking, most emphatically agree. The builder, who is a somewhat rough, obstreperous fellow, disclaims all responsibility as he asseverates that he used Riddoppo, by my orders which—I need hardly tell you—I did not hesitate to give him after so strong a recommendation from yourself.

It will, as you will perceive, be a very great advantage to me under these distressing circumstances if you would grant me the privilege of consulting you and availing myself of your abundant stores of experienced knowledge; and if you could spare us the pleasure of your company at Honeywood for a week-end—or longer if possible—or can at any time concede us a single night of your valuable time, Lady Brash and myself would have most extreme pleasure in entertaining you.

It is a considerable interval since I had the good fortune to meet you, but I often hear from friends of the activities of your busy life which, I trust, continue to prosper.

Believe me, my dear Mr. Swatmug,
Ever yours sincerely,

(ENCLOSURE 5) BRASH TO SWATMUG

My dear Mr. Swatmug,   27.6.26.

I ventured to indite a missive to you some three weeks ago anent the Riddoppo paint you were so very kind as to recommend for the interior decorations of an unpretentious house I was building. As I have received no expected reply, it occurs to me either that possibly you never received my letter or that, by some unfortunate disaster, yours to me has gone astray.

Lady Brash and myself have been looking forward to the pleasure of offering you the hospitality of Honeywood Grange, and live in hopes that the enjoyable event will not long be delayed.

Ever, my dear Mr. Swatmug,
Yours very sincerely,

(ENCLOSURE 6) SWATMUG TO BRASH

My Dear Brash,   4.7.26.

Yes, I received your "missive" and must apologize for not having answered it before, but what with being much abroad and having several flotations in hand, and then this wretched divorce action which you must have heard of, I am afraid your letter escaped my attention.

I am pleased to have been of service to you so think nothing more about that, but I am not clear what the matter is you refer to. However, I have nothing now to do with the Riddoppo Company as I resigned from the Board when they wrote down the capital, so I fear I can be of no further use to you; but in any case I know nothing whatever about paint, though I always understood Riddoppo was a sound proposition and what you say is news to me.

I should only be too delighted if it were possible for me to accept your and your good Lady's charming invitation, but, alas! that is quite out of the question, I am sorry to say.

Yours sincerely,

A charming letter: the letter of one who knows no virtue that will not pass the test of "Does it pay?" and who has sold the goods (and the buyer) and sees no more profit in the miserable, grovelling Brash.

(ENCLOSURE 7) BRASH TO SWATMUG

My dear Mr. Swatmug,   5.7.26.

Permit me to thank you in acknowledgment of your communication anent Riddoppo. I anticipated that, as it was at your urgent personal recommendation I adopted the use of Riddoppo, you would be desirous of assisting me in securing elimination of consequent defects; however, I comprehend that you have now no connection with the Company and that I need have no apprehension that you will interpret any action I take to secure restitution from the Company as in any way involving yourself.

Lady Brash and myself are extremely disappointed to know we may not immediately anticipate the enjoyment of a visit from you, but we still live in hopes that eventually your divers engagements may permit you to give us that pleasurable gratification.

Believe me, dear Mr. Swatmug,
Yours sincerely,

(ENCLOSURE 8) BRASH TO SECRETARY, RIDDOPPO CO., LTD.

Dear Sir,   5.7.26.

About twelve months ago you supplied me with a quantity of your New Novelty Riddoppo Super-Paint for the interior decoration of Honeywood Grange. I regret to inform you that a very brief period after the painting was completed it commenced to disintegrate and peel away from the surface. I shall be glad if your representative will call at an early date to view the disaster, and to know what proposals you will make for immediate renovation.

Yours faithfully,

(ENCLOSURE 9) BRASH TO RIDDOPPO, CO., LTD.

Dear Sirs,   12.7.26.

Permit me to call your attention to my communication of 5th July anent failure of your Riddoppo paint, and to politely request the favour of an immediate reply without any further procrastination.

Yours faithfully,

(ENCLOSURE 10) RIDDOPPO, LTD. (AND REDUCED)
TO L. BRASH, ESQ.

Dear Sir,   19.7.26.

We do not find that at any time we have supplied any goods to your order.

Yours faithfully,

We now may begin to understand why there was an interval of four months between the day Brash referred the question of responsibility to Russ, and that on which he wrote telling Spinlove liability lay at Grigblay's door.

It will be noticed that the Riddoppo Company describes itself as "Ltd. (and Reduced)." This means that the Company has, as Swatmug mentioned, written down—or cancelled—part of its share capital. This writing down is equivalent to cutting losses, and will enable the Com-

pany to pay that small available dividend on the reduced nominal share value which would have been swamped as a percentage on the original share capital. *The fact suggests that the Riddoppo Company is struggling to keep its head above water.*

(ENCLOSURE 11) BRASH TO RIDDOPPO, LTD.

Dear Sirs,   20.7.26.

I beg leave to communicate the obvious intimation that your Riddoppo super-paint was not ordered by myself, nor am I aware that it is a customary habit for private gentlemen to order materials for building operations. The paint was appropriately ordered by my builder, Mr. John Grigblay, of Marlford, as—will you permit me to politely remind you?—you could perfectly well have informed yourself had you so desired.

It is also expedient you should clearly comprehend that attention to this matter brooks no further protracted delay, and that unless I immediately receive a satisfactory proposal for the restoration of the defective paint I shall employ other persons to carry out the necessary undertakings and hold you liable for the cost as well as for the disbursements I have already incurred in *augmentation of the domestic staff* necessary to the prevention of deleterious effects upon carpets, curtains and furniture.

I have also to ask your permission to intimate that you are not addressing "Mr. L." but Sir Leslie Brash Knight Bachelor, which information you could have immediately acquired from the most cursory reference to *Dod's, Who's Who*, the Post Office and Telephone Directories and numerous other publications.

Yours faithfully,

(ENCLOSURE 12) RIDDOPPO TO SIR L. B. K. BACHELOR

Dear Sir,   5.8.26.

We regret error in name, which was new to us, and signature hard to decipher.

We have now communicated with Mr. Grigblay and enclose copies of correspondence, which kindly note as this closes the matter so far as we are concerned, and oblige,

Yours faithfully,

(ENCLOSURE 12A) RIDDOPPO TO GRIGBLAY

Dear Sir,   26.7.26.

Sir Leslie Bachelor of Honeywood Grange has written complaining our N.N. Super-Paint ordered by you has gone wrong there, and shall be glad of particulars as this is the first we have heard of same.

Yours faithfully,

(ENCLOSURE 12B) GRIGBLAY TO RIDDOPPO

Gentlemen,   27.7.26.

We painted out Honeywood with your Riddoppo super because we were so ordered, and if you want to know what it looks like better go and see as we only carried out architects orders and it is no more business of ours and we will have no more to do with it. You may like to know we did not french polish or put fire to it or squirt any acid at it or boiling water or super-heated steam or molten lead, but if that is what is wanted there is still a bit of it left for you to get to work on.

Yours faithfully,

The last paragraph is a characteristic comment of Grigblay's on the advertisements of "Riddoppo New Novelty Super-Paint," which held out, for the encouragement of house-owners and decorators, that it was "fire and acid proof, not to be damaged by jets of boiling water and super-heated steam and capable of receiving a high polish."

(ENCLOSURE 12C) RIDDOPPO TO GRIGBLAY

Sir,   30.7.26.

We suppose your cheeky letter is because you do not know better and want to insult us because your painters do not know how to read instructions when they are printed in clear print on the tins for everyone to see and go by. The paint we sent you was in perfect condition as supplied to others, and if you have made a mess of things by not following instructions, well, that is your affair and not ours, which kindly note as this is the last we have to say to you or anyone else on this matter and oblige

Yours, etc.,

(This ends correspondence covered to Spinlove by Brash's letter of 18.9.26.)

SPINLOVE TO GRIGBLAY

Dear Sir,   29.9.26.

I enclose copy of correspondence on the subject of failure of Riddoppo, which I have to-day received from Sir Leslie Brash who considers it to be demonstrated that the defects are due to the painting not having been properly done, and instructs me formally to call upon you to clean off and repaint forthwith.

Will you return enclosure by Friday morning at latest, and let me know what answer I am to give Sir Leslie, as I am meeting him to discuss the matter on Saturday.

Yours faithfully,

Spinlove has no business to send what are, in fact, Brash's private papers to Grigblay. By doing so he takes Grigblay behind the scenes and puts him in possession of his client's "case"—as the lawyers call it.

The detachment Spinlove again displays in his letter can now only be expected. The time has gone by when any architect could hope to adjudicate.

SPINLOVE TO BRASH

Dear Sir Leslie Brash,   21.9.26.
I am in receipt of your letter and enclosures and have written to Grigblay. He will, I fear, without doubt refuse to make good the paint-work, and for the reasons he before gave—namely, that he only painted with Riddoppo when you undertook to accept responsibility for the results. I inspected the painting on several occasions while the work was in progress and could find no fault with the way it was being done; in fact, Grigblay put his foreman decorator in charge so that it should have special attention.

I will set aside Sunday morning to go into the matter with you, as you ask; but as Grigblay will certainly refuse to go back on his decision to have nothing more to do with the painting at Honeywood, and I have no experience of Riddoppo—the composition of which is, as you know, a trade secret—I am afraid I shall not be of much help to you.

Yours sincerely,

We here see Spinlove again writing a letter that is not only unnecessary but the very soul of tactlessness. The mention of his name by Brash's solicitors as possibly liable, jointly with Grigblay, has made him eager to exculpate himself and consolidate Grigblay's position.

GRIGBLAY TO SPINLOVE

Dear Sir,   21.9.26.
Correspondence *re* Riddoppo returned herewith. We have nothing to add to what we have already said and shall be glad if your client will note same.

Yours faithfully,

And so Sir Leslie Brash is left hanging in the air, which is just what we have been expecting, and no more than he deserves for overriding the advice of his architect and the objections of the builder. If Spinlove had specified Riddoppo and Grigblay had used it without protest, Grig-blay—and possibly Spinlove—would have been responsible to Brash; and as Brash holds a substantial sum as security for Grigblay's perfor-mance of his covenant to make good defects, he could, if Grigblay failed to restore the work, employ someone else to do so and deduct the cost from moneys to become due to Grigblay, so that his position would have been secure. A claim for damages, in that case, might still lie against the paint company for supplying defective paint; but this would be Grigblay's affair entirely and no concern of Brash's.

BRASH TO SPINLOVE

Dear Mr. Spinlove,   23.9.26.

With a view to obviating the painful necessity of giving unpleasantly frank indications of my feelings when I receive you, I write to intimate that when I give instructions to my professional adviser I anticipate they will be performed *without* unnecessary refractory comment.

The whole of this infernal muddle anent Riddoppo is suffi-ciently exasperating without the additional vexation of disparag-ing opinions which—may I be allowed to asseverate?—I have not invited, and do not desire.

For perfectly logical reasons I require Mr. Grigblay's final answer to my demands, which I apprehend I shall in due course receive; but I do *not* desire to be informed what in your opinion that answer is eventually likely to be; I do *not* ask to be told that Mr. Grigblay has previously obstinately refused restitution; I do *not* ask to be reminded that the fellow obstreperously desires to put the blame on me; I do *not* require to be instructed that the composition of Riddoppo is of a secret nature, and I do *not* ask you to reiterate over again that you know nothing of the paint, and for the very obvious and comprehensive reason that I am already redundantly informed upon the whole of those matters.

The only intimation that your communication conveys with which I was not previously conversant is that you espouse the contentious representations of Grigblay in opposition to your employer's interests; and that though you profess to have no acquaintance with the ingredients of which Riddoppo is composed, you asseverate complete confidence in your ability to decide the appropriate method of applying it. This—you must permit me to intimate—causes me considerable astonishment.

Yours sincerely,

We can imagine Spinlove aghast at this reception of his letter, and asking himself, "What on earth have I done now?" but although Brash's expression of irritation may not be excusable, his annoyance certainly is so. We have before observed an engaging frankness in old Brash of which this letter seems only another example. Spinlove's smug letter has exasperated him, and he acts on an impulse to let Spinlove know what he feels about it so that there need be no sour reserves in his greeting of his guest. It may be, of course, that his native pepper got the upper hand and that he let fly as we have often seen him do before; but, even so, there is a simplicity about the old boy which is disarming.

SPINLOVE TO GRIGBLAY

Dear Sir,   27.9.26.

 I saw Sir Leslie Brash on Saturday and gave him your answer to his demand that you should repaint. I understand he is going to review the whole question.

Yours faithfully,

THE STATEMENT OF ACCOUNT

Dear Sir,   29.9.26.

We have now further considered the items of the Statement of Account which remained in dispute after your interview with Mr. Grigblay, and as we wish the account to be now settled we offer to reduce certain of our charges, but only supposing you meet us by allowing the others to stand; failing which we must withdraw our offer and hold to our full claim, as we consider our charges fair and we have already met your views in a reasonable way, and think we are entitled to a little consideration, as all give and no take is not the treatment we are accustomed to receive from architects, and one way and another this job has not been much profit to us and if we see ourselves clear when all is done it is about as much as we can expect.

MAKING GOOD DRY ROT

We must refuse to withdraw this item. If we did we should be agreeing it was a defect under the contract, which we have all along disputed and cannot take responsibility for.

If Grigblay met the cost of this work he would involve himself in liability for all further dry rot due to the same cause. It should be remembered, also, that the Courts have decided that a builder's liability for defects is not limited by the date named in the contract as terminating his liability when it can be shown that the defect existed, or was latent,

before the expiration of the time fixed by that date. It is therefore of
special importance to Grigblay that the architect should, by passing the
item as an extra, acknowledge that the cause of the dry rot is not a defect
for which the builder is responsible. It is, of course, equally important
for Spinlove that he should not exonerate Grigblay by allowing the item
to rank as an extra: but Spinlove, who is apparently unconscious of the
dreadful disaster the dry rot may portend, is probably also unconscious
of the consequences of agreeing that Brash shall pay for restoring the first
manifestation of it. The cost of restoring is likely to be only ten or fifteen
pounds, but if it were only as many shillings Grigblay, who understands
well how he stands, would be just as obstinate in claiming payment.
The case, in fact, is a good instance of the considerations of policy with
which architects must temper discretion—and sometimes even moral
justice—in settling up building accounts. The bearing of each detail
upon the interpretation of the contract as a whole is always in the mind
of the experienced man.

RAKING JOINTS AND SPECIAL POINTING AFTER FROST

We are willing to knock off £17, making the charge £32 6s. 3d.,
which is, as near as we can measure, 4½ d. a foot for special.

SPECIAL POINTING IN LIEU OF PLAIN STRUCK JOINT

This claim we cannot withdraw. We were willing to finish flat
point where frost pulled out joint, and to finish new to match in
place of striking off as specified; but you ordered a special pointing, and we are entitled to extra cost of special over ordinary flat,
as already pointed out.

Apparently Spinlove specified that the faces should be finished press-
ing the mortar out of the joints and striking off surplus with the edge
of the trowel as the bricks were laid. A sharp frost spoilt some of this
work while it was new, and the joints had to be raked and pointed which
made it necessary for the whole of the brick faces, afterwards built, to be
pointed to match. Spinlove, it seems, required a method of pointing which
Grigblay claims was more costly than what properly could be required of
him under the contract. The justice of this claim seems decidedly doubt-
ful, but it is necessary to know the whole of the facts before forming an

opinion. *The sum involved, as shown in the Interim Statement (see page 72), is £134 3s. 0d.*

ALTERATION TO GROUND-FLOOR WINDOW HEADS

We regret we cannot accept your view of this matter. Your half-inch joinery detail figured height from ground floor, but this varied from datum level as the floor had been lowered 1½ in. by your orders, and we cannot accept responsibility for same.

As recorded in "The Honeywood File," Spinlove forgot that the floor had been lowered, and figured the dimensions wrongly; but he always contended that it was Grigblay's duty to see that the frames were made to fit the building. Grigblay's refusal is so worded as to support his repudiation of dry rot: he makes clear that he accepts no responsibility for the lowering of the floor.

RENEWING TWO CATCH PITS

We are willing to cut this out.

We have given the whole of these matters close attention and this is the last we have to say and hope you will now accept our offer, and not oblige us to withdraw it, since we understand Mr. Tinge has been waiting for your decision on outstanding points for a long time and has had the whole of account ready several weeks, so that this will now settle everything.

Yours faithfully,

SPINLOVE TO GRIGBLAY

Dear Sirs,   4.10.26.

I have considered your offer and decided to accept it and settle the account on your terms. I saw Mr. Tinge to-day and he says he can have the statement of account ready this week.

Yours faithfully,

Spinlove seems to have contested every inch of the ground in this long battle of the extras in a way that does justice to his conscientiousness and native tenacity. At the same time he appears to have been a little hard on Grigblay who, like every builder that takes a craftsman's pride in his work, has given a good deal more than his contract demands of him. However, the figure arrived at is likely to be a fair one, for Grigblay is well able to take care of himself, and Bloggs knows how to take care of him too—in fact, appearances are that no fly of any kind has ever settled on Bloggs.

TINGE, QUANTITY SURVEYOR, TO SPINLOVE

Dear Sir,   8.10.26.
Enclosed please find Statement. Copy has been sent to Mr. Grigblay.

Yours faithfully,

Tinge, at any rate, does not waste words. The Statement of Account, which must be long and intricate, is not in the file. It is no doubt put away with the contract documents.

SPINLOVE TO GRIGBLAY

Dear Sir,   9.10.26.
I have received Statement of Account from Mr. Tinge showing total £20,242 11s. 9d. I shall be glad if you will confirm that you accept this figure.

Yours faithfully,

As Spinlove has already agreed with Grigblay the items making up the account, and Tinge is in the position of auditor, valuer, or assessor; Spinlove's invitation to Grigblay to agree the figure Tinge has arrived at is little more than a formality though, as a matter of business, a necessary one. Tinge is expressly appointed under the contract to determine the total figure; and neither Grigblay nor Spinlove can object to the account unless it should appear that Tinge has misunderstood instructions or made any mistake.

SPINLOVE TO BRASH

Dear Sir Leslie Brash, 9.10.26.

I have just received the Statement of Account and am very glad to be able to tell you that I have succeeded in saving nearly *three hundred and fifty pounds* off extras. The exact figure is £337 3s. 5d., making the account £1,555 11s. 2d., instead of £1,892 14s. 7d., which, you will remember, was the total originally shown. To this have to be added certain items which have come in since the original account was drawn up, totalling £54 2s. 2d.; and a few others that Grigblay accidentally omitted—value £112 1s. 8d., so that, after allowing certain profits (£22 4s. 9d.) on the new items, the total figure shown is £1,753 19s. 9d., which, after including quantity surveyor's fees (£58 12s.), gives a final total of £ 1,802 11s. 9d. I thought you might like to know the figures at once. With kind regards,

Yours sincerely,

Brash must have been glad Spinlove's letter ended when it did, for the vaunted three hundred and fifty pound gain had already dwindled to £90, and, at the pace Spinlove was keeping, another half-dozen lines would have brought him to a three hundred and fifty pound loss. Whether Spinlove's is the best method of making a saving on a building account appetizing to a client I am not psychologist enough to determine; but I am disposed to doubt it. If I wanted a hungry lion to receive the highest possible gratification from the gift of a cutlet, I should not first offer him a leg of mutton and then snatch it away.

We have before noticed an adroitness in Spinlove on these occasions, which is so excessive as to be almost unholy. His persistency has no doubt saved Brash money; but the amount for which Spinlove claims credit is the whole of the difference between the totals of the Interim Summary and of the totals of corresponding items in the Final Statement. This difference, however, is not due to Spinlove, but mainly to Grigblay's wisdom in affixing full covering figures to those items in the Summary the exact value of which remained to be ascertained; and it is due to his foresight that, after the inevitable omissions and additions have been set against one another, the Final Statement shows a saving, and not an excess, on the Interim Summary. Spinlove, however, is perhaps unaware of this. With characteristic impulsiveness he rushes in front of the curtain without waiting to reflect whether he deserves the plaudits he invites. In view of his air of masterly elucidation, it is a pity he has made a slip of ten pounds in his manipulation of the figures. An architect who originates or passes inaccurate figures does himself very great damage for, obviously, his client would not entrust him with his affairs at all unless he had confidence in their being handled with exact care. It is to be understood that Spinlove is dealing only with the total of extras—£1,802 11s. 9d. This, added to the contract sum, £18,440, makes the total of the account £20,242 11s. 9d., which it may be mentioned is almost exactly the figure of probable least cost when the house was first projected.

GRIGBLAY TO SPINLOVE

Dear Sir,   14.10.26.
    We agree Account and Mr. Tinge's figures of total cost, £20,242 11s. 9d., and balance due, £1,242 11s. 9d. As we shall be entitled to said balance on 10th November we shall be glad to have list of any defects outstanding so that we may now get contract completed.
Yours faithfully,

Grigblay has been paid by instalments a total of £19,000, and this balance due is, in main part, money held back as security for making good defects appearing within nine months of the date of of the work, which has been acknowledged by Spinlove to be 10th February. Grigblay evidently means to have his money directly it is due on 10th November and his intention is no doubt braced by the dispute about Riddoppo. What we have to expect is that Grigblay will demand his balance on 10th November, and that Brash will refuse payment on the ground that Riddoppo is a defect for which Grigblay is accountable.

THE SMELLS RETURN

LADY BRASH TO SPINLOVE

Dear Mr. Spinlove,   10.10.26.

They have all come back again and *more than ever*, even Phyllis says so now, and what is to be done I really do not know as after the gentleman who came about them they all went away and Leslie said that was the end, but now I do not know what he will say as Mrs. Godolphin, who is staying here, notices them very much at night and it affects her *breathing* and I am the *same*, so it must be very bad and something must be done about it, but you will know best so will you say *at once* as it is so very unpleasant for everyone and cannot be allowed.

How very cold the weather has been of late.

Yours sincerely,

SPINLOVE TO LADY BRASH

Dear Lady Brash,   11.10.26.

I understand from your letter that you still think there is something wrong with the drains, but that cannot possibly be the case as you will remember the question was definitely settled when the sanitary experts tested the drains five or six months ago. If there had been anything amiss they would certainly have discovered it, so you may dismiss the idea entirely and think no more about it. What you noticed is no doubt some smell from the kitchen. Are you sure the servants, to save trouble, do not use the range as a refuse-destructor—that is, burn fat and kitchen residues and rubbish there, instead of throwing them into the dustbin? They may do this before they leave the kitchen at night, and it may give rise to most unpleasant smells and should not be allowed, as it burns the fire-bars and cheeks.

Yes, the weather has been wretchedly cold.

Yours sincerely,

This seems a most inadequate reply to Lady Brash's letter.

LADY BRASH TO SPINLOVE

Dear Mr. Spinlove,   14.10.26.

It is very kind of you to advise me not to trouble about them, but it is not the kitchen range, for I would never allow it and cook says she never does and it is much more in her bedroom which is why she complains so, and something must be done at once as poor Mrs. Godolphin left the house in a terrible fit of coughing as I knew she would, and even the doctor feared asthma and told her she should if it affected her so. It may still be the *drains*, he says, only no one will decide though I have spoken to Leslie time after time, but he comes home tomorrow I am thankful to say for something has got to be done or we shall all have to leave too.

How chilly it is for this time of year, but the radiators are a godsend! Would it cost much to put one in the Ideal Attic—I wonder? The fire gives out *no heat* up there, I find, but then there are no smells *there!*

Yours sincerely,

MISS PHYLLIS BRASH TO SPINLOVE

Dear Jazz,   14.10.26.

Is it the *architecture* of the house that smells? If so, you ought to choose a different style: the Free Tudor, as you call it, is altogether too rather. Mum is getting herself into one of her states over it and you ought to come down and nose around. It is no good sounding the "all's well" any more. "All's wrong" is the tuney, for we none of us like living in a third class in a S.R. tunnel. You must take this seriously, please, for it *is* serious.

Yours,
PUD.

SPINLOVE TO GRIGBLAY

Dear Sir,   15.10.26.

I enclose list of various small defects which have been standing over so that they might all be dealt with together. Sir Leslie Brash agrees with the list, and I have sent him a copy of it. Failure of Riddoppo was added by his orders. He understands, of course, that you do not intend to touch the paint.

I have had further complaints of smells in the house. It seems that they are the old "drain" smells, but they are now stated to be much worse than they were before. I wish Mr. Grigblay would go to the house on an early day, as he is often in the neighbourhood, and see what it all means.

Yours faithfully,

Spinlove, as we remember, has held back the making good of defects until they should have fully developed, and so that all might be dealt with at one time, and he then, quite properly, obtained Brash's agreement to what Grigblay was to be required to do. This is a most necessary step, not only as making sure that the client's ideas will be satisfied and protecting the builder who is entitled to know definitely and finally what is required of him, but as putting the client in mind of a fact he is liable to forget—namely, that the builder is not at his beck and call, but that there is a strict limit to the demands that can be made upon him.

It is the duty of the architect to decide what work a builder shall be called upon to do in fulfilment of his covenant to make good defects. The list represents Spinlove's requirements in this particular, and as he does not hold Grigblay to blame for the failure of Riddoppo, he ought not to include that item. It is important for an architect to maintain always a definite position and to be consistent and to act in exact accord with the forms prescribed by the contract, but when, as in this case, he knows he may have to justify himself to lawyers, he cannot be too cautious and circumspect. These miserable contests, however, invariably lead to cross-purposes and confusion, and we may suppose that if Spinlove had declined to put Riddoppo on the list he would have fallen out with Brash, and that he accordingly took the line of least resistance by including it and telling Grigblay it was understood he would ignore it. This is consistent with Spinlove's policy, throughout the whole of the affair, of sitting on the fence; but he will cut a poor figure when lawyers begin pressing their questions.

SPINLOVE TO LADY BRASH

Dear Lady Brash, 15.10.26.

I am so very sorry to know you are troubled with this unpleasant smell, and have arranged for Mr. Grigblay to call on an early day and make a thorough investigation of the cause which I am convinced cannot be far to seek.

Yours sincerely,

In spite of Pud's endorsement of her mother's complainings, it is clear that Spinlove still refuses to believe that the reported smells can be due to any defect in the building. In this, his native tenacity seems a little misplaced. He is wise, however, to make no reply to Lady Brash's suggestion of a radiator in the converted boxroom, for such a radiator would be likely to develop the same defect as the fire does, and "give out no heat." "Jazz" seems to have answered Pud's letter in his own hand, for there is no copy of his reply on the file. He has disappointed us in this way, before.

GRIGBLAY TO SPINLOVE

Dear Sir, 16.10.26.

We are obliged for list of defects requiring attention to complete contract and will put same in hand next week, except making good Riddoppo which, as we have stated, is no business of ours and which we respectfully refuse to do.

Mr. Grigblay regrets he cannot take any further action re reported smells as he has already obliged once and could find nothing amiss except mischievousness by the servants, which has since been put right.

Yours faithfully,

Grigblay's refusal to investigate the smells is natural. It is not many months since he put himself to some trouble to get to the bottom of complaints for which he could find no justification, and Spinlove's peremptory manner of calling upon him to pacify Lady Brash a second time—which, in any case, is Spinlove's job and not Grigblay's—would properly dispose Grigblay to refuse the favour even if he were otherwise inclined to grant it.

LADY BRASH TO SPINLOVE

Dear Mr. Spinlove,   16.10.26.

I do not want Mr. Grigblay to call any more; he does not wait to listen to me but only says there is nothing wrong and it will be all right in the summer, and goes away and nothing is done and all getting worse and worse every day and the fire giving out no heat no matter how much coal so that I cannot sit there it is so *freezing*, with the cisterns making a new noise and I lie awake and keep wondering what is happening when I am not there, so will you send some *proper* person *at once* to say what it all means, as Leslie comes home to-morrow and will naturally want to know why it all is when he hears about it. You have been *most* kind and considerate I know, but now at last it must really stop for I cannot bear any more.

So depressing with the leaves falling and this cold wind!

Yours sincerely,

The poor lady is fast getting into one of her "states." In spite of her rambling ambiguities we may understand that it is the smells that are

*the trouble. There seems to be no doubt that something is wrong; and
it may be that if Spinlove had applied himself to mastering the cause of
the complaint when it was first made, instead of discountenancing it
and allowing the tough sensibilities of Grigblay to discredit the delicate
perceptions of the lady, he would have saved his clients some annoyance,
and himself much trouble.*

BRASH TO SPINLOVE

Dear Mr. Spinlove,   19.10.26.

I returned yesterday from the Shire [*sic*] where I have been
engaged in company with various sporting acquaintances in
beguiling the wily partridge. A number of hares also fell to my
bag, and I was fortunate in securing a polecat—an exploit which
my host is commemorating by having the creature set up by Row-
lands. The event is the subject of a paragraph in this week's *Field*,
you will notice.

Your communication anent extras was forwarded on to me,
and I now write to intimate my satisfaction at the amount of the
final total. I confess that I anticipated that the previous summary
would again be eventually increased, and my gratification at your
intimation that there is a reduction of £90 on the previously estimated figure, is considerable. There is also, I have noted, the additional saving of £92 in respect of overpayment for bricks which
you previously reported, making £182 in all. May I point out that
the figure £1,753 should be £1,743? This error does not, however,
affect the ultimate total of extras £1,802 11s. 9d., which I take to be
final and to represent my inclusive liabilities excepting the resid-
ual balance of your own outstanding fees of which I shall be glad
to receive particulars.

Anent the list of defects, the question of responsibility for the
Riddoppo failure has the further attention of my solicitor from
whom I expect shortly to receive a communication.

I must now, I regret to intimate, request your attention to a
serious matter. On my return home I find that the malodorous

emanations have returned with such virulence that the whole domicile is involved, our domestic staff almost in revolt, and Lady Brash so affected in health that immediate change of air is imperative and she is leaving for Brighton to-morrow.

In the past there has been some doubt as to the existence of unsavoury effluviums, but that doubt no longer persists as both my daughter and myself have experienced disgusting vapours in various parts of the house, which are particularly obnoxious at night and in the early morning. The matter now brooks no further protracted delay and, as a first step towards elimination, I request that you will on the earliest day possible come and sleep in the house and apply your trained discernments to the identification of these nauseating savours the repulsiveness of which, if they continue, will render the house permanently uninhabitable. I shall therefore anticipate a telephone message from you to-morrow signifying the earliest day on which we may expect you.

Yours sincerely,

A remarkably urbane letter under the circumstances! Brash's beguiling of the wily partridge, and his newly acquired polecat fame, seem to have given ballast to his moral equilibrium; but his surprising acceptance of the extras account must be due to other causes, and supplies an instance of the entirely unexpected that so commonly happens. It was not to be expected that a reduction of £182—as he supposes—would reconcile Brash to the claim for £1,900 which he had so hotly repudiated; yet this appears to be the case, and the explanation, stripped of the subtleties with which the psychologist would load it, seems plain. First, Brash has already exhausted his indignation at the extras; blown off all his steam; fussed away all his available fuss: he is heartily sick of the subject and, having had a respite of some weeks, has no wish to lash himself into a renewal of his grievance. This is a common weakness in men who have not the habit of self-control. Second, as he tells us, he had made up his mind that the estimate of extras supplied him would prove to be a mere stepping-stone, or half-way house, to a much larger final claim as, except for Grigblay's honest good sense in preparing the Interim Summary, it might well have been; and the fact that the worst is revealed to be so much better than was expected, has reconciled Brash to the figure and led him to forget how unacceptable it once seemed. Third, with the serious contest over the paint unsettled and the new trouble of the inexplicable smells to be disposed of, he is glad to be quit of the question of extras.

SPINLOVE TO BRASH

Dear Sir Leslie Brash,   20.10.26.

This is to confirm arrangement by telephone, that I will meet you at Charing Cross on the 5.25 to-morrow. I am astonished at what you tell me. Why these smells should suddenly reappear, and worse than formerly, is extraordinary—as indeed is the fact that there should be any smells. I will do my best to get to the bottom of the matter, though I cannot think that the trouble can be due to any defect in the work.

I have also to thank you for your letter. I will let you have particulars of my charges. The final payment to Grigblay falls due on 10th November, as you know.

I should mention that the refund of £92 from the brick manufacturer *is included* in the Statement of Account. I will bring the Statement with me to-morrow, for you to see.

Yours sincerely,

We may hope, for Spinlove's peace of mind, that it has not occurred to him that the smells may be those associated with extensive dry rot, but, in point of fact, the early manifestation of the smells, their complete disappearance and their sudden return, does not indicate such a source.

We may also hope that the reflection that this was the last of Spinlove's snatching exploits reconciled Brash to the vanishing of the £92 with which he had endowed himself.

SPINLOVE TO GRIGBLAY

Dear Sir, 22.10.26.

I went yesterday to Honeywood at the urgent request of Sir Leslie Brash to investigate the smells complained of. I am at a loss to understand Mr. Grigblay's report to me earlier in the year that there were no smells; for there is no doubt whatever that the house is pervaded by a sour, stuffy atmosphere. What the cause of this is I have no idea. The smell was described to me as like that of a third-class carriage in a tunnel on the Southern Railway, and I was myself once or twice reminded of a smoky chimney; but there were no fires in the house except the heating and hot water furnaces and the kitchen range, and the smell is most noticed at the opposite end of the house, particularly in the bedrooms; in fact, the stuffy odour can be at once detected in Nos. 9, 10, 12, 15 and 16 if they are kept shut up for a few hours, but it is scarcely noticeable—if at all—anywhere downstairs. I slept in the small spare room (No. 9 on plan) with the windows shut, and the disgusting atmosphere was proved when in the morning I opened the windows and breathed fresh air. I was conscious of an oppressive sensation in my chest and a listless enervated feeling when I first got up, and I had a slight headache.

I may say that Sir Leslie Brash naturally expects that the state of affairs shall be put an end to at once, and I will ask Mr. Grigblay to meet me at Honeywood either at 3.30 tomorrow afternoon, or in the course of the following day, and I shall expect to hear from you by telephone in the morning. Yours faithfully,

If we had not such frequent cause to resent the peremptory, ill-mannered tone in which Spinlove addresses those under his direction, I should call attention to this instance of it. It is particularly to be regretted when he is addressing Grigblay to whom he has been in the past greatly indebted.

A CONSULTING CHEMIST

Sir,   23.10.26.

I was away all to-day, but your letter was sent up to the house so I should see it to-night. I understand they rang up from the office to let you know I could not meet you to-day, and I now write to let you know I cannot meet you to-morrow and for the following reason.

I may have as good a nose as most, but I don't hold out to have a better and there is no use my joining in any sniffing match up at Honeywood, for that, if you will pardon me, is all it would amount to. If what you say is fact—and I do not doubt it is, for you will find that I dropped a hint of the same in the report I made last spring—I can make a guess what is the matter, and it is no small matter either; but the first thing is to find out whether the trouble is what we think, and to do that we want something a lot better than any nose, and that is a "detector," and my advice, sir, is to ask Mr. F. T. Pricehard, Consulting Analyst (somewhere in Westminster he used to be), to send down and test the air same as they do in mines, and he will tell us what the fumes are—if there are any—or if it's dead mice he will tell us that. He will not charge a large fee, and if the trouble's any fault of mine I will pay it, and if not I take it the old gentleman will.

You will excuse me telling you what I think best, but if Sir Leslie wants the trouble put right the first thing is to find out what trouble it is, and if Pricehard can't say, nobody can.

I am, sir,

Yours faithfully,

In the report referred to, Grigblay attributes a stuffy smell he noticed to down-draught in the flues carrying smoky air from adjoining chimney-pots into certain rooms: and it now seems that he suspects the present smells to derive from smoke fumes. The "detector" he refers to is a simple apparatus for the ready measuring of the deadly monoxide gas that accumulates in sewers, coal mines, and other places. Pricehard's methods, however, would be more exact than those made possible by the use of such an instrument.

SPINLOVE TO GRIGBLAY

Dear Mr. Grigblay,   25.10.26.

Thank you for your letter. I have spoken to Sir Leslie, and have to-day sent instructions to Mr. Pricehard.

Yours truly,

SPINLOVE TO PRICEHARD

Dear Sir,   25.10.26.

In confirmation of arrangements made over the telephone to-day, I enclose the full history of the "smells" at Honeywood and particulars of the construction of the building. Plans showing drains and all service pipes are hanging in the kitchen passage.

Sir Leslie Brash has arranged for doors and windows of bedrooms to be kept shut on Thursday, and will send his car to meet the 2.5 from Charing Cross at Wedgefield Junction.

Yours faithfully,

PRICEHARD TO SPINLOVE

Dear Sir,   6.11.26.
I enclose report which gives analysis of samples of air taken in the rooms at Honeywood Grange specified in the report, at the times and under the conditions described. The slight trace of sulphur dioxide (SO_2) would account for the smell noticeable. The presence of sulphuretted hydrogen (H_2S) was not revealed by the ordinary tests used. Carbon dioxide (CO_2) 0·048 is scarcely more than would be found in normal air. Carbon monoxide (CO) 0·015 (in the worst sample) would be likely to produce headache, giddiness and oppression, after some hours.

I am of opinion that fumes from closed coke fires are present in all the samples of air I took. There are two such coke furnaces in the house, that of the heating service and that of the hot-water supply, either of which might be the source of such fumes; but I am not in a position to say how those fumes are dispersed through parts of the house remote from the furnaces.

I enclose note of my charges.

Yours faithfully,

So Lady Brash is vindicated at last! Carbon monoxide, which is colourless and without smell, is in high favour with suicides who find their most exacting needs supplied at a quite trifling cost by the public gas companies, but an architect who lays on a continuous supply of it to the bedrooms is likely to be regarded as officious. If the percentage Spinlove appears to have arranged for at Honeywood had been 0·15 instead of 0·015, no one would be likely to have survived one night.

Pricehard's investigation probably took the form of drawing samples of the suspected air through burettes with ball-bellows until the original air in the burette was displaced by the tainted air, and then closing the cocks at each end of the burettes. The contents of the burettes, each of which would have a capacity of about 200 c.cs., would then be analysed in the laboratory.

(HOLOGRAPH) GRIGBLAY TO SPINLOVE

Sir,   6.11.26.

I write confidentially to let you know, as I don't suppose you have any hand in the matter, that I have received a letter from Russ & Coy., solicitors, threatening proceedings for the failure of this new novelty patent supercrawling and crocodiling paint your client insist I use; but there are others can employ solicitors besides Sir Leslie Brash as he will find out. I never put anyone into Court myself, and never was brought there except for once, and the man who put me there has been sorry ever since and so will this one be; for I have learnt a bit, these last months, about the successes of the Riddoppo Company with their wonderful extra super face-cream, or whatever it is, and if they have any customers left now, they won't have any after I have done with them. No one had ought to be better pleased than me for the old gentleman to go on and see what he will get for his trouble; but I am a poor man and have my work to attend to, and it will do me no good being in all the papers and I think it hard I should have all this trouble put on me because I used the stuff on the understanding I was not responsible, which I should never have done except to oblige; so I just take the liberty to write and ask you, sir—as you know how things are—to drop a hint to Sir Leslie and put him in better mind of where he stands, for this Riddoppo soup of his has given the belly-ache to near everyone who has tasted it, and he will surely lose his case if he tries to make me responsible for the mess at Honeywood.

You will pardon me writing, but thought just as well as it will save a lot of trouble for everyone if the old gentleman can be persuaded to see reason just for once.

I am, sir,

Yours truly,

(CONFIDENTIAL) SPINLOVE TO GRIGBLAY

Dear Mr. Grigblay,   7.11.26.

As you know, I am entirely on your side in this dispute about the painting. Sir Leslie Brash well understands this, but he shows extreme impatience whenever I refer to the matter. However, he certainly ought to be told of the general failure of Riddoppo of which you speak, and I will drop him a hint of it.

I have just received Mr. Pricehard's report and will write to you to-morrow.

Yours truly,

I have several times expressed the opinion that it was long ago Spin-love's duty, as architect, to take control of the position and guide his client's discretion; and have deprecated his policy of sitting on the fence—though, in point of fact, his was no policy, but a mere instinct of weak evasion. I have now to confess, however, that his inertia has given him a position of neutrality which astute diplomacy might well fail to effect; he has avoided falling out either with Grigblay or with Brash, and has still an opportunity—if he can but use it—of intervening to prevent the miserable disaster of an action at law.

SPINLOVE TO GRIGBLAY

Dear Sir,   8.11.26.

I enclose copy of Mr. Pricehard's letter covering his report of the tests he made. The question is, How do the fumes get into remote bedrooms when they are not noticeable downstairs; and how is the nuisance to be cured? It is clear there must be some serious flaw in the building of the house, and I must call on you to find out what it is and to let me have your proposals for putting things right, and without delay; for this is a serious matter as you will see from what Mr. Pricehard says of the poisonous effect of the fumes. I am not writing to Sir Leslie on the subject until

I can give him your explanation and tell him the defect is being remedied.

Yours faithfully,

Spinlove's readiness to dissociate himself from the disaster and to deny all sympathy to Grigblay, is not only wrong in policy, but has the appearance of being thoroughly bad-natured. For two years Grigblay has served Spinlove as a devoted colleague, and on many occasions has helped him out of difficulties with his wise advice and kindly forethought; and Spinlove must know perfectly well that this defect in the building, whatever it may be, is not Grigblay's fault but his misfortune. Grigblay has before endured similar treatment from Spinlove, with patience, and he no doubt understands that these gaucheries are merely due to want of self-confidence in the person he probably regards, and perhaps speaks of, as "the young gent."

MR. SNITCH TRIES IT ON

Dear Mr. Spinlove,   8.11.26.

I herewith transmit enclosed communication I have received from Mr. Cohen Snitch. This is the gentleman—may I remind you—who endeavoured to foist upon me fraudulent plans of cottages which, it eventually transpired, were a purloined illegal infringement of another practitioner's copyright.

You may have observed that within the last few months a number of wretched little common villas have been springing up like mushrooms—or rather I should more appropriately say like *toadstools*—on either side of the Honeywood Hill Road after it leaves Thaddington Village. These abortions must represent the Honeywood Garden Estate the fellow speaks of. The villas so far built are all exactly similar replicas of one another, and we have been greatly annoyed to observe that they reproduce the form of the bay window, chimney and gable of the little pretty Den projection of Honeywood Grange which, as you know, is visible from our entrance gates; and the names all up the road, "Honeywood House," "Honeywood Lodge," "Honeywood Manor" are also an intolerable violation of my rights! Has it come to this, that a gentleman may scarcely call his house his own? It is clearly evident that Mr. Snitch intends to retaliate on my refusal to submit to his attempted fraudulent extortion of fees, and I shall have no hesitation whatever in taking all possible necessary steps to stop his proceedings and compel him to alter his designs or even to pull the places down. I therefore desire you will be so obliging as to notify me exactly what are the liabilities for the infringement of my copyright, of which this must be a most flagrant example.

I am even more disturbed at this threat of Mr. Barthold—who is an auctioneer and house-agent in Marlford—of covering the land up to the eastern boundary of my Honeywood property with the insupportable eyesore of shoddy bungalow abominations, though I apprehend that the whole proposal may be a monstrous pretext for bluffing me into extortionate disbursements. The price this saucy fellow asks is nearly three times the rate at which I acquired my Honeywood estate, and approximates to nine times the agricultural value—a most unheard-of proposition. The whole thing is intolerable and beyond bearing, and I have still to consider what suitable reply I can make to the man. If you have any views on this matter I shall be grateful if I may have the advantage of knowing them.

I regret to intimate that the repulsive emanations continue to cause us considerable discomfort, and shall be obliged by the anticipated early communication from you anent the ascertained reason of the odoriferous conditions.

Yours sincerely,

(ENCLOSURE) SNITCH TO BRASH

My dear Sir,   4.10.26.

Re Honeywood Garden Estate. I beg to think you may be interested to know that my client, Mr. Vincent Barthold, who is taking an active local line in this national housing proposition, is considering extending his development up Honeywood Hill to boundary of your property as preliminary to layout of back land with Rural Bungalow Allotments the same as has proved so popular below Westerham Hill, as extension of motor bus service to Wedgefield Junc. offers fascinating rural amenities to Londoners.

As adjoining owner, Mr. V. Barthold begs to hope you might be interested to support same and join small syndicate he is contem-

plating with a view to flotation of a Honeywood Dainty House-
lets Co., and will be glad to hear from you privately *re* same.

Mr. Barthold is willing to dispose of part or whole of same,
freehold, at from £170 (back) to £450 (front) per acre according to
location.

If this proposition interests you, shall be glad to hear from you
at early date as other investors are in the market, and will supply
further particulars on application.

Yours faithfully,

"The Honeywood File" recounts how Brash, with the idea of reduc-
ing cost, employed this same Mr. Snitch—who practises locally as an
architect and surveyor—to build a block of cottages, and how Mr. Snitch
sold Brash the design of another architect which he copied, for the pur-
pose, from an architectural magazine. Spinlove warned Brash that if he
used the plans he would make himself liable to an action for infringement
of copyright, and this is what Brash has in mind when he notices features
of his own house travestied in the villas of "Honeywood Garden Estate."

It is no new thing for commercial enterprise in housing to find profit
in the execration its achievements provoke, by acquiring land and then
coercing the owners of adjoining houses to buy it at an enhanced price
under threat of building on it, and just as the highwayman was obliged
sometimes to shoot so that his formula "Your money or your life" might
be respected and yield a due harvest, so "Buy or we build" is by no means
an empty threat, even when there is no intention of building. A cottage,
however hideous, can readily be let, and is a profitable investment when
it serves as a warning to rebellious mansion-owners. I know of a remote,
solitary, bleak, raw red brick labourer's cottage compromising four stark
walls and a drain pipe, set in a break of the hedge on a country road. Its
position—which would be readily understood if cottages were jettisoned
from passing aircraft—is explained by the entrance drive to a large pri-
vate house on the opposite side of the road, up which the cottage stares
unwinkingly like a village idiot entranced. It is there, as is notorious, in
fulfilment of a threat, because the owner of the mansion refused to buy the
field in which it stands.

This is the happy instance of the way commercial enterprise advances the cause of civilization by establishing blackmail as a recognized source of revenue and of increase to the wealth of the Empire. By building cheaply and rapidly instead of in the old-fashioned way, not only are larger profits immediately accrued, but future profits are secured by the early need for renewal, and good money earned merely by refraining from building.

GRIGBLAY TO SPINLOVE

Dear Sir,   10.11.26.

What Mr. Pricehard says is pretty much what I feared. Of course there is some stupid thing been done somewhere and it will be a job to find out where, for what has happened is that fumes from the heating furnace get into the hollow of the outside walls, and one of those places it gets out again is, in my opinion, where the joists of upper floors bear on the 4½-in. inner thickness of outside walls, and so lets the air be drawn from the hollow into the space between joists and through joints of flooring into the bedrooms. I have had a look at the plans and you will find that those particular bedrooms is just where it can get; for the joists in those rooms run across to the outer wall and not parallel with it; and another thing that fixes it is the way these fumes came on worse than before when the heating furnace was started up again a few weeks ago, for as the work dried out in the summer the ends of joists, where they were built in, would shrink and leave a bit more room for the fumes to leak through than when the work was newly finished. The joints of flooring will not lie so close now, either. Well, we know the fault is in the heating flue, for the complaints stopped just when the fire was drawn for the summer; but where the fault is, and what to look for, is the difficulty—unless we open up the flue till we find out. I have never had the like of this happen in any building of mine. None of my bricklayers would play hanky-panky with a chimney flue or leave out a brick, which is what looks like; and Bloggs would not let them if they tried it. However, there cannot be many places where a little thing wrong would make all that difference, and Bloggs will be likely to say. I have written him to-day.

Yours faithfully,

Here, then, is the explanation of the famous "defective drains"—otherwise "odoriferous effluviums"; but the defect giving rise to the nuisance is still a mystery; for carelessness which would leave an opening from a chimney flue into a hollow wall-space would seem impossible of men employed by a builder of Grigblay's standing, or in work overlooked by Bloggs.

The subtlety with which smoke will find its way through brickwork has long ago established the parging—or plastering—of the interior of flues, and until quite recently the parge was always worked up with a proportion of cow dung which prevented it from developing cracks as a lime and sand rendering is apt to do. Fifty years ago bricklayers began to resist using this traditional parge—probably because its composition seemed ignominious; and as the mortar in which the bricks are laid, now commonly used to parge the flues, seems to be all that is required, it may well be that the traditional parge was, like so many craft-methods, a survival of an immemorial custom.

BRASH IS FOILED

Now Mr. Spinlove,   12.11.26.

I desire that you will be so obliging as to carefully peruse the enclosed copy of a letter I yesterday received from Mr. Russ anent Riddoppo, and of correspondence therein referred to, which I transmit herewith preparatory to your meeting me for the purpose of discussing the position of affairs on an early day. You will observe that I refrain from all comment. Such views as I have to communicate are, I apprehend, more fit to be the subject of verbal rather than of literary intercourse; but you may tell that infernal scoundrel Grigblay that if he or any of his damned workmen put so much as their noses inside my gate I will have them thrown out into the road.

Yours sincerely,

P.S.—Pray excuse a pardonable asperity of diction.

Dear Sir,   10.11.26.

In accordance with the instructions you gave Mr. Russ in your interview with him on 28th September, we entered into communication with Messrs. the Riddoppo Coy., Ltd. (and Reduced), and subsequently, on receipt of the Company's reply, with Mr. Marston Grigblay, and we enclose copy of the correspondence.

Before we received the letter from Mr. Grigblay's solicitors, of 3rd October, it came to our knowledge that a receiving order had been made out against the Riddoppo Coy. The firm is in liquidation and from information in our possession we are of the opinion that reorganization is extremely unlikely; that the assets will be sold for the benefit of the debenture holders, and that there will be little or nothing left for the unsecured creditors. In the circumstances we do not consider the company worth powder and shot.

In view of the position Mr. Grigblay takes and the difficulty of showing him to be responsible without the evidence of the Riddoppo Company of the soundness of the paint supplied; and in view also of the opinion given us by Mr. Chawlegger, we do not consider that you could succeed in an action against Mr. Grigblay. It seems to us, therefore, that the only course for you to take is to withdraw.

Yours faithfully,

So the end of this matter is that, for his sins, poor old Brash is left high and dry. Riddoppo, Ltd. (and Reduced) has gone bankrupt, a fate that overtakes not a small number of such ventures and which offers an additional reason why architects should be wary in experimenting in untried materials. The company's property will be sold to pay the debenture holders, creditors will get little, shareholders nothing, and the only person who is likely to have done well out of Riddoppo is perhaps Brash's influential commercial friend Mr. Ziegfeld Swatmug, who may have bought the rights from the inventor for a small sum, sold them to the public for a large one, and afterwards resigned from the board of directors and disposed of his holding.

(ENCLOSURE 1) RUSS TO SECRETARY, RIDDOPPO COY.

Dear Sir,   30.9.26.

We are instructed by Sir Leslie Brash, of Honeywood Grange, Marlford, Kent, that certain paint manufactured and supplied by your Company to Mr. John Grigblay, builder, of Marlford, for the decoration of Honeywood Grange, has proved seriously defective; and have to say that unless you can make satisfactory explanation showing the said defects not to be due to any fault in the paint you supplied or, alternatively, will at once give an undertaking to restore, renew or repaint as may be necessary for the proper completion of the work, we are instructed to take you for breach of warranty.

Yours faithfully,

(ENCLOSURE 2) RIDDOPPO TO RUSS

Dear Sir,   2.10.26.

The paint we supplied to Mr. Grigblay a year ago, which we understand is the cause of complaint, was our well-known New Novelty Riddoppo, Super-Paint (Matt) and was in perfect condition as taken out of stock and same as supplied to others. We can demonstrate the superior quality of our Riddoppo Super-Paint, and produce evidence of painting carried out with paint taken from our stock before and after same supplied to Grigblay.

The defects are due to neglect of painters to follow instructions which we now enclose as sent to Mr. Grigblay and all others and clearly printed on the tins.

We have no intention to renew defects, as same are due to neglect to follow instructions, and not to Riddoppo Super Paint and which is no business of ours.

Yours faithfully,

(ENCLOSURE 2A) PRINTED LEAFLET

NEW NOVELTY "RIDDOPPO" SUPER-PAINT

IMPORTANT See the word "RIDDOPPO" (with 2 "d's" and 2 "p's") on every tin. NO OTHER GENUINE and if noticed should be informed at once.

N.B. These instructions must be followed if best results desired.

INSTRUCTIONS FOR USING RIDDOPPO

1. Use at a temperature of 55 degrees or over which should not be less than 40 degrees but in damp weather a higher temperature gives best results particularly for last.

2. Keep air-tight lid hermetically sealed and well stir before transferring and at once replace.

3. If copper-bound tools are used must be protected as RID-DOPPO acts as solvent and same may affect appearance.

4. All tools to be used first immerse and thoroughly cleanse in "RIDOP" (pink tin) supplied with all orders only after careful drying.

5. No paint must on any account be returned but specially in damp weather and if left overnight to be removed from pot carefully cleansed after with "RIDOP" (pink tin) before same is again re-used.

6. As damp takes longer to dry close windows or similarly open and shade from sun if same is not.

7. If ropy add "RIDOP" (pink tin) unless affected by frost though only a small amount and not otherwise or results will be unsatisfactory.

ALL TINS ARE THE PROPERTY OF THE RIDDOPPO COMPANY WHICH WHEN NOT RETURNED WILL BE CHARGED 2S.

(Issued by Riddoppo Lid.)

———

The seven golden rules of Riddoppo!

One disadvantage of a Public School and University education (however lightly faced) is that it prevents a man from understanding directions, such as these, which offer no difficulties to Bloggs and his painters, and which Grigblay could probably read aright if he stood on his head to do it.

(ENCLOSURE 3) RUSS TO GRIGBLAY

Dear Sir,   4.10.26.

We are instructed by Sir Leslie Brash to point out that certain painting carried out by you at Honeywood Grange under your contract has developed serious defects, which you have declined to remedy after being required to do so.

The Riddoppo Company, who manufactured and supplied the paint in question, state that it was taken from stock and was in perfect condition, as supplied to other customers, and sent you full instructions for applying the paint, which instructions were also printed on the tins.

We are instructed to inform you that unless you can show that the failure of the paint-work is not due to defective workmanship or other fault for which you are responsible; or, alternatively, will give an undertaking immediately to restore or renew the defective paint-work to the satisfaction of the architect; Sir Leslie Brash intends to have the necessary renovations carried out by some other person and to deduct the cost of such renovations, together with certain expenses he has already incurred as a result of the defects, from the balance ot moneys retained by him as security for the completion of your contract.

Yours faithfully,

(ENCLOSURE 4) GLAUBER AND WALSH (SOLICITORS) TO RUSS

Dear Sir,   8.10.26.

Our client, Mr. John Grigblay, instructs us to say, in reply to your letter to him of 4th October, that he strongly objected to use Riddoppo paint and only did so to oblige your client after receiving the written undertaking of the architect that your client accepted full responsibility for the result of the experiment; that he placed his foreman painter in charge of the work and employed only skilled decorators upon it; that the instructions supplied with the paint were exactly followed, or if not exactly followed, then followed as exactly as the ambiguous and confused wording made them possible to be understood or, if understandable, then as exactly as painters and decorators can, or could be expected to understand and follow them; or if the said instructions were not ambiguous, then that they were redundant and fastidious and such as no practical men could observe, or if they were not, then that no warning of such defects as have occurred was given, so that these defects tie not due to any failure to observe instructions, if clear instructions were given, which my client denies, but were due to the omission of warnings of dangers of which my client could have no knowledge as the paint was composed of "new and secret ingredients."

Furthermore, my client's case is that the said instructions are worded and designed to be, and in fact are, a mere device to enable Riddoppo to shelter themselves from liability for defects in their paint; which paint my client has evidence to prove is generally discredited by the building trade as a worthless imposture.

I am further instructed to say that my client contends that he has carried out his contract to paint in a skilful and workmanlike manner, and that he refuses to renovate or restore or renew or have anything more to do with any painting at Honeywood of any kind whatsoever or for any consideration whatsoever; and that my client regards the threat of an action by your client as the malicious attempt of a rich man to bully and browbeat a poor one, and will defend any action which your client may bring, to his last penny.

Yours faithfully,

(Here ends the correspondence enclosed by Russ to Brash.)
As Grigblay said—"There are others who can employ solicitors besides Sir Leslie Brash."

GRIGBLAY TO SPINLOVE

Dear Sir,   12.11.26.
As promised, we wrote to our foreman Bloggs on the subject of the run of the furnace flue, and his report is as follows:

"She start off left hand pretty quick but only as far as the top of fire lump at back. . . . Then she make a sudden turn and rise up straight, but going away backwards eight courses I reckon or may be ten, till she have nine inches to face of cellar wall. . . ."

Bloggs says this was done by your orders to prevent wine from getting chilled, and that it made the flue very tight just above so that he had difficulty in getting it over. He goes on:

"After that she start off and away she go left hand over the door of fuel and past soot door till that girder under kitchen hearth stop her; but she just lean over right hand to clear and off she go again nice and easy right up to stalk and a good one for a brush all the way after she pass the soot door. She was a bit tight below I admit, but I did the best I could and she swept beautiful and draw a treat and so I left her and do not know what the trouble can be since."

We are afraid the above does not help us much, but Mr. Grigblay is arranging to go over to Honeywood with the plans on Thursday and see what he can make.

Yours faithfully,

It is apparent that Bloggs's authentic chirp is in part lost to us by the editorial conscience of the typist. I picture the omitted passages as recording Bloggs' views of the architect's demands.

He speaks of the flue as "she" out of respect and affection for flues, and for somewhat different reasons than when he used the same word to designate Lady Brash.

SPINLOVE TO BRASH

Dear Sir Leslie Brash,   14.11.26.

I have been away from the office on important business and found your letters of the 8th and 12th awaiting me on my return yesterday.

I am very sorry to hear of the building activities and really do not know what to advise. I am afraid however, that no question of infringement of your copyright arises. In the case of the block of cottages you proposed to build last year, the entire plan—which was the material part of the design—was, you say, "purloined"; but I do not think there can be any copyright in an architectural feature, and though the villas may imitate, they cannot attempt to *reproduce* any part of your house. I am afraid, too, that you have no copyright in the word "Honeywood," as it is a place-name which was in use long before you adopted it.

As regards the proposed bungalow allotments, I do not know what to say. The only thing seems to be to buy the people out. It was, I think, considerate of them to give you the opportunity of acquiring the land. They perhaps thought you might not like to have buildings of that kind close up to your boundary.

I have received the analyst's report. He says the smells are due to fumes from the heating furnace. These must somehow get into the space of the hollow walls and are by that means distributed to remote parts of the house. I cannot understand in the least how this has happened. However, Mr. Grigblay has agreed to make no charge for putting things right, as it is a defect for which he is responsible.

I was sorry to learn the result of your negotiations for settlement of the Riddoppo dispute. I have always felt, as you know, that Grigblay could not be held responsible in view of his objection to the paint and of his consenting to use it only after you accepted responsibility for the result. This was also Mr. Chawlegger's view, you will remember, and now Mr. Russ evidently feels the same about it. It will be impossible for me to see you this week, but I will ring up early next week and arrange a meeting. I am extremely busy just now.

You asked me some time ago to let you have particulars of my charges. These I now have the pleasure of enclosing.

Yours sincerely,

This letter seems to have been written on one of the very worst of Spinlove's "bad days." Except for the directions it gives Brash on the matter of copyright, it is futile to the point of exasperation. If he had no advice to

*give he should have said so, instead of elaborating vacuity. Brash is well
aware that he has acquired no rights in the word "Honeywood"; that he
can rescue himself by "buying the people out," and that the one entirely
impossible explanation of the proposal made him by Snitch is consideration for his feelings or his interests.*

*Spinlove's comment on the Riddoppo fiasco—"I always told you
so"—and his bland assumption that the whole nuisance of the smells is
satisfactorily disposed of by Grigblay's putting it right "without charge"
is the very cream of tactlessness; and why he should choose this occasion
of all others to tell Brash, twice over, that he is too busy to give him full
attention, and to send him particulars of his charges, is beyond understanding.*

*As regards this matter of architectural copyright, it is only in recent
years that the thing has been recognized in English Law, and there have
not been enough judgments to determine how the Courts apply the text of
"colourable imitation"—which establishes infringement—to plans, elevations, and architectural features. There are, however, from time to time
claims by architects whose published designs for small houses have been
adopted by private building-owners. Such claims are usually settled by the
author of the design being paid the fees he would have earned as architect
for the work, and the making of them must be among the most lucrative
activities of architectural practice; but the generality of architects have a
natural repugnance to taking advantage of simple souls whose attachment
to the great ideal of something for nothing has been a little too fervid.*

*Appearances are that Spinlove is not anxious for Brash to see Price-
hard's report. This is not surprising.*

SPINLOVE TO GRIGBLAY

Dear Sir,   15.11.26.

    I write to confirm telephone message: Mr. Grigblay to postpone
visit Honeywood till further communication from Mr. Spinlove.

Yours faithfully,

R. S. PINTLE.

Pintle is Spinlove's assistant and is presumably acting on instructions Spinlove gave before he went away on this "important business" of his. Brash's threat to have Grigblay "thrown out into the road" if he came again to the house would seem to make this intervention by Spinlove no more than merciful. What, however, must quite properly have weighed with Spinlove is that Brash has still to unburden himself of some deep grievance against Grigblay and, that being the case, Spinlove cannot make himself a party to an act by Grigblay which Brash for any reason has said he will not tolerate. In human affairs things are not unimportant because they are childish and silly: in fact, the chief burden of life is the importance of trivialities.

GLAUBER AND WALSH TO SPINLOVE

Dear Sir,   18.11.26.

We are instructed by Mr. John Grigblay to call your attention to the fact that the final balance under our client's contract with Sir Leslie Brash fell due on the 10th of this month and to request that you will at once issue the necessary certificate for the amount of £1,242 11s. 9d., as shown in the Statement of Account agreed by you on behalf of Sir Leslie Brash.

Yours faithfully,

As Grigblay has been called upon by Spinlove to make good the defect to which the escaping fumes are due, he is not yet entitled to this final balance which only becomes due after he has completed his covenant to make good defects; and as Grigblay has agreed to make good the defect it must be assumed that his solicitors wrote this letter on instructions Grigblay gave them before the defect was established. Grigblay no doubt so instructed Glauber and Walsh at the time he employed them to answer Russ's threatening letter, in view of the fact that the withholding of the certificate by Spinlove, or the refusal by Brash to honour it, would bring the Riddoppo conflict to a head by compelling Spinlove either to range himself in opposition to Brash or to join issues against Grigblay.

SPINLOVE TO GLAUBER AND WALSH

Dear Sirs,   21.11.26.
I am unable to draw certificate for final balance under Mr. Grig-blay's Honeywood contract as there are still outstanding defects which he has been called upon to make good.

Yours faithfully,

This letter is either clever to the point of being cunning, or it is merely the result of shortsightedness, and from what we have seen of Spinlove the latter explanation seems the more likely. If Spinlove perceived that Glauber and Walsh wrote in ignorance of the fumes defect and for the purpose of bringing the Riddoppo dispute to a head, his reply is a most adroit evasion; for had he stated plainly that the defect which prevented his issuing the certificate was that of the fumes, he would have implied that the Riddoppo defect was not an obstacle to the issue. He has answered Glauber and Walsh and yet still retains his firm position on the fence.

MISS PHYLLIS BRASH TO SPINLOVE

Dear Jazz,   20.11.26.
Well really, thingys are getting a bit *too* rather, don't you think? Why not jump in and do something! Poor Dad exploded when he got your letter the morning he went away, and knocked over his coffee. You should not do that. What did you say to upset him so? He told me the smells were fumes from the heating furnace; and since he went it has been like living in a refuse destructor here, and I had to tell the servants to let the fire out or I should not have been able to keep any of them in the house, Mum is pining in exile and I dare not go to her for fear of finding the house empty when I get back; Dad is thoroughly displeased with you, and I do not know what he will think if he comes back and still finds nothing done. It is just as if you did not care a blow. You really ought to get a move on.

PUD.

As there is no reply to this letter in the folder, we must suppose Spinlove answered it privately. In point of fact the delay is due rather to circumstances than to any neglect on his part.

SPINLOVE TO GRIGBLAY

Dear Sir,   21.11.26.

I write to confirm telephone message asking that you will at first opportunity go to Honeywood with the plans, as you proposed, and find out where this defect in the furnace flue is. Something really must be done without delay as the inconvenience is increasing and great dissatisfaction is expressed.

Will you telephone which day Mr. Grigblay will go; and let me know result of the investigation by wire or telephone?

Yours faithfully,

BLOGGS LENDS A HAND

21.11.26.

Reply paid. Can you say where defect furnace flue likely to be.—Spinlove.

SPINLOVE TO BLOGGS

Dear Mr. Bloggs,   21.11.26.

I wired to you to-day and enclose confirmation. I have seen your report on the run of the furnace flue, but what is wanted is information of the cause of the escape of fumes into the hollow wall, and of the position of the defect. Can you recall any circumstances which will throw light on the subject?

Yours truly,

It is irregular for an architect to write personally to any servant of a builder, but as Grigblay failed to tap the appropriate vat of Bloggs' garnered memories, Spinlove, in his ambition to "get a move on," is impelled to make the attempt.

(TELEGRAM) BLOGGS TO SPINLOVE

21.11.26.

Sir try Williams sweep Thadford may likely know.—Fred.

207

If Spinlove had no other feeling than surprise on reading that last word I do not envy him. Bloggs is known to everyone about buildings as "Fred"; he regards himself merely as "Fred," and his modesty holds him from the assertiveness of using his patronymic.

GRIGBLAY TO SPINLOVE

Dear Sir, 21.11.26.

Mr. Grigblay will arrange to go to Honeywood Friday. Please note delay is no fault of ours as Mr. Grigblay proposed to go over last week, but we had message from you we were to wait your further instructions.

We should like to explain that Messrs. Glauber and Walsh's letter to you of 18th November was under a misapprehension.

Yours faithfully,

Glauber and Walsh no doubt wrote to Grigblay reporting Spinlove's refusal to issue the certificate, and asking further instructions.

The following letter has been written under the conditions of extreme torment imposed by the absorbent back of an old blue print—embossed by the hobnails of someone who once stood on it—and a pen of unimaginable antecedents. Bloggs has evidently made haste to reply by return.

BLOGGS TO SPINLOVE

Sir, 22.11.26.

Now I come to think there wehre a lanky chap Williams by name come hanging about to get the job to sweep the chimblys, I sent off but two or three days after there he was come back and says her Lady ship add give him the order, well I give you the order not to touch no fleues I says but I'll give you a nice easy job I says and that thire is the quick job of clearing off from wehre you have no call to be I says and wehre your not wanted I says.

He sauce me and says I dursent let him has the half could never be rodded, but I dident think no more till one Tuesday dinner after the day the riging come and took the gate post, and there was the little hand cart he had standing—What's this here I ask some of them—Oh thats the chap too sweep the fleues they says and theire I found him right up the furnice acause she told him to, and grined dirty at me acause he could not pass is rods with a grate big coreing iron he had haeving and pokeing and never thinking thire wehre a soot door. It made me fare mad with half a bussel of parge and mortar he had raked down and I prety near had to frog marsh him before he would take himself off. Well thire it was been and done and had to be left you cant get inside a fleue to parge but never thought no harm would come.

Yours respectfully,

"The Honeywood File" recounts how, during Brash's absence on holiday, Lady Brash became the dupe of a touting chimneysweep, and it now appears that the defect which has been the cause of her continued complaints, and the source of so much trouble to so many persons and for so long a time, is due to no remissness on the part of either architect or builder or of anyone else, but to the lady herself, who ignored the assurances of Spinlove and allowed the vigilance of Bloggs to be eluded. It is only fair, however, to regard the catastrophe as the lady's misfortune rather than her fault.

SPINLOVE TO WILLIAMS, CHIMNEY SWEEP, THADFORD

Dear Sir,   23.11.26.

I understand you were employed by Lady Brash to sweep chimneys at the new house at Honeywood and were stopped after you had begun on the furnace flue, and that you found an obstruction you could not clear.

I should be glad if you could tell me where the obstruction was.

Yours faithfully,

No purpose is served by Spinlove asking this question, for now it is known that the defect is probably due to violent attempts to clear the flue of an imagined obstruction, the damage is to be looked for at the place where a set-off, or bend in the flue, prevented the rods from passing. This place will probably be above the soot door spoken of—the purpose of the door being to give access when bends in a flue prevent its being wholly swept from the fireplace opening.

SPINLOVE TO GRIGBLAY

Dear Sir,   23.11.26.

I enclose copy of letter received from Bloggs, contents of which I communicated by telephone to-day.

I have written to the chimney-sweep, but perhaps Mr. Grigblay will be able to get in touch with him before going to Honeywood to-morrow.

Yours faithfully,

"MR. WILLIAMS, PRACTICAL CHIMNEY-SWEEP (CHIMNEYS SWEPT)" TO SPINLOVE

Sir,   25.11.26.

Replying *re* your favour, we operated on Her Ladyship's furnace as per instructions. On endeavouring to pass 18 in. brush, obstruction was encountered after six canes. Following our usual practice with refractories from fair to medium, we then made attempt with No. 1 iron, but received instructions to desist from contractor's representative before desired results obtained.

Said flue belongs class 1 unsweepables, in our opinion, being carried over too sharp at six-and-a-quarter canes.

Yours respectfully,

MR. WILLIAMS (*Chimneys Swept*).

GRIGBLAY TO SPINLOVE

Dear Sir,   25.11.26.

We beg to report we had furnace flue opened up yesterday
and found defect due to damage by sweep employed by Sir Leslie
Brash. We have left the flue opened up for your inspection and
instructions.

Yours faithfully,

SPINLOVE TO GRIGBLAY

Dear Sirs,   26.11.26.

Please make all necessary repairs to flue at once, so that heating furnace may be brought into use. To be charged *extra*.

Yours faithfully,

GRIGBLAY TO SPINLOVE

Dear Sir,   27.11.26.

We must decline to restore damage to flue until we have
received your acceptance on behalf of Sir Leslie Brash that we are
in no way responsible for same.

Yours faithfully,

*This sort of thing is the natural consequence of bringing solicitors
upon the scenes: without good faith and mutual confidence in a common
purpose it would scarcely be possible ever to get any building contract
carried out at all. Brash, by his conduct of the Riddoppo dispute, has
made it no less than necessary for Grigblay to protect himself as he does.*

(HOLOGRAPH) GRIGBLAY TO SPINLOVE

Sir,   27.11.26.

I saw your letter at office to-day, and you will have received my
reply, but I will just take leave to send you private word and ask
you to have a look at that flue, for where shall I be if I build up and

all evidence destroyed and only my word that the damage is no business of mine but the work of the sweep acting on your client's orders? It would be a good thing if the old gentleman had a look as well, for he has been over ready to lay trouble that is nobody's fault but his own to other people's doors, and seeing is believing, and believing may save a few solicitors' letters of which there have been more than enough wasted already. Sir Leslie is expected back in a few days they tell me, so no harm to wait a bit.

From what Bloggs wrote you I broke into the flue about five feet up in the corner of the scullery, and there it was plain enough, the handy work of "Mr. Williams"—as he calls himself—who carefully raked away about two feet of the new parging, clawed the mortar out of the joints and punched a bit of a closer, that happened to come nice and handy, clean through into the hollow wall so as to leave a proper hole you can put your hand through comfortably without rubbing any skin off your knuckles. I never saw the like of it in all my experience: he would have ended by raking the house down if Bloggs had not stopped him. It is lucky it is an easy matter to put right, though it will mean a bit of pulling down before we can get at the job.

You will pardon me writing, but thought you ought to know how things are.

Yours faithfully,

Although a building owner has no right to expect, as some do, that an architect shall give up the better part of a day to viewing one or two insignificant defects in a completed house, it is clearly Spinlove's duty, under the special circumstances, to inspect this flue so that he may satisfy himself that the damage is as Grigblay reports and, if it is, that there has been no contributory negligence in the building of the flue. Grigblay's reference to a "closer"—which is a small piece of brick built in for the purpose of overtaking the break of the joints and making the end brick of the course finish to a fair face—indicates that the bricklayers may have been at fault, for a closer would scarcely be rightly used in the position indicated. The defect may be the occasion, as Grigblay foresees, of adding fuel to

Brash's grievances; and it is incumbent on Spinlove thoroughly to master the facts so that his apportionment of responsibility may be authoritative. Strictly speaking, he had no business to decide that the sweep was to blame as he did when he authorized the repairs as an extra—without satisfying himself of the fact by an inspection of the work. It would serve no purpose for Brash to view the damage, for he could not use his eyes unless someone were at hand to direct him in the evidence of them, and it is only Spinlove who could well give him that direction.

BRASH EXCEEDS

Dear Mr. Spinlove,   2.12.26.

Your communication of the 14th reached me on the day of my departure and I now, on my return, sit down to indite my reply in the hope that you are by this time so far relieved from the pressure of your extreme preoccupation with various other interests as not to be entirely prevented from perusing it with the attention which, as your employer, I apprehend I am entitled to expect.

My unavoidably protracted delay in replying will, I conceive, be no disadvantage to the matter I have to expound, as the extreme *insouciance* of your last communication—if I may diverge into a foreign tongue to express my sense of the inappropriateness of the epistolary style you think fit to adopt—might have precipitated a more forcible rejoinder.

The explanations I must request you to furnish, as I have already intimated, anent your attitude to the Riddoppo dispute, and anent your approval of extortionate "profits" and "fees" added in the builder's Statement of Account, and anent also your own astonishing claim for fees—I desire to postpone to the occasion of a personal interview to be conveniently arranged at Mr. Russ's office. I now address myself to you exclusively on the subject of the noxious emanations which have continuously tormented us ever since we first took up residence at Honeywood Grange. After ten months of elusive evasion and dilatory procrastination you now inform me the house has been so built that coke fumes from the heating furnace are dispersed to all parts of it, and that we are being slowly poisoned; and you intimate with a bland assurance which—you must permit me to remark—causes me most amazed astonishment, that the whole matter is now satisfactorily disposed of *because* Mr. Grigblay has signified his willingness to carry out the necessary preventative measures *"without charge."* You must permit me to asseverate that I cannot subscribe to any such fantastically preposterous view of the matter. As a consequence of Grigblay's contemptibly shoddy building and—you must allow me to point out—the negligent supervision of my architect, and his dilatory indifference to the appalling discomfort attendant on the disgusting effluviums of which we are the victims, Lady Brash has suffered in health, the domestic staff has been on the verge of revolt, and I have been involved in heavy disbursements on account of fees incurred by the necessity of recourse to the advice of medical practitioners and to the employment of sanitary consultants.

During these months you have had numerous intimations of the repulsive odoriferous conditions, and have repeatedly reiterated assurances that no unsavoury emanations could possibly eventuate in so carefully built a house as Honeywood, and have excused yourself from the trouble of ascertaining the cause of complaint by sending Grigblay to persuade us nothing was wrong so that he might save himself the trouble of having to put anything right. Our complaints have been met by nothing but evasive procrastinations; and when, eventually, on my urgent insistence, you condescended to investigate and were compelled to admit the presence of olfactory effluviums, what did you do? You did nothing! After weeks of delay I return expecting the necessary ameliorations to have been effected in the interim of my absence, and find only that under your directions men have knocked a hole in the scullery so that the furnace cannot be used, pushed some dirty sacks into it and vacated the work.

The position of affairs is perfectly intolerable and beyond all bearing: I do not precisely know what my rights are, and I apprehend that since my architect is in the opposite camp it is not to be anticipated that he will exactly inform me of them; but it is beyond the bounds of credulity that I am to be subjected to these persistent annoyances and refractory oppositions without power to extricate myself; and unless my architect and his builder *immediately* bestir themselves to make this house a human domicile instead of a lethal chamber for cats and dogs, I shall exercise my own resources and employ others who can be depended on to carry out what they engage to perform. My eventual demands on Grigblay for compensation are a matter for contingent consideration.

Yours faithfully,

Brash is certainly deserving of sympathy, for he is gloriously unaware that the whole of the trouble is due to his wife's interferences; he also, I think, deserves sympathy in that his manful effort at self-control has not proved equal to the length of his letter; but most of our sympathy must lie with Spinlove, who has the task of answering the letter.

SPINLOVE HITS BACK

Dear Sirs,   4.12.26.

I enclose copy of letter I have received from Sir Leslie Brash, and also a copy of that to which it is a reply. As your client, by objecting to my style, appears to require me to answer him in his own, I am replying to you. It was a great shock to me to get his letter, as no doubt he intended since it is the result of ten days' reflection; and what his immediate more "forcible rejoinder" would have been I do not know, for such studied misrepresentation and abuse must need deep thought.

You are acquainted with the facts of the Riddoppo dispute, and will be able to point out to your client that I was *right* in advising him not to use the paint; *right* in supporting Mr. Grigblay's objection to using it; and *right* in saying Mr. Grigblay could not be held responsible for the failure—which was also Counsel's opinion and is your own view. Further, that it is a mere quibble to say I took sides with the builder; that if your client, at any point in the dispute, had acted on my advice he would have saved himself wasted trouble and expense; and that everything I have done has been in his interests, which, if I had acted differently, would not have been the case. The truth is that what your client resents is my being right and he wrong.

You will also be able to explain to your client that the "profits" and "fees" charged in the Statement of Account are according to

217

custom; that every detail of the account has been audited by the Quantity Surveyor, Mr. Tinge, after authorization by me, according to the stipulations of the contract; and you can remind him that I offered to explain any points upon which he was not satisfied.

I enclose copy of the official Scale of Charges issued by the Royal Institute of British Architects, so that you will be able to show your client that my charges are in accordance with it except where they are less. I find, however, that I omitted certain services for which I am entitled to additional fees: I therefore enclose amended account in substitution for that previously sent in error.

With regard to the leakage of coke fumes, you will be able to tell your client that his ardour in abusing me for what is no one's fault but his own, outruns discretion unless he can explain: (1)—how his household has been "continuously tormented by disgusting effluviums ever since the house was occupied," when no one but Lady Brash was able to detect any smell at all, and the furnace that caused it was out of use for more than six months, and (2)—in what way I was guilty, also "continuously," of "elusive dilatory procrastination" for giving assurances that there was nothing wrong with the drains, when there was nothing wrong, or in failing to recognize a smell which it required the services of a chemist to determine.

The facts are, as your client knows, that early in the year it was suspected something was wrong with the drains. The builder investigated and found unsanitary conditions due to neglect to keep traps clear. The drains were subsequently proved sound, and there were no more complaints of smells till the 10th October. An indeterminate stuffy smell was then noticed, and at my instigation a consulting chemist was called in who, four weeks ago, reported fumes from coke fires. My dilatoriness has since then consisted in determining what and where the defect was, and in getting the work opened up. In this I have been delayed fifteen days by your client's prohibiting the builder from entering the house, and by the refusal of the builder to make good until your client accepted responsibility for the defect, which is revealed *to be a hole knocked in the flue by a chimney-sweep employed by your client*, and who eluded the foreman after being told not to touch the flues. You will, therefore, be able to point out to your client that he has misstated many facts perfectly well known to him, and that he alone is responsible for any annoyance he has suffered.

In this letter I have tried to confine myself to the business of settling up; but as Mr. Grigblay cannot answer for himself and my silence might imply acceptance of the aspersions on him, I wish to say that Mr. Grigblay has from first to last done his duty—and more than his duty; that he is a scrupulously honourable and self-respecting man and a conscientious and capable builder; that the whole of the trouble during the past months has been made by your client; and that Mr. Grigblay has far more cause for grievance against the building owner than the building owner has against him.

You will note that your client has had the forethought to write in his own hand so as to escape the consequences of libel—a most wise precaution. It may be, however, that his sense of obligations is not entirely regulated by fear of legal proceedings, and therefore, although he has made it impossible for me to enforce a withdrawal and apology, I will nevertheless pay him the compliment of demanding both.

Yours faithfully,

We have noticed before that the highly temperamental Spinlove has a bit of the Old Adam in his make-up. Like other temperamental persons, he becomes a different being under different circumstances, and it is this that explains the exuberant folly of some of his letters, the stiff-necked superciliousness of others and the passionate resentment he sometimes, as here, displays. He must have had the devil at his elbow when he wrote and rewrote and polished up and altered the first typescript of the above, for it is clear he could not have produced the thing off-hand. The stored depths of bitterness it reveals are dreadful, and it is the sort of letter that may be said to be scarcely ever written, for those who are capable of writing them know better than to indulge themselves. The arresting thing about the letter is the deliberate uprooting of the plant Spinlove has been tending for two years with such solicitude, and the discarding of Brash's esteem and friendly offices just when they were ripe for garnering. This seems inexplicable; for if Spinlove were characteristically unable to control his temper he could not have arrived at the position he has reached. The only explanation that seems possible is that there are matters affecting the relationship of Brash and his architect which this correspondence has not revealed.

The wild folly of Spinlove's action does not, however, prevent us from admiring his courage in writing the letter, and there is a manly disregard of consequences which shows him to be of finer metal than we have hitherto had reason to suppose. That the letter is not quite fair to Brash is of no consequence: the only impediment at the prospect of Brash's reading it is that Spinlove is but little over thirty and Brash is advanced in middle age—for I imagine Grigblay's "old gentleman" to be no indication of senility, but provoked by a humorous perception of frontal luxuriance, tight boots, and similar abnegations of youth.

We also may sympathize with Spinlove. In what way ought he to have replied to Brash's outrageous letter? It is a very difficult question. He might, of course, have flattered Brash into reason by being submissive, giving a diplomatic answer to the various complaints, appealing for a more tolerant view of the facts and a recognition of what was due to himself; or he might have risked a letter of passioante protest, such as in early days Brash once provoked from him; but he could scarcely have done either except at the loss of his own self-respect and his claim on Brash's—and why should he make any surrender whatever?

When a letter is written under a genuine misapprehension and without any intention of offensiveness, a diplomatic answer removes the misapprehension and prostrates the offender with the realization of his transgression; but when, as in Brash's case, there is a deliberate intention to affront, and facts are wilfully distorted to bolster abuse, the problem is how best to hit back, and to hit back with effect, for it is easy for the hitter to do more damage to himself than to his adversary—as, indeed, Spinlove seems here to have done. Spinlove must have been tormented with the difficulties of his task before he struck the happy idea of addressing his reply to Russ; and if he had written coldly instead of with feeling, made no attempt at retort, and suggested the expedience of an apology without appearing to care whether it were conceded or not, he would probably have hit Brash the harder and disarmed him of the deeper grievance he has now given him cause to feel. The things that will hurt Brash are—Spinlove's disdaining to reply to him; Russ's seeing the letters; and the humiliation of being told that his various grievances are without foundation and that he is wrong and Spinlove right. Spinlove's sarcasms were not necessary, and may be expected to do him more harm than they will Brash.

A FRIEND IN NEED

Dear Jazz,   7.12.26.

What have you been doing to Dad? He is utterly furious with you and I am afraid he is going to see Mr. Russ to-day. Why do you make all this trouble? It was never like this when the house was being built, and afterwards he was so blown out and pleased with everything—but now everything is horrid. He *shouted* to-day—he hardly ever does that. Do please have a reconcilly, or I don't know what will happen. Why is not the flue put right?

Yours,

P.

P.S.—Mum comes home to-morrow, in spite of all cold and comfortless. She took the leap at Brighton—not into the sea but into a psycho-merchant's bosom, and Aunt G. says it has done her good already.

Solemnly, it is not my fault. I am most terribly sorry about it and would do *anything* to have a reconcilly, but he wrote me a most horrible letter; abusive and misrepresenting all the facts—not troubling to understand them, and actually insulting. I could not possibly take it lying down and did not know how to answer without making matters worse; so, as he proposed to refer matters to Russ, I replied to Russ. I suppose this has upset him, but Russ will put things right, I am sure. The flue will be patched up directly the word is given. I can do no more.

RUSS TO SPINLOVE

Dear Sir,   9.12.26.

On receipt of your letter and enclosures we communicated with our client who has since called to see us and has instructed us to say that his letter to you of 2nd November was written under a misapprehension as to certain facts. He now realizes that his criticisms of your conduct were not justified, and he withdraws them and expresses his regret that he made them.

We shall be glad if you will make an appointment with Mr. Russ at this office on an early day for the purpose of explaining one or two matters arising out of the Statement of Account, and your own charges.

We have also to direct you to instruct the builder to make the necessary alterations to the flue at the earliest moment, and to inform us directly you know definitely the date when the work will be completed.

Yours faithfully,

It will be noticed that, by ignoring Spinlove's violence, Russ's formal letter conveys a more effective rebuke than any retort or comment would be likely to do. Russ has evidently persuaded Brash to a more reasonable state of mind.

SPINLOVE TO MISS PHYLLIS BRASH

10.12.26.

Since you rang up this morning a letter has come from Russ which puts everything right so far as business is concerned—apology and everything. Will you keep a lookout to-morrow morning

and let me know how thingys are at your end, as I am writing him
a really nice letter that I hope will put everything right. Excuse
typewriter.

For "him" I read "your Father."

SPINLOVE TO RUSS AND CO.

Dear Sirs,   10.12.26.
I am much obliged for your letter and gladly accept without
reserve Sir Leslie Brash's withdrawal and apology. Of course, I
was bound to ask for it.

I will call and see Mr. Russ at 11 on Thursday if that will be
convenient to him.

I have arranged by telephone with the builder to put the repairs
to flue in hand at once. They will be finished next week, and there
is no reason why the furnace should not be lighted on Friday.

Yours faithfully,

*In writing "Of course, I was bound to ask him for it" Spinlove raises
a doubt whether he was justified in asking, and disparages both the apology and Brash's wisdom in conceding it.*

SPINLOVE TO BRASH

Dear Sir Leslie Brash,   10.12.26.
I have to-day received a most satisfactory letter from Mr. Russ
which I have, of course, suitably acknowledged; but I am impelled
to thank you and to tell you the great pleasure I received from the
message he sends from you. I do hope that everything is now all
right between us. I was in great difficulties when I received your
letter as it was really altogether "too rather," as Phyllis says, and
misrepresented the facts in such an extraordinary way that I could
not trust myself to reply direct; and as you had threatened to call
me to account with Mr. Russ I thought the best thing would be to

take the bull by the horns (I am not referring to you, of course) and see if *that* would do any good—as it *has*, I am thankful to say.

I have arranged with Grigblay to get on with the flue, and you will be glad to know that he will definitely finish the work next week and that you will be able to light the furnace on Friday, certain. I understand you agree that the damage was caused by the sweep Lady Brash employed, and that no question will be raised on the point after the work is restored. As you know, Grigblay refuses to touch the flue except on the understanding that you accept responsibility for the damage.

With kind regards and best wishes,

Yours very sincerely,

So this is Spinlove's idea of a "really nice letter"! He would have been entirely right in telling Brash he received his message with great pleaure and accepted it fully and without reserve, and a light comment on some remote subject to show the quarrel as over and out of mind; but he appears—as usual—to have written out of the feelings of the moment without any regard for the effect of his words, which will open every wound that Brash's vanity has suffered in his interview with Russ.

MISS PHYLLIS BRASH TO SPINLOVE

Dear Jazz,   11.12.26.

I spotted your screed at breakfast this morning, but I do not think Dad is going to wear it next his heart *immediately*. He put it back in the envelope after he had read it, and said nothing, but he lobstered—he does that sometimes; not anger—sort of bashfulness, don'tcherknow? What was it you said to make him? Mum is wonderful, but, odds architects and builders, when are we going to have the heat on? The whole household is suffering terribly from a chilblain on Mum's little finger. She is writing to you. *It's all right.*

Yours,

P.

Mem: *Go and get psychoed.*

SPINLOVE TO GRIGBLAY

Dear Sir,   17.12.26.

I kept an appointment with Mr. Russ, Sir Leslie Brash's agent, yesterday, and am glad to tell you that there is no intention against you for the Riddoppo failure. The matter has been dropped and all suggestions that you were in any way responsible withdrawn.

I enclose certificate for £1,242 11s. 9d. being final balance due under the contract as shown in the Statement of Account. The account for restoring the flue, including analyst's fee, should be rendered separately.

Yours faithfully,

BRASH TO SPINLOVE

Dear Mr. Spinlove,   13.12.26.

I am gratified by, your intimation that you have received and fittingly acknowledged a communication from Mr. Russ, and that that communication meets with your approval.

The matter you refer to as in dispute between us is I apprehend anent the furnace flue; in which it appears we are eventually in agreement and I accordingly observe with satisfaction that you have succeeded in obtaining Mr. Grigblay's consent to undertake the work, as the result of his protracted decision in this matter has been of interest to us for a considerable time.

I suffer, I apprehend, from a certain unavoidable confusion of mind anent the various building operations which Mr. Grigblay objects to perform, and anent those others for which he refuses to take responsibility; but any compliances on his part which offer expectations that we will shortly see the last of him are most welcome.

Yours faithfully,

Brash, is sulky. Spinlove has won!

THE CAT JUMPS

My dear Mr. Spinlove,   13.12.26.

Here I am again you will see, after a most enjoyable stay at Brighton with my sister, but all the time I wished I was at home which rather spoilt my visit in spite of not having a *dreadful* chilblain when I was there.

First about the *heat*. Leslie says it will never be finished, but the men are at work now so will you tell them to be a little *quicker*. There, I knew I had forgotten something. I nearly wrote to you from Brighton but it is so much easier when one is closer. Mrs. Cooper tells me they are *all the rage* just now but of course only young people do it in public and I should never *dream* though Phyllis always does. Now what would it, all cost? I should like it on the roof so as to be near the sun, and down and all closed in to make it invisible, so will you tell me and then I will ask Leslie.

Phyllis is having some friends on Saturday to celebrate the hot water she says and we hope you will stay the night. Please excuse writing, I have such a *dreadful* chilblain on my finger.

Yours very sincerely,

And Sunday night.—P.

Apparently the lady has in view a sun-bath. The benefits of psychoanalysis are not as pronounced as might have been hoped.

SPINLOVE TO GRIGBLAY

Dear Mr. Grigblay,   18.12.26.

I had a long talk with Sir Leslie during the week-end. He is sending you a cheque in final settlement to-day and with it a letter which I hope will end all memory of the upset over the painting. He now admits that he ought to have taken our advice the first instance, and realizes that the failure of Ridddoppo is in no way your fault. There has been no complaint of fumes since the furnace was relighted, and I slept for two nights in the house with windows shut and noticed nothing; so the matter is disposed of, at last!

What I am particularly writing to you about is the restoration of the paint. It is, as you know, in a dreadful state, and what is left of it will have to be thoroughly rubbed down and the whole painted anew. The family is going abroad for two months after Christmas, Sir Leslie will not be much at home and it would be a great satisfaction to him to feel the work was in your charge. I know also that, for personal reasons, it would be a pleasure if you would undertake the work; and it would also relieve me of great anxiety. I trust, therefore, that you will reconsider your decision to have nothing more to do with it.

Believe me,
Yours sincerely,

P.S.—Sir Leslie has decided not to have the bedrooms painted out each in a different colour, as now, but uniformly in duck's-egg white as I originally designed.

Spinlove seems to have made good use of his week-end visit.

(HOLOGRAPH) GRIGBLAY TO SPINLOVE

Sir,   19.12.26.

I am not going to say I was not glad to read your letter or that I do not know I have to thank you for the very considerate one I received yesterday from Sir Leslie Brash with his cheque for final balance. The old gentleman expresses himself in a remarkably handsome manner to one so far below him in station, and I have written him that nothing remains to be said.

The job of building Honeywood Grange has, one way and another, perhaps been a bit more of a trouble than it had any call to be; but that is what we have to expect sometimes in the building trade, and so long as the owner is satisfied, and the architect, that is all I ask, for the house is a good one and if it wasn't it wouldn't be for want of everyone concerned having had a try at making it so.

About the painting, of course I will take on the work as asked; but I shall not be able to give an estimate and I shall want a free hand to do what I think well, and I cannot guarantee perfect results although I will do my best to secure them. If you care to have it like that, it would I think, sir, be a good thing to have a talk over. I shall be in town to-morrow and can arrange to call at any time convenient after two o'clock.

Yours faithfully,

Grigblay evidently found Brash's "handsome expressions" more gracious and condescending than he had stomach for, and his sly reminder of obstruction due to the architect's solicitudes and the owner's interferences tells its own tale.

SPINLOVE TO BRASH

My dear Sir Leslie,   21.11.26.

Grigblay called to see me about the painting yesterday. He is glad to oblige us by doing the work, but as he does not know what is involved in it he cannot give an estimate. The work will be done as Day work—i.e. at net cost plus 15 per cent to cover establishment charges and profit. This is an offer that ought certainly to be accepted.

He says he cannot actually *guarantee* perfect results, but he will spare no pains to secure them, and as he proposes to clean the existing paint entirely, and sand-paper all vestiges of it from the wood, there is no doubt all will be well. He will arrange with. you about dismantling the rooms. He would rather not undertake this.

I spoke to him about the threatened extension of villa building up Honeywood Hill and the proposed development of the back land. He ridicules the whole idea, and says it is merely a trick to induce you to buy the land at a high price. He says that some of the villas already built are standing empty and that the work has been stopped, and that the land Barthold offered you does not belong to him. He only has a twelve months' option on it from Mr. Rallingbourne who parts with no land without particular restrictions as to the buildings to be put on it. Were there no restrictions as to the number and kind of buildings that might be put on your land when you bought it? I recall that you asked me for a set of plans to send to Mr. Rallingbourne's solicitors. Besides all this, Grigblay says there is no chance for a "Bungalow Town" anywhere near Marlford, and if there were, nothing could be done unless the Building Byelaws were revised which the District Council would never agree to.

I saw my friend to-day, and he says the appliance I spoke of is Wealdstone's New Radio-Active Spleen and Liver Pad, made in two strengths, "strong" and "extra." He recommends latter. They can be re-charged from any electric light plug stocked by Spedding, 92 Fountain Street, St. James's. My friend swears by it.

Ever yours dutifully,

BRASH TO SPINLOVE

23.12.26.

My dear James—(to indite the new nomenclature),

I am much gratified and also relieved in mind at the intimation that the building propositions of Mr. Barthold are a fraudulent pretension, and as I have to-day received a peremptory reminder from Mr. Snitch, asking a reply to his previous communication, he will be sufficiently answered by my continued silence.

I had quite forgotten, as in my case it was a mere formality, that Mr. Rallingbourne makes it a prohibitive condition in his conveyances that only private houses of due importance and refinement of design shall be erected on the land.

Will you, since no alternative course seems expedient, be so obliging as to complete the necessary arrangements for Mr. Grigblay to undertake the renovation of the painting? We shall be unboundedly thankful—as you may imagine—to see a termination put to the disgraceful state of affairs which deforms the domicile and is no better than an unsightly eyesore.

I am obliged by the information you give anent the Radio Pad. I shall certainly test the efficacy of the device.

I have the pleasure to enclose cheque in final settlement of your fees. You will observe that I have augmented the amount to a round figure, but you will not, I hope, resent my indulging this friendly impulse as I apprehend that in giving me the right to do so you surrender the right to object!

The gong! I must hence and array me for the feast!

Ever, my dear boy,
Yours affectionately,

P.S.—I am requested to remind you that the performance tomorrow is timed to commence at 8.15 and *not* at 8.30 as originally intimated.

We have long suspected that something of this sort was going to happen. Apparently, in the stress of a "reconcilly" staged by Pud, barriers went down and consciences were unloaded all round; and appearances are that Brash, filled out with a son-in-law and a (soi-disant) radio-active liver pad, will take on a new lease of that benevolence which lies beneath his weakness and follies; for Brash, despite his irascibility and pomposity, is a simple soul at heart. His simplicity is well borne out if we accept to hilarious implication of the liver pad; namely, that during the unbosomings of that eventful week-end Brash was led to confess to a discontented liver, whereupon his architect promptly recommended a cure for it.

This letter, the last in the folder, by explaining itself explains also those not infrequent signs of a relationship which the correspondence did not reveal and of which Spinlove's reckless retort on Brash's strictures is the outstanding example. We cannot decide that no man would act as Spinlove did towards his prospective father-in-law, while we have no means of knowing under what circumstances he so acted. The matter, however, seems clear enough if we remember the months of badgering to which Spinlove has submitted, and suppose that when the young people's early friendship ripened to deeper feelings, Brash, finding himself in hopeless opposition to an only child and a neurotic wife, vented his irritation on the architect, and that Spinlove, secure in his position and unable to support the humiliation thrust upon him or go hat in hand to a man who considered himself at liberty to affront him, yielded to an impulse to have the thing out. In this elemental matter of pursuing a wife a man who follows his impulses at least keeps faith with his manhood; and in no other affair of life does his manhood better recommend a man.

In wishing Spinlove the best of luck we must not forget that this affair of his holds out new terrors to some who may be toying with the idea of employing an architect; and it is therefore desirable to make clear that Spinlove's behaviour in this matter is entirely "unprofessional."